First Lieutenant

First Lieutenant

Kenneth Maynard

St. Martin's Press
New York

Library of Congress Cataloging in Publication Data

Maynard, Kenneth.
  First lieutenant.

  1. Great Britain—History, Naval—18th century—
Fiction. I. Title.
PR6063.A8883F5 1985   823'.914   85-11729
ISBN 0-312-29244-9

First published in Great Britain by George Weidenfeld & Nicolson Ltd.

First U.S. Edition

10 9 8 7 6 5 4 3 2 1

First Lieutenant

Chapter 1

Winter had started early and hard, and this morning, as for many mornings past, England lay beneath cloudless skies and a glassy cover of deep-driven frost. The sun shone brightly but without heat on the sparkling waters of the Spithead roadstead, riffled by the arctic breath of a brisk, north-east wind. Ice glistened in the scuppers and rime gleamed from the rigging of the frigate *Adroit* as she tugged at her moorings. Lamb vigorously rubbed his chilled hands and performed a little dance on the quarterdeck for the benefit of his circulation, his breath smoking in the air.

'A fine, bright morning, Latimer,' he remarked cheerfully to the quartermaster who was acting as officer of the watch.

Latimer wriggled his frozen toes. 'Aye, sir, it is,' he agreed without enthusiasm, morosely reflecting that if the first lieutenant had also been on the quarterdeck for close on two hours, instead of a bare five minutes, he would not be so bloody cheerful.

Lamb gave his hands a final rub, clasped them behind his back and began his customary slow pacing to and fro beside the quarterdeck rail. Behind him, his neck hunched against the chill wind, Midshipman Bird, duty signals midshipman but with little prospect of any signals to entertain him, eyed the tall officer's antics with an amused smirk and burrowed his hands deeper into his armpits, in lieu of his warmer but forbidden pockets. A thin scrap of a boy of some twelve years, his diminutive frame housed the appetite of one three times his size and his solitary musings were largely given over to food. At this time of the morning, exactly midway between breakfast and dinner, it loomed large in his mind and as he dwelt lustfully on huge pies and massive cakes he began to sniff, loudly and wetly. Lamb considered himself to be a tolerant, kindly man and he allowed the first indrawn, bubbling snort to pass with no more than a narrowing of his eyes; the second made him hesitate in his walk and the third spun him on his heel.

'Mr Bird! Kindly stop that disgusting noise. Use your damned handkerchief – and do not lounge on the quarterdeck!'

'Yes, sir. Sorry, sir.'

Bird removed his back from the shelter of the bulwark beside the carronade and pretended to fumble for a handkerchief. As soon as Lamb had turned away he ran his sleeve along his dribbling nose and hastily transferred the tell-tale smear to his hip.

Lamb resumed his slow, thoughtful pacing. The captain had been due on board some five minutes ago but in the few weeks since he had joined the ship Lamb had learned that he rarely managed to keep to the time he promised. The reason, Lamb suspected, having once had occasion to visit the captain's lodgings, lay with his wife, a formidable woman who had made it plain that Captain Slade's loyalty and attentions should be to her rather than to his ship, a misapprehension which doubtless placed a strain on their loving ties. Lamb smiled as the thought crossed his mind that if Mrs Slade could be a little sweeter at home then perhaps Captain Slade would be a little less sour on board.

The receiving-ship was also overdue but Lamb was not concerned. The Impress Service was notoriously inefficient and if the last batch of pressed men arrived before noon he would be pleasantly surprised. He had made arrangements to receive both the captain and the new men; a dozen scarlet-clad Marines were huddled against the scanty shelter of the forecastle under the unkindly eye of Sergeant O'Keefe, and the boatswain was to hand, bent over the lashings of the ship's boats in the waist; below Lamb, against the break of the quarterdeck, chairs and a table had been set up and ink, pens and the muster book waited under a scrap of canvas.

A faint shout caught Lamb's ear and he turned and glanced over the starboard side at the *Leander*, a fifty-gun two-decker moored half a cable away. A figure on her poop-deck shook a fist in Lamb's direction and he grinned, raising an arm in return. It was an old friend, Basil Hall, the *Leander*'s second officer. His captain was as hungry for men as was Captain Slade and both had sent boats to the approaches to the roadstead last night in the hope of picking up a few men from incoming merchantmen. It had been a bitterly cold wait and when at last a brigantine had been sighted there had been a desperate race to be the first to reach her. Lamb's boat had won by a matter of yards, much to Hall's loud and coarsely expressed disgust, but Lamb had not found rich pickings. The brigantine had been stopped in the Channel a few hours earlier by a man-of-war and Lamb was able to take no more than three seamen from her, leaving her furious master with scarcely enough men to see her into Portsmouth.

'The captain's gig is approaching, sir,' announced the quartermaster.

Lamb glanced over the side and saw the boat rounding the stern of a nearby sloop, the captain's hat clearly visible over the heads of the oarsmen.

'Side party, Mr Bird.'

'Aye aye, sir.'

Bird clattered down the quarterdeck ladder at breakneck speed and Lamb followed at a pace more in keeping with his rank as the challenge rang out from the deck and the coxswain of the gig shouted the reply.

'*Adroit!*'

Lamb removed his hat as Captain Slade heaved his fleshy bulk through the entry port to the clash and thud of the Marines' muskets and the scream of the boatswain's pipe. He gave a cursory salute to the quarterdeck and turned his large nose towards Lamb.

'The press tender is late again, I see. Damned slackness! Four bells in the forenoon watch is four bells in the forenoon watch, *I* was always given to understand. The Service is coming apart at the seams these days.'

'Yes, sir,' said Lamb, sensibly forbearing to point out that the captain himself had been due on board some thirty minutes ago. Slade began to walk aft, still talking, and Lamb fell into step beside him.

'How many men have we been promised today, did I say?'

'Thirty, sir.'

Slade grunted. 'If we get twenty I shall be astonished. Well, let us be optimistic and say thirty. That will bring our total complement to – let me see – one hundred and eighty-eight plus thirty is two hundred and twenty-eight. Not too far short, Mr Lamb.'

'Excuse me, sir – two hundred and eighteen.'

Slade shot Lamb a sharp frown. 'Do not contradict me, sir. I was about to correct my reckoning, if you had but waited half a second. Yes, as I was about to say, two hundred and eighteen. I had hoped for a few more but we must be content. Time presses, Mr Lamb, time presses.'

'Yes, sir.'

A major worry for Slade since the frigate's brief refit had been finding sufficient men to man her, especially experienced men, and much of Lamb's energies since he had joined the ship had been devoted to that end. The posters he had put up around the town, offering a life of well-fed ease, grog, glory and guineas galore had competed with other posters with similarly exaggerated claims and had produced no more than a handful of seamen, all of whom had taken the posters' claims with a pinch of salt but were willing to try their luck with a captain who was not known as a flogger. Inward-bound merchantmen had reluctantly yielded up a number of prime seamen and some of Slade's old hands had turned up of their own accord, grinning shyly at his enthusiastic welcome. The standing officers – the gunner, boatswain and carpenter – managed to persuade a few old acquaintances aboard and with her nucleus of prime seamen and petty officers padded out with quota men, pressed men and green volunteers, the *Adroit* was now not far short of her full number. Her deck was guarded by armed Marines night and day to make sure the number did not diminish.

'So far as our stores and spares are concerned,' continued Slade, 'we are all complete, are we not, apart from water?'

'Almost, sir. The hoy is due this afternoon and then we are only waiting for Mr Freed's number-four canvas.'

'Well, he won't get it. I told the bloody man yesterday that there is no number four to be had for love nor money. He will have to make do with what he has.'

'Yes, sir.'

'I shall inform the Port Admiral that we will be ready to weigh on tomorrow's early tide. It will be a relief for us both.'

Slade paused as he reached the break of the quarterdeck and

looked at his shoes for a moment. When he spoke it was in a surprisingly diffident tone.

'Mrs Slade has expressed a desire to entertain the officers and midshipmen to supper tonight. I – um – I promised that I would add my weight to her invitation. The wardroom has nothing planned for tonight, I take it?'

'No, sir, nothing. We shall be delighted, sir.'

'At eight o'clock then, at my lodgings. It will be a very small, homely affair, you understand.'

'Mrs Slade is very kind, sir.'

'Yes. Run your eye over the midshipmen before you leave. Make sure they are half-way to being clean – the parts that show, at least. I don't want my daughters squirming in disgust; you know how fastidious young females can be.'

'I shall make a point of it, sir.'

Slade gave a nod of dismissal and turned to enter his quarters but stopped abruptly as he caught sight of Bird on the quarterdeck, his head turned to the shore, absently delving an industrious finger into his nostrils. The captain's eyebrows rose alarmingly and he turned an outraged face to Lamb.

'Look!' he exclaimed, pointing. 'There is a – a person picking his nose – picking his bloody nose on my quarterdeck!' He raised his voice in a furious bellow. 'You, sir, on my quarterdeck, sir! Come down here at once!'

Bird jerked his mind away from the delights of the shore as the captain's roar hit his ears. He removed the offending finger and trotted hastily down the quarterdeck ladder to stand quaking in front of Slade. The captain glared down at the boy.

'What the devil do you think you are at, you disgusting young animal? Eh? Eh? Littering my quarterdeck with gobbets of snot! Have you no sense of decency, sir? Report to Mr Clegg at once and obtain a bucket and a scrubbing brush. You will scrub the entire quarterdeck – on your hands and knees! See that he does it thoroughly, Mr Lamb.'

Slade gave Bird a final shrivelling glare and turned towards his cabin.

'Young animal,' he muttered. 'Must have been reared in a bloody sty.'

The door slammed shut behind him. Lamb nodded at the pale midshipman.

'Off you go, Mr Bird. I shall be keeping an eye on your efforts, remember.'

The scrubbing brush was still being vigorously applied when the tender from the receiving-ship came alongside an hour later. Lamb stood by and ran a critical eye over each man as he leaped or fell or climbed gingerly down from the side. Perhaps a dozen or so really useful men in the lot, he decided, and of those he doubted if more than half could tell the taffrail from the beakhead. Of the rest, dross, men too stupid or too drunk to conceal themselves from the roaming press-gangs. Well, each man had two arms at least and under the gentle guidance of the boatswain and his mates would soon learn to run to his allotted station and haul on his rope.

The last man came aboard and scurried to join his colleagues in the waist, encouraged on his way with a blow from a rope's end. Lamb eyed the shivering group with a degree of sympathy; a naked, cold-water scrub on the upper deck of the receiving-ship in this bitter wind would have done little to boost their spirits.

The master, gunner, carpenter and purser had taken their seats at the table, the purser, Mr Littlefield, endeavouring to induce some liquidity to the frozen ink by rolling the bottle between his hands and breathing on to it.

'Let us have the first one, Mr Clegg,' Lamb called to the boatswain and strode aft to join the officers at the table.

'God damn it, Matthew,' said Rank for the third or fourth time in the past few hours as the officers made their way through the Portsmouth streets, trailed by the *Adroit*'s midshipmen, 'it really is too bad. I had other plans for my last evening in England and they did not include making small talk with Mrs Slade and her ghastly daughters.'

'How to you know they are ghastly?' enquired Lamb.

'If they take after their father in the smallest degree they are bound to be. I can see them now – stout, big-nosed, booming voices, a trio of Captain Slades in dresses!'

Lamb chuckled. He had not seen the captain's daughters but he had met his wife and she resembled her husband in looks, build and voice.

'Take heart,' he advised. 'They may all be absolute stunners and you might find yourself quite smitten. Who knows, one day you might find you are the captain's son-in-law.'

'Heaven forbid!'

The captain's lodgings were three rooms at the top of a narrow house in a quiet side street half a mile from the harbour. A tiny servant girl opened the front door and retreating to the stairs bellowed 'Cap'n Slade!' in a voice that would have done credit to any self-respecting boatswain. Slade came down the stairs while the echoes were still resounding and ushered his officers and midshipmen up. He seemed a little subdued, thought Lamb; perhaps he viewed the next hour to two with as little enthusiasm as his guests.

'Mr Lamb! How very nice to see you again,' said Mrs Slade in her deep, harsh voice. 'I swear George has been keeping you boys prisoners on your little ship. If I have asked him once I have asked him a dozen times to bring you here; but no, it is always the same. "Too busy," he says. "They are all far too busy. Time presses!" Never mind that his poor family languishes in these horrid little rooms with rarely a fresh face or a little social conversation from one week to the next and with nasty, drunken sailors lurching about at every corner when we venture out. These past few weeks have been a positive trial, Mr Lamb – you cannot imagine. But we have put up with them without a murmur and now the time has arrived for my poor girls' father to leave us yet again we all feel quite tearful. You must forgive a woman her little emotions, Mr Lamb – we were all born to suffer.'

The captain stared stonily with folded arms at a bottle garden in the corner of the room during his wife's little speech, giving Lamb the impression that her feelings about their lodgings, the town and their restricted social life did not come to him entirely afresh.

Lamb bowed over her plump hand. 'It has been a very busy time for us all, ma'am, and it was with keen pleasure that we received your kind invitation. We, too, have been much cut off from social intercourse.' He caught Slade's sharp, warning glance and went on hastily: 'Allow me to introduce my fellow officers and midshipmen to you, ma'am.'

Mrs Slade raised her hand. 'No, no, let me guess. I am acquainted with all their names, of course, if not their faces, but

7

knowing how the Navy arranges things I am quite certain they have lined up in order of seniority. Now this will be Mr Rank, am I right? And Mr Ball? And Mr Collier? There, George!' she smiled triumphantly. 'Did that not surprise you? And these delightful boys must be your midshipmen, of course. My, how very spruce they are – they positively shine!'

Lamb's lips twitched. After his first inspection of their initial efforts it had taken the threat of a cold-water scrub under the head-pump to produce the trio of pink-skinned, damp-haired young gentlemen shifting and blushing under Mrs Slade's maternal hand.

The daughters, Amanda, Alice and Anne, dark, slim and demure, the two eldest of an age to cause Mrs Slade to look hungrily at most eligible males, rose briefly from their chairs to bob their curtseys, carefully graded from a deep one for Lamb to a mere dip of the shoulders for little Bird. The captain shifted uncomfortably in the background while these pleasantries were taking place, large and silent, an uneasy smile on his broad, red face.

'Give the gentlemen some sherry, George,' smiled Mrs Slade, sinking into a chair and plumping out her skirts. 'My, need I remind you?'

Slade attempted to play the part of the easy host as he gave out the sherry. 'Did you know, my dear, that Mr Lamb was on the *Sturdy* – the frigate that took the *Trompeur* off Madagascar?'

'Really, Mr Lamb? Madagascar, indeed. That it not a place I would wish to visit. The thought of all those yellow men with slitty eyes and their hands hidden up their sleeves quite turns my blood cold.'

'I think you have China in mind,' growled Slade.

'Have I? Well, they are much the same, are they not? Do not split hairs, George. Anyway, you told me all about Mr Lamb before; you remember, I remarked on his brownness. You have your tan still, Mr Lamb. It is very becoming to you – do you not think so, Amanda?'

'I am sure I had not noticed, Mama,' replied the girl, tossing her head and darting a furious glance at young Anne who had let out a small shriek of amusement.

There came an awkward little silence, made more marked by the loud ticking of the ormolu clock. The lieutenants thoughtfully swirled the sherry in their glasses and the midshipmen, who had nothing left to swirl, pursed their lips and gazed at the ceiling.

'Shall we eat?' asked Slade abruptly.

'Of course, dearest, if you are ready,' replied his wife sweetly, shooting him a glance of an entirely different flavour. 'Would you ring the bell, Anne?'

The table was not large enough to accommodate twelve diners and supper was served from a trolley brought to the room by the diminutive servant girl and eaten from plates balanced on the knees. The captain had clearly overdone his warning of the extent of young men's appetites because his wife had provided enough food to make even the midshipmen's eyes go round with astonished delight. Lieutenant Ball was seated next to his hostess and he manfully shouldered the task of entertaining her. Plump, jovial, ready-tongued and possessed of a cruel wit on occasion, he soon had Mrs Slade almost bursting with pleasure. Lamb listened to some of his efforts with sardonic amusement, albeit not without some anxiety that the captain might later take objection to his more outrageous flattery.

'Are you acquainted with Lady Chalfont, ma'am. No? You surprise me. But I am sure you must share the same dress-maker. Lady Chalfont was wearing almost the spit of yours when I dined with the family last month. I remember it particularly. I venture to say, ma'am, that it did not suit her nearly so well – the style is a little young for her, I think.'

Mrs Slade went pink with delight. Was Mr Ball well acquainted with her ladyship? Second cousin, indeed! Did Amanda hear that? And where was Mr Ball's family seat? Shropshire? A lovely county, she had heard.

The captain attempted some small conversation with Lamb, concerning the state of the *Adroit* and the weather, but mainly he sat in gloomy silence over his plate as Ball and his wife chattered on. Amanda, for reasons of her own, sulked and refused to eat a morsel, her sisters tittered at their mother's foolishness and the midshipmen concentrated their attention on their plates and ate steadily. The trolley was circulated again, emptied, removed and refilled, and passed round once more until even Bird's indomitable appetite was crushed into defeat.

9

Mrs Slade and Ball were still in full flow when over the rim of his coffee-cup Lamb caught the captain's significant stare and rose with a cascade of crumbs on to the carpet to express astonishment at the way in which time had crept up on them. The officers could not thank Mrs Slade enough for her hospitality and the midshipmen muttered something to the same effect. Mrs Slade expressed her delight at the conviviality of the evening, with a particularly warm smile at Ball. The captain shuffled his feet while he stood at the door leading to the stairs and Bird stole a large seed cake with which to supplement his breakfast.

Lamb was the last to leave the house as Slade saw his guests to the front steps.

'Thank you again for a very pleasant evening, sir.'

The captain nodded with the weary air of one who has successfully completed an unpleasant but necessary duty.

'Tell Leyton to have my gig at the steps at four o'clock. Good night, Mr Lamb.'

'Good night, sir.'

The night was dry and very cold. Lamb turned up his collar and glanced up at the pale moon, swimming in a clear sky. There would be a heavy frost tonight, he thought, as he hurried to catch up with the others. They were waiting for him around the corner, the lieutenants conferring in a little huddle of steaming breath, the midshipmen at a nearby shop doorway leering at an indifferent Portsmouth Poll. Rank turned a questioning eye at Lamb as he came up.

'We are all for going on to the Benbow for an hour or two. What say you?'

Lamb had been turning the same thought over in his mind. With the captain due on board shortly after four o'clock and the frigate set to weigh on the early tide he had almost decided against it but the stultifying past two hours had swung him the other way. He fished in his pocket and examined his finances. He had spent heavily in the past few days; a new gold-braided hat, shoes, half a dozen shirts and several books, including the very expensive, recently published translation by Thompson of D'Antoni's masterly work on guns and gunpowder, much superior to Lamb's tattered copy of *The Practical Sea-Gunner's Companion* and a book he had lusted after for some months.

'Why not?' he grinned, noting the gleam of gold amongst the handful of silver and copper. 'Our last night ashore for many a week – let us make the most of it. Bear in mind, though, that if young Sal is free, she is mine.'

'Huh! She's yours and welcome,' said Rank. 'Young Bird has a bigger chest than that skinny scrub.'

Lamb ignored the jibe. 'I'll just send those young Turks on their way. Mr Hopper!'

The senior midshipman, engaged in earnest bargaining with the whore for a peep at her bosom, returned his sixpence to his pocket and trotted back to Lamb.

'Sir?'

'I want the three of you back on board in one hour. Report to the officer of the watch and have the time of your arrival noted. If you step out smartly you should just make it. Off you go.'

Hopper's cheerfully expectant expression had vanished with Lamb's first few words. He was a very large young man, a year older than Ball and unlike the other two midshipmen his appetites were not completely satisfied by food alone. With a few shillings jingling in his pocket he had been looking forward to much the same sort of pleasures that his seniors intended enjoying.

'Aye, aye, sir,' he said reluctantly. He hesitated and gave what he fondly imagined to be a winsome smile. 'You could not make that two hours, could you, sir, please?'

Lamb was unmoved. 'You heard me, Mr Hopper.'

'You were a little hard on him, Matthew, were you not?' commented Rank as the three midshipmen made off, their footsteps ringing on the cobbles. 'Another hour would not have made that much difference.'

'Perhaps not,' agreed Lamb. 'But with a bellyful of beer and his hand up the skirt of a young doxy would it have stopped at one hour? We sail on the early tide, you remember, and I would be grievously saddened if we sailed without the wit and talent of Hopper to enliven the long weeks ahead.'

The others chuckled. Midshipman Hopper might have been many things but witty and talented he was not.

The landlord of the Admiral Benbow reserved his large upper room and several adjoining smaller rooms for the exclusive use of officers and their female companions. It was a favourite haunt for many of the junior officers from the ships in the harbour. Trade was a little slack tonight but not so slack that Sal had been unable to find herself another admirer for the evening. Lamb was not left disconsolate for long and as he sat with a steaming glass of mulled wine before him and the soft buttocks of a pretty, red-haired doxy squirming warmly on his lap he felt supremely content.

The girl stroked his thigh expertly. 'How did you come to lose your little finger, dearie?' she asked, putting a curious finger to the short stub on his left hand.

'It was chopped off by a French axeman in the Indian Ocean,' replied Lamb, reaching for his wine.

'Fancy! He didn't cut nothing else off, did he?'

Lamb chuckled and squeezed her waist. 'I'll let you find out a little later,' he leered.

The Union flag was snapping bravely from the *Adroit*'s jackstaff and the capstan-bars shipped ready to raise the anchor from Spithead's litter-covered bed when the captain mounted the quarterdeck a little after first light. Lamb and Collier, the officer of the watch, touched their hats and moved to the lee side of the quarterdeck, leaving the other side clear for Slade's august tread. The captain looked around the anchorage and glanced aloft.

'Are we ready to weigh, Mr Lamb?'

'Yes, sir. The tide is just on the turn, sir.'

'I am perfectly aware of that. Get under way, if you please.'

'Aye aye, sir.'

Slade turned and gazed at the distant harbour wall. A small group of women were huddled in their shawls against the cutting wind, some with children at their side and babies in their arms. A few brave souls waved at their unseen men. A little to one side stood the captain's wife and daughters and Slade lifted his hat slowly into the air and replaced it carefully on his head before turning away.

Lamb strode purposefully to the quarterdeck rail, his brisk manner concealing his unhappy state. He had only narrowly beaten the captain's gig back to the ship and lack of sleep, a sour, churning stomach, a sharp pain over the eyes stabbing rhythmically through his head and a deep sense of alcoholic guilt combined to render him as miserable as the grey, dreary, windswept surroundings of the anchorage.

'Weigh anchor!' he called to the idlers and Marines waiting expectantly at the capstan.

'Stamp and go! Stamp and go!' roared the boatswain's mates.

The pawls clanked on the drum, slowly at first, then faster and faster as the men increased their pace, toes digging in and elbows locked as they leaned their weight against the bars and the swifters.

'Loose foretops'l, spanker and jib.'

The forecastle men and the afterguard had been waiting ready for Lamb's order and the canvas billowed out with a rush in the fresh east wind, setting the frigate in motion as the anchor broke clear of the sandy bottom. Slowly she began to slide past the Spit Sand and the brooding forts overlooking the sheltered water of the anchorage, heading along the channel between the quiet hulls of sleeping ships thrusting their hundreds of bare masts into the chill, morning air like a leafless forest. The small group of women and children receded slowly astern, patiently and bravely waving until the movement of their hands could scarcely be seen.

'Ease her a point, quartermaster.'

'Ease her a point it is, sir.'

Clear of the roadstead, the topgallant masts were swayed up, the foremast staysail and flying jib set and the courses loosed. The frigate rounded the wooded hills of the Isle of Wight and headed past the Needles with a brisk wind on her larboard quarter. A passing Indiaman, beating against the opposing wind, dipped her foretopsail in salute, her poop crowded with passengers eager for the first view of their homeland after years beneath an Indian sun.

'A word with you in my cabin, if you please, Mr Lamb,' said Slade.

After the chill morning air of the open deck, the captain's cabin struck warm and bright; sunlight streamed through the broad stern-windows, throwing a shifting pattern on the black-and-white painted squares of the canvas-covered floor, and dust motes danced merrily in the wide, slanting rays. Slade tossed his hat on to the leather-covered bench seat beneath the window and lowered himself heavily into his chair.

'Sit yourself down, Mr Lamb. I want your opinion of the provisional watch list and gun-crews that I have made out, since you are rather better acquainted with the new hands than I.'

For close on an hour the two worked through the lists, transferring men from one watch to another and occasionally moving them back again. At last it was done, with no more than the odd, muttered curse from the captain as he scratched out one name and added another. He threw down his pen and blotted the list with powerful thumps of his fist.

'I hope you are quite content with that now, Mr Lamb.'

'Oh, yes, if you are, sir.'

'I was quite happy with the lists as they were, but you are quite entitled to put forward your recommendations and far be it for me to disregard the opinions of my first lieutenant, even if it will cost me an hour's work rewriting the damned things.'

He shook his head sadly at the deletions and alterations, little curving arrows and qualifications written sideways in the margins, and tapped the gun-crews lists with a large forefinger.

'We are somewhat fortunate in that we have a fair number of experienced gun-captains and quarter-gunners but we also have a great many green hands and Marines. I would be obliged if you would assemble the crews at their guns as soon as they have had their dinners and give them a brief instruction as to their duties. I doubt if many of them can tell the difference between a worm and a rammer and the sooner they find out the better. I have instructed Mr Winter to prepare sufficient cartridges from his most dubious powder to give three rounds to each gun and we will see how the men shape up. I shall feel happier once they have all had a taste of gun smoke.'

He tucked the lists beneath the punishment book and leaned back in his chair, drumming his fingers on the table as if gathering his thoughts. Lamb eyed him covertly, thinking not for the first time that Slade was fairly old to be a frigate captain. He must have married quite young to have a daughter of marriageable age and Lamb guessed he must be in his early forties. It was clear that promotion had come late to him but it did not show; authority sat naturally with him and it was difficult to imagine Slade as anything but a post-captain sporting two epaulettes. The notion of him ever having been a mid-shipman, true as it must be, seemed too ridiculous to contemplate.

'I am sorry we have not had time to get better acquainted, Mr Lamb,' said Slade, giving his first lieutenant a quick glance and immediately looking away as if touching on the personal gave him some unease. 'Refitting and re-manning is always a busy time and when added to domestic affairs ashore – ' His voice tailed off and he drummed thoughtfully on the table for a few seconds. 'No matter. We have many weeks in front of us and long before we reach Antigua I am sure you will know precisely how I like my ship to be run. Providing we do not deviate in that direction I am certain we will get along very well. Thank you, Mr Lamb, that is all.'

Apart from a distant blink of sail to the north-west the Channel was deserted of shipping when the gun-crews took their places in the early afternoon. The lieutenants and midshipmen stood by their batteries and Lamb paced slowly to and fro just forward of the mainmast. The sentry at the door to the captain's quarters slammed to attention and Slade emerged, to mount the ladder to the quarterdeck.

'Carry on, Mr Lamb,' he boomed.

Lamb touched his hat and faced forward.

'For the benefit of the green hands,' he shouted, 'we shall go through the procedure slowly, one step at a time. You have all been assigned your duties so pay particular attention to the task that befalls you. Now watch the men at this gun.'

He flung out an arm to the gun on his left, manned for this occasion by experienced gunners.

'Open ports! Cast loose your guns!'

The gun-port was swung up and secured by its lanyard and the deck rumbled to the weight of the gun on its carriage as it was hauled inboard on its squealing wooden wheels to the limit of the breeching ropes.

'Loaders – load your powder!'

The cartridge slid down the barrel.

'Rammers – first wads!'

The wad was rammed down on to the cartridge.

'Load roundshot!'

The twelve-pound ball rang and rumbled its way down the barrel.

'Second wads!'

The rammer tamped the wad hard on to the ball.

'Run out your guns!'

The men clapped on to the side-tackles and ran the gun down the slight slope of the deck, hauling it hard up against the ship's side, the black-painted muzzle questing out over the cold green water.

'Handspikemen – train hard forward!'

The crowbar dug in and levered, inching the gun rapidly round until the muzzle was pointing as far forward as the gun-port would allow.

'Adjust your quoins – maximum depression!'

The gun-muzzle dipped as the wedge lifted the breech. The gun-captain crouched over his flint-lock, waiting for the final order.

'Fire!'

The lanyard jerked, the spark flew, the muzzle belched flame and smoke and thunder and the gun hurtled backwards, brought up sharp by the breechings.

Lamb waited a second or two for the silence to settle over the ship again.

'You will have noticed the recoil of the gun then. If you want to keep all your toes you will make sure your feet are well away from the trucks.' He turned to the gunners waiting beside the smoking muzzle. 'Worm out! Sponge out! Secure the gun!'

'Thank you, Mr Lamb,' bellowed Slade from the quarter-deck. 'You new men should all now know your duties. There can be no reasons now for ignorance or incompetence. The more observant amongst you will no doubt have noticed that there are very few men on the larboard guns. I want you to take a good look at the gun-captains on that side and remember the face of the one opposite you, because that is where you will run to when the order is given to man the larboard guns. We shall now fire three rounds from each gun. Stand by! Open ports! Cast loose your guns!'

The first broadside was very ragged, not the fault of the new men who performed surprisingly well, but because two guns missed fire on the first pull of the flint-lock and the lanyard of a third snapped before it produced a spark. These matters put right – Slade immediately ordered the doubling-up of the flints

– the exercise continued, the broadsides sounding almost as one. Gun smoke billowed along the deck and swirled off to leeward, obscuring the bright sea. The captain's eyes missed nothing, his outstretched hand pointing out incompetents and slackers.

'That man on number four – the one with the bald head; he is not pulling his weight. Take his name, Mr Lamb! The sponger on number six – see where he has placed his rammer, the stupid man, right behind the truck. Take his name! That man standing beside number two with his arms folded – does he think he's a bloody audience? Take his name!'

When the men had run across the deck to join the gun-captains at the larboard guns Slade descended from the quarterdeck and roamed up and down, continuing to roar and gesticulate but as the last broadside echoes died away and he returned to the quarterdeck he was smiling broadly.

'Close ports!' shouted Lamb. 'Swab out! Secure the guns!'

He left the men busy about their guns and climbed to the quarterdeck, touching his hat to Slade standing at the top of the ladder.

The captain nodded at the activity on the maindeck. 'Well, that all went very well, Mr Lamb. I am very pleased at the new hands. Given an hour or two at the guns every day they will soon be down to a two-minute broadside and less. They all seem to be good, willing fellows and a little more work will soon put a polish on them.'

'Yes, sir,' said Lamb, thinking of the eleven names of the good, willing fellows he had on his list of defaulters, all placed there at the behest of the captain. He removed the list from his pocket, wondering if Slade's present good humour would persuade him to give summary punishment rather than the formality of a hearing in front of the assembled hands at the next punishment day, a duty which would involve Lamb with a good deal of work.

'Do you wish these names to go forward as defaulters, sir?'

'How many are there?'

'Eleven, sir.'

Slade seemed surprised. 'Eleven, eh? Oh, I think I can afford to be a little magnanimous on their first exercise. Put them to cleaning roundshot for an hour, off watch. But from now on I shall not be so lenient.'

The wind remained steady and brisk on the larboard quarter as the *Adroit* continued along the Channel on a south-westerly course designed to take her round the island of Ushant on the north-western corner of France and south to Madeira before she struck out westward along the Trades to the West Indies. The Channel remained quiet; there was some coastal traffic far off to starboard but few merchantmen were prepared to risk alone the privateers that in the past few years had become such a menace in these waters. An armed cutter passed about a mile to leeward, beating close-hauled against the wind, a suspicious-looking lugger hovered far off to windward, and towards the end of the afternoon watch a barque was sighted broad on the larboard bow.

'What is this?' cried Lamb as he ascended the quarterdeck ladder, from which vantage point he could see some sweepings trapped beneath the truck of the larboard carronade. He pointed an accusing hand. 'Sweepers, there, if you please, Mr Collier.'

'Sweepers to the quarterdeck!' bellowed Collier.

'Deck there!' came the hail from the masthead. 'That there barque be now abeam with two luggers a-chasing her.'

The sweepings were instantly forgotten. Lamb and Collier climbed into the mizzenmast shrouds and directed their telescopes towards the unseen French coast. The barque was directly abeam, heading eastward close-hauled, with a lugger to windward and another coming up astern, large, two-masted vessels. He saw the red wink of a gun fired from the deck of the merchantman and as he jumped to the deck and beckoned to the duty midshipman he heard the low, faint grumble of its discharge.

'My respects to the captain, Mr Bird. Two privateers engaging a barque three miles off the larboard beam.'

'Two privateers engaging a barque three miles off the larboard beam, aye aye, sir,' gabbled Bird and hurled himself down the quarterdeck ladder. As he raised his fist to rap at the captain's door it was suddenly opened from within.

'Are you raising your fist to me, sir?' demanded the captain, with a ferocious glare.

'No, sir, sorry, sir,' squeaked the terrified midshipman and stepped hastily out of the captain's way, cannoning into the sentry at the door.

'Steady there, you clumsy young oaf,' growled Slade. 'Don't knock my Marines about.'

He strode past Bird, ignoring his stuttering attempts to pass on Lamb's message and made his way up to the quarterdeck. Lamb touched his hat in salute.

'Two luggers engaging a barque off the larboard beam, sir,' he said, having heard every word that had taken place at Slade's cabin door.

Slade nodded. 'Luff up, quartermaster. Hands to the braces, if you please, Mr Collier.'

The duty watch ran to their places, urged on by the strident shouts of the boatswain's mates and as the wheel spun to bring the bows nearer to the wind the yards were hauled round to narrow the angle of the sails.

'Keep her so,' said Slade to the helmsmen. 'Beat to quarters, Mr Collier; we will not bother to clear for action. Your glass, if you please, Mr Lamb.'

He moved to the weather shrouds and trained his telescope forward as the Marine drummer began his rapid, blood-warming call to action stations. Men erupted from the forward hatchway and ran to their guns, hauling them inboard; others began to busy themselves about the deck, scattering damp sand, erecting water-soaked screens around the hatchways to guard against stray sparks finding their way below, filling the water buckets beside the guns and ferrying shot from the racks round the hatch coamings and along the sides.

Slade moved away from the mizzen shrouds and handed the telescope back to Lamb. 'It will be touch and go for that merchantman, touch and go. We must offer her some encouragement. Hoist our colours and let fly with the bow-chasers, Mr Lamb. It will do little good at this range but it may stiffen the master's backbone and spread a little alarm amongst the Frenchmen.'

The six-pounders barked away at two-minute intervals as the frigate gradually closed the range, battling close-hauled through the deepening dusk. Lamb glanced at the western sky; in half an hour or so the darkness would be complete. The sound of the intermittent gunfire from ahead, heard now to the accompaniment of faint musket-fire, suddenly increased in tempo as the privateers closed the barque in a desperate attempt to snatch the prize before the man-of-war came within range. Slade and Lamb stood together on the quarterdeck peering forward at the red gun-flashes and the dozens of tiny sparks from the muskets on board the barque as she struggled to prevent the luggers from closing.

'Extreme range, Mr Lamb, extreme range,' muttered Slade, 'but we must try a couple of our for'ard long-guns. Quartermaster, starboard your helm two points.'

'Two points to starboard it is, sir.'

Slade leaned out over the quarterdeck rail and raised his voice to carry forward. 'Mr Collier! Try your two for'ard guns at maximum elevation. Fire when you are ready.'

The two guns thundered half a minute later, the twin explosions sounding as one. Lamb estimated the range to be about a mile, the very limit of the twelve-pounders. He gazed intently forward, hoping to see the fall of shot but the light was now so poor that he could see no evidence of the accuracy of the gunners' aim. They were as likely to hit the barque as the luggers, he thought, but it was more probable that the roundshot had plunged into the sea short of their target. The long-guns sounded again and before the echoes had died away Lamb saw to his delight the distance between the privateers and their prey suddenly widen. Beside him Slade grunted with satisfaction.

'Ha! We have frightened the buggers off! Now let us see if we cannot wreak a little slaughter amongst them. Luff her, quartermaster, luff – luff – steady. Keep her so.'

The frigate was now sailing as close to the wind as she was able, the yards braced sharp round. Lamb kept his eye on the two luggers, their rectangular sails on their odd, angled yards now an indistinct blur as they headed for the coast of France on widely diverging courses. The *Adroit* sailed past the merchantman at a distance of half a cable and the cheers of her crew echoed thinly across the water. The frigate's crew cheered and waved in reply and Slade removed his hat and brandished it slowly and solemnly in the air. Lamb ran his eye over the barque as the *Adroit* ploughed by. Her canvas was lacerated, peppered with holes; there was some damage on her side and rail but from what he could see it was superficial. He was not surprised; he doubted if the privateers carried anything heavier than a one-pounder and in any case their crews would gain nothing in capturing a ship that was foundering beneath them. Slade gave a last slow wave to the upraised hat of the barque's master and replaced his hat firmly fore-and-aft on his head.

'Brave fellow, that, Mr Lamb,' he remarked, nodding in the direction of the merchantman. 'It must have seemed hopeless for him with a Frenchman on either side and yet he continued to hammer away with his little guns and muskets.'

'Yes, sir. It was lucky for him that we happened along but then luck often has its own making, I've been told, sir.'

'Well, he certainly helped it along in this case. I have no great opinion of merchant captains in general – and I've known some cowardly buggers in particular – but I take my hat off to that one.' And he did so, lifting it a generous inch into the air.

It was now very nearly dark, the red blaze at the western horizon shrinking and giving way to the steady creep of blue-black sky from the east. Lamb strained his eyes to keep the sails of the luggers in view. One was heading east and the other due south, straight for the hidden coast of France, doggedly followed by the frigate. The *Adroit* sailed well close-hauled but the lugger's rig, with its double jib and running bowsprit, enabled it to sail much closer to the wind than the square-rigged frigate and Lamb knew that barring an accident to the privateer's spars they stood no chance of gaining on her. Her sails were no more than a faint grey blur and suddenly they were not even that; she had been lost to distance and darkness.

Slade grunted and turned away from the side.

'Secure the guns, Mr Lamb, and stand the men down. Wear ship, Mr Collier; steer west-sou'-west.'

He waited in silence until the guns had been secured and the ship was on her new heading and then gave orders for the topgallantsails to be furled and the topsails double-reefed. As soon as the sails had been shortened for the night he left the quarterdeck and disappeared into his quarters without another word. Lamb watched the indistinct figures of the topmen swarm down, dismissed the off-duty watch below and made a round of the gun-deck, satisfying himself that the guns were securely snubbed tight against the ship's sides. He returned to the quarterdeck as the ship's bell sounded four times for the end of the first dog-watch and watched in silence as the helmsmen were relieved.

'Steer west-sou'-west.'

'West-sou'-west, aye.'

The off-duty watch scampered below, anxious not to lose a minute of their two hours' rest. The duty watch settled down into the little nooks and crannies out of the wind and the *Adroit* sailed on into the darkness to the never-ending song of creaking spars, slapping sea and the sighing of wind through the rigging. Lamb checked the compass heading in the dim light of the binnacle, had a final word with Collier and went below, ravenous for his supper.

If Lamb had been serving in a fine, three-decked, hundred-gun ship of the first rate or even on a fifty-gun fourth-rate he would have descended to the spacious magnificence of the wardroom directly below the quarterdeck and eaten his supper at a long, broad table beneath windows that stretched the width of the stern and with a servant hovering behind each chair. On a fifth-rate frigate, however, with no poop-deck to house the captain's cabin, the wardroom was shunted below to the gunroom, and the unfortunate midshipmen and master's mates were ousted to the narrow confines of the forward cockpit. Lamb ducked his head and entered the gunroom; even here he was unable to stand upright for fear of cracking his head against the low deck beams and with his superior height he was in more danger of this than most. He made his way to his chair at the head of the table and sank into it with a sigh of pleasure as he took the weight off his legs.

The gunroom was warm and stuffy with the warmth and fumes of the lanterns and candles and the body heat of its occupants. There was only one vacant chair, Lamb noted; that of Collier, the officer of the watch. Even Vaughan, the lieutenant of Marines who had complained of feeling ill in the moderate motion of the sheltered Spithead anchorage was in his chair, greenish in complexion but valiantly determined to have his supper for the honour of his uniform. The room was noisy with a cheerful buzz of relaxed conversation as the officers discussed the inconclusive skirmish with the luggers and recalled previous brushes with privateersmen in the Channel. Sykes, the wardroom steward, put his head round the side of the door and raised a questioning eyebrow at Lamb, who gave a brief nod in reply. Sykes withdrew his head and a moment later the two young Marines who doubled up as wardroom waiters entered and laid out cold beef, pickles and fresh Portsmouth bread.

'You cannot accuse them of being shy,' said Goode, the master, a black-browed, heavy man in his fifties, much addicted to his Bible and possessor of a foul tongue and a fine singing voice. 'It was in ninety-five or ninety-six that I saw as pretty a piece of work as you could wish to see. I was second master in the old *Rapide*, convoying a couple of dozen merchantmen to Halifax. We get into the Channel, they are all milling about at sixes and sevens as usual, shaking their fists at each other and damning their escorts, when all of a sudden down swoops a little brig, comes alongside one of them, a dozen men climb across and within a minute the pair of them are fast vanishing across the Channel. By the time the escorts had woken up and the Commodore had confused everyone with his signal flags it was too late. And this didn't happen the once – oh, no, five ships that brig took before we rounded Ushant. It was the Commodore's fault, the bone-headed fool, for not deploying his escorts properly. Billy Brett, he was – Sweet William we used to call him, on account of the perfume he drenched himself with. He never flew his pendant again after that and no more he should, the useless bugger. But all credit to that Frenchman, nevertheless. For sheer daring and persistence he is hard to beat, privateer or not.'

'Well, they make a profession of it, of course, and a damned good living out of it, too, many of them,' said Lamb. 'Not only in the Channel but in the Baltic, the Indian Ocean and the Caribbean. With luck, we may be given an independent cruise once we get to the West Indies and perhaps reduce their numbers a trifle.'

'Have you been that way before?' asked Goode.

'No. The Mediterranean, the Cape, the Indian Ocean and the Bay of Bengal but never the Caribbean.'

'Well, you haven't missed a great deal. If you like pretty sights it looks pretty enough, I dare say, but the weather can be bloody nasty at times in the hurricane season, and if you survive that you've got yellow jack to contend with. There is a spit of sand between Kingston and Port Royal and there are so many jacks and jollys and soldiers buried in it that there are more bones there than there is sand.'

Sykes and his two helpers came in and cleared away. The King's health was drunk and the port began to circulate. Lamb pushed back his chair a little to stretch his legs. After the bitter cold on deck the heat of the gunroom and his full stomach were making him drowsy. He loosened his stock and stretched, yawning.

'By the by, Matthew,' said Rank. 'We have still to hear your account of the fight with the *Trompeur*. You can carry modesty too far, you know.'

'I did start to tell you of it a few nights ago, you remember, but we had that little interruption when the cockpit nearly went up in flames.'

'Yes, that's right. Bloody careless little snotties!' snorted Rank. He was a dark, hard-faced young man, pleasant enough in the gunroom but disliked by the lower deck for his harsh, bitter tongue.

'I was only the fourth lieutenant,' said Lamb. 'The real credit for the *Trompeur* must go to Tom Kennedy, the second. He took command after Captain Cutler and the first lieutenant were killed.' He cleared a space on the table and reached for a couple of walnuts from the dish. 'We were thirty miles north of Madagascar, heading west for the Mozambique Channel with the wind from the north when a sail was sighted off the starboard beam.' He told his story in simple, undramatic terms, moving the walnuts about the table to illustrate the movement of the two frigates. The others listened in enthralled silence, nodding to signify their comprehension as the walnuts moved. The admiration of the junior lieutenants was wholehearted, but a ship-to-ship action between frigates was a rare-enough event to tinge their feelings with a little envy as they reviewed their own remote chances of earning such glory.

'It sounds as if it was a very bloody affair,' said Rank. 'How did you get the Frenchman to port? There could not have been too many whole seamen left.'

'Our casualties were surprisingly light compared to the losses on the *Trompeur*. We had twenty-eight killed and about twice as many wounded. Kennedy let me have what hands he

24

could spare and all the Marines, plus a midshipman and a master's mate by the name of Irving. The midshipman was useless but Irving was a godsend, a right seaman and a damned good navigator. The Frenchmen were battened down below and that is where they stayed until we reached Simon's Bay. We lost contact with the *Sturdy* on the second day in a gale and also our mizzentopmast and most of our canvas. The pumps were going night and day and we very nearly foundered again in strong winds in the Mozambique Channel. It took us eleven days to get to Simon's Bay, by which time most of the hands were near dead from exhaustion and I was nigh the same for lack of sleep. It was not the most pleasant of journeys.'

'And the *Trompeur* – was she bought in?' asked the purser from the other end of the table, his mind being naturally more attuned to the tangible rewards of the victory rather than the glory.

'Yes, after a great deal of iffing and butting, mainly because of her condition. She had suffered a good deal from our carronades but after a good deal of chin scratching she was finally bought in. They deducted a vast amount for repairs, though and we ended up with a paltry sum in the end. By that time Kennedy had his own sloop in the Mediterranean and I was third on the *Barfleur*, Lord Keith's flagship. I met up with Tom Kennedy again for a while when the fleet called in at Leghorn.'

'Ah, Leghorn!' cried Goode. 'Did I ever tell you what happened to me off Leghorn?' He launched into a rambling tale of storm, fire in the hold and a hazardous boat journey, in each case of which his own heroic activities loomed large. Rank caught Lamb's eye and closed one of his own in a slow, significant wink, at the same time helping himself to a large pinch of salt from the silver cellar. Ball gave a quick laugh, immediately stifled as the master's angry eye fell on him and Lamb rubbed his cheek to hide his own grin. Goode ploughed dourly on with his saga which ended, it was strongly hinted, with the Commander-in-Chief of the Mediterranean Fleet fairly beside himself with gratitude and the shy hero modestly refusing enormous rewards and recognition. The sole reaction to the master's colourful tale was a strangled grunt from the ashen-faced Vaughan who pushed back his chair and made a crouched dash for the door with a hand clapped to his mouth. He was followed by a loud volley of advice.

'A nice piece of fat pork will soon settle you.'

'Go and sit under a tree – it never fails.'

'Make for the weather side.'

'Strange fellows, these Royal Marines,' said Lamb, looking puzzled. 'Was that one of their ancient, after-dinner customs we have just witnessed? Have we been privy to –?'

'Shame on you all!' cried the surgeon, 'to mock a man when he is ill. What wretches you are, to find humour in a poor fellow's suffering.'

'Suffering, you say, Andrews? He would put it a sight stronger than that, I fancy. He'll be feeling near to death now, I'll warrant, ha! ha! ha!' laughed Rank.

'Yes and praying to God he will not have long to wait!' roared Ball and the pair of them dissolved in tearful, rocking laughter.

The surgeon shook his head reproachfully. 'Och, you pitiless devils,' he said, struggling to maintain a stony face in the midst of the laughter bubbling around the table. 'Wickedness always finds its retribution. Just you wait until you have need of my services – I will remind you of your amusement tonight, before I dose you with the blackest, vilest draught I can make.'

'It amazes me, you know, in this day and age when we read of the huge strides medicine has taken of late, that you doctors are unable to find a simple little cure for seasickness,' observed the purser, turning his long, pale face towards Andrews. 'You can make pills for this, draughts for that, for almost any ailment under the sun but simple *mal de mer* has you beat.'

Andrews was quick to defend his profession. 'Seasickness is not an illness; it is not a condition of the body proper, like the ague or the pox. Seasickness is brought about by the motion of the ship on the stomach, which in turn affects the eyes and brings on the sweats, much as a child finds when it rolls over and over down a hill and jostles the stomach juices. The effect is the same and so is the cure. Nature has her own remedy and that is time. Time will reconcile Vaughan's stomach to the movement of the waves in a day or so, as it will with all the other poor wretches suffering below. Why interfere with Nature when she performs so well on her own?'

'Yes, but Nature can be helped, surely? responded the purser. 'Now if you were to mix together a bit of this and pinch of that and come up with a cure, why, your fortune would be made. You could retire to a grand house in Scotland and spend your days with your paints and brushes and bits of canvas, as happy as – '

'I am not a quack, sir,' snapped the surgeon angrily. 'Let other people foist their worthless potions on to a gullible public – I take my profession a little more seriously. I will have you know my father worked with Fothergill, whose treatises on the putrid sore throat shook the medical world. I myself have listened to Huxham describing his work on epidemic fevers. I have even shaken the hand of the great Edward Jenner himself, of whom even you, sir, may have heard. Do not talk to me of quack cures, sir.'

Andrews reached for his glass with a trembling hand and sank back into his chair with a final, defiant glare at the purser. Littlefield was not in the least abashed.

'Of course the name would be all-important if you wish to catch the imagination of the gullible public. How about "Andrews' Anodyne and Antidote for Seasickness Sufferers"?'

'Pah!' snorted the surgeon.

Lamb had been told of Andrews' passion for painting and he had seen one of his latest efforts attached to the bulkhead of the surgeon's cabin, a mud-coloured daub that he had taken to represent a spindle-legged dog but had later learned was a horse. He suspected that Andrews' ire would not have been aroused but for the slighting reference to his artistic endeavours. Lamb drained his glass and stretched, suddenly bone-weary. The activities of the day and the previous night had caught up with him and brought on a longing for his cot. He pushed back his chair.

'It is time I did my rounds and turned in,' he announced, ducking his head with unconscious habit as he rose.

'And it is time I relieved Collier,' said Rank, rubbing his eyes and giving a sleepy shake of his head.

The two ascended the aft companionway together and parted on the cold, windswept deck, Rank to the quarterdeck and Lamb to make his round of the dark maindeck and forecastle. After the heat of the gunroom the cold wind cut like a knife and Lamb's mind leaped forward several weeks and as many thousand miles to dwell with pleasure on the warmth and sunshine of the West Indies station.

Chapter 2

It was almost dawn. The slow spin of the earth had yet to roll the Atlantic Ocean into the full light and heat of the sun but already the sky astern of the *Adroit* was paling to the deepest turquoise as the Marine at the ship's bell sounded the first of the eight chimes that signified the end of the middle watch and the start of the ship's day. Lieutenant Ball, eager for his sleep after four long hours as officer of the watch and revelling in the perverse delight of summoning others from theirs, was roaring from the quarterdeck as the second chime sounded.

'Turn the starboard watch up, Mr Clegg!'

Clegg and his mates had been licking their silver whistles in readiness for the order and the hideous shrillig of 'All Hands' immediately vied with the sharp notes of the ship's bell.

'All hands ahoy!' screamed Clegg, poking his hairless head down the forward hatchway.

'All hands ahoy!' screamed his mates as they ran below with their knives in their hands ready to slash the lanyards of the hammocks of men still too stupefied by sleep to spring to the deck. 'Out or down, there! Out or down! Rouse out, rouse out, rouse out! Rise and shine! Show a leg, show a leg!'

Back in Portsmouth Harbour, before paying off, a hundred female legs might have been displayed and earned their owners exemption from summary eviction from their frowsty blankets but today the tender susceptibilities of the boatswain's mates were spared and the only legs that sprang or crept reluctantly to the deck were all of the hairy, muscular, non-female variety. The men tumbled up on to the deck, most of them bare to the waist, displaying here and there ugly patches of pink, peeling skin on bodies exposed too eagerly to the unaccustomed sunshine, the more fastidious amongst them dry-washing their faces as they ran. The last man from the hatchway was sped on his way with an encouraging cut across the buttocks with a

29

rope's end as a sleepy Marine sentry took up his position beside the hatch in order to discourage the hands from creeping back to their hammocks.

Lamb, shaving by the dim, yellow light of his lantern in his cell of a cabin, heard the roaring of the petty officers on the deck above and the clanking of the pumps as the decks were wetted. Captain Slade was an early riser and although Lamb kept no watches it would not do for Slade to be striding the damp, early-morning deck of his ship whilst his first lieutenant was still snug in his cot. Amongst his many duties, Lamb was responsible to the captain for the upkeep of the ship's fabric and its appearance; a smart ship was a credit to her captain, but anything less and a finger would be pointed at her first lieutenant. Lamb's intention was to make sure that there could be no fingers levelled at him by the time the captain put his first foot of the day on the maindeck. He wiped his razor and put it into its little case; it had been pulling a trifle this morning – he must remember to hone it before he used it again. Bending to peer into his shaving mirror as he dabbed the soap from his face he smiled as he heard Ball pum-pumming his way untunefully through something that closely resembled 'Greensleeves' from the cabin across the narrow way. Ball was an inveterate romantic; he had confided to Lamb that he had fallen in love regularly every few months since he was about eleven years old, each time more passionately than the last. Such liaisons had avoided Lamb, brought up by a widowed father in the harshly masculine confines of the bachelors' mess in a military depot, and sent early to sea where the opportunities for romantic dalliance were so limited as to be non-existent. He had frequently taken his pleasure from women's bodies but not, so far, without coin being passed and of late, ashore, he had often found himself gazing wistfully at passing couples, laughing happily together, arms entwined, uncomfortably aware that he was missing something in his life. Women's minds were closed books to Lamb; on the few occasions when he had met them socially he had found that women tended to fall into two classes – those that prattled endlessly on topics he found incomprehensible and those that sulked and pouted and said almost nothing. Perhaps there was a third class, one that neither prattled nor sulked but fell engagingly between, able to converse intelligently and amusingly on things unconnected with gloves and hair and fashion and other females' complexions, perhaps to gaze with increasing interest into Lamb's eyes, perhaps to edge a little closer, perhaps . . . ? Here his perceptions became a little clouded; the mechanics of sex he understood – the intangibles of love and romance were a mystery. He peered at the face frowning thoughtfully at him from his little mirror. Was that a face that women would find attractive? It was not, he had long ago decided, handsome in the classical sense – the nose, perhaps, a trifle too long, the grey eyes a little deep set – but it could hardly be thought of as ugly, even from his own subjective viewpoint. He gave his image a friendly wink and stretched out his hand for his shirt.

The sun had heaved its uppermost tip above the eastern horizon as Lamb reached the maindeck and picked his way through the lines of kneeling men busy with their holystones. He mounted the quarterdeck and bade Rank a good morning before going to the binnacle and checking the compass against the course marked on the slate. He gave a brief nod to the quartermaster and made his way to the forward rail where he could look out along the maindeck, observing the men below him inching their way over the wetted, sanded planks. Beside him Rank stood in silence, for which Lamb was grateful. He had never been one for talk before breakfast and until his tongue had tasted the first mouthful of coffee he preferred to exercise it as little as possible.

The last faint stars in the western sky vanished as the sun climbed higher into a cloudless sky, giving early promise of another warm day. The boatswain and the carpenter made their separate ways to the quarterdeck and made their reports to Rank in loud, formal voices. The master, pale of face, his arm in a sling, made his slow and painful way up the ladder.

'Hello, Ralph, what the devil are you doing here?' asked Lamb. 'I understood from Andrews you would be confined to your cabin for a day or two yet. How are you feeling?'

'How do I look?' countered Goode.

'Like bloody death!'

'And that is how I feel!' He eased his arm in its sling and winced. 'A pox on all bloody midshipmen!'

The master's misfortune had occurred a few days earlier, a

31

week out of Madeira where the frigate had stopped briefly to top up her water and wine supplies. From a clear sky a sudden squall had sprung up and there was a hasty scramble to reduce the sail area. Midshipman Allwyn, a year or so older than Bird but at sea for the first time, was on duty on the quarterdeck and the sudden, violent motion of the ship immediately renewed his acquaintance with the seasickness which had brought him low for a week after leaving Spithead and which had hovered close ever since. He struggled manfully for a few minutes with his heaving stomach and then, white-faced, staggered blindly for the lee rail. The captain chose that moment to move backwards from the forward rail, his eyes fixed on the men busy on the maintopgallant yard and Allwyn, head down, cannoned into him. The midshipman's hand was clamped firmly over his mouth as he strove to keep his stomach contents behind his teeth and he bounced off Slade's well-cushioned body, staggered to one side and continued his desperate dash for the rail. Slade was outraged, both at the bodily contact and the lack of apology. He flashed out a long arm and spun the midshipman round to face him.

'What is this then, sir?' he roared, shaking Allwyn by the collar. 'What the devil to you mean by bruising your captain and walking on without so much as a by your leave or a kiss-me-arse? Eh? Eh?'

Allwyn looked up at Slade, his eyes wide. He shook his head dumbly, not daring to part his lips. The captain's brows lowered dangerously and a dark flush spread over his cheeks.

'Will you give me an answer, you insolent young sod?' he bellowed and shook the midshipman so violently that his feet left the deck. Allwyn's teeth unclenched themselves and a pint or so of malodorous liquid shot over the captain's sleeve and splashed on to his shoes. With a roar of rage Slade swung his arm and caught Allwyn a mighty buffet around the side of his head. The boy careered across the wet, tilting deck and slammed into the legs of the master who promptly crashed to the deck on his back, bumped head first down the quarterdeck ladder and ended up in a heap in the lee scuppers.

Slade was almost dancing in his fury. 'Get that – that thing out of my sight before I hurl it over the side!' he shouted, pointing a quivering finger at the unfortunate midshipman sitting in a pool of vomit and tears. He strode to the rail, unbuttoning his coat as he went and slammed it disgustedly on to the maindeck in front of his cabin door.

'Donovan! Donovan!' he bellowed, leaning out over the rail. 'My other coat and shoes up here this minute, do you hear me? Stir yourself!'

Lamb bent over the unconscious master. Blood ran from his nose, there was an ugly swelling over his eye and his arm was tucked at an awkward angle beneath his back.

'Call Mr Andrews,' he said to the boatswain's mate hovering with deep interest nearby.

'How is he?' called down Slade.

'Unconscious, sir, and I think he has a broken arm. I have sent for the surgeon.'

'Jesus Christ!' growled Slade. 'The damage that one snot-nosed little midshipman can do!'

Concussion and a broken humerus was the surgeon's verdict and Goode was carried away to the sick-bay in the forecastle. Isherwood, a master's mate, was given temporary promotion to the quarterdeck in Goode's place. He was a bright, cheerful, competent young man, a one-time midshipman who had decided the odds against him ever obtaining a lieutenant's commission were too high and had opted for a sideways move to master's mate as another avenue to the quarterdeck. Navigation and mathematics were his passions and playthings, both subjects a constant source of nagging guilt to Lamb who had barely scraped through them in his examination for lieutenant and had promptly forgotten much of what he had learned immediately afterwards.

'How is it now?' asked Rank.

Goode poked a finger inside his sling and gave his binding a cautious scratch. 'It itches. How has young Isherwood been performing – not too well, I hope? I don't want him exposing any of my little deficiencies.'

'It is strange you should ask that,' said Lamb. 'Mr Rank and I were just discussing that very point and agreeing how very pleasant it has been these past few days with Isherwood on the quarterdeck – were we not, Bob?'

'Indeed we were,' agreed Rank. 'And also how comforting it is to have as master a man who can translate our midday sights into an actual position instead of making a blind stab at the chart.'

'Impudent buggers!' growled Goode. 'Right, that settles it. It's back to the maindeck for Isherwood, the young upstart. He can confine his fucking talents to looking after the tops'l sheets and a-serving of the beef.'

He made his way to the wheel and peered closely into the binnacle, as if to reassure himself that the compass was still present and working after his absence. Straightening, he gave each of the grave-faced helmsmen a long, suspicious glare and turned his attention aloft to the spars and yards. He gave a grudging nod as he completed his tally and stumped his way forward to the quarterdeck ladder where he paused with one foot on the top step.

'If Isherwood comes up here be so kind as to direct him to his old duties on the maindeck. I shall be back as soon as Sykes has given me a shave – if the ham-fisted clod manages not to cut my windpipe.'

'Oh, heaven forbid!' murmured Rank.

Goode shot him a glance, grunted and resumed his careful descent to the maindeck. The two officers looked at one another and grinned. Goode was too easy a mark – his lack of any sense of humour was notorious.

By four bells the holystoning was finished and as the damp patches on the planks rapidly shrank under the influence of the wind and the climbing sun the men were sent below to lash their hammocks and to scrub out and make all shipshape in their quarters.

'Up all hammocks!'

The men erupted from below carrying their numbered hammocks carefully lashed with the regulation seven turns of their cords. Lamb stood by as the demoted Isherwood saw to their stowage in the nettings suspended between the brackets along the bulwarks, his eye alert for a slipshod lashing. He saw none; the knowledge that the first lieutenant would be scrutinizing each hammock was sufficient to ensure that every one was brought to the side rolled and lashed to perfection. With the hammocks stowed to Isherwood's satisfaction and his own nod of approval, Lamb set the hands to cleaning their boarding weapons in the short time remaining before they were dismissed below for their breakfasts. He set off on a slow round of the ship to assure himself that all was as it should be for the captain's nit-picking eye. He resumed his place at the quarter-deck rail beside Rank, waiting for the hour to be struck, gazing over the spotless boards with all the pleasure and satisfaction of a wife surveying her freshly scrubbed kitchen flagstones.

Sharp on six bells Slade emerged from his quarters, shaved and fully dressed with his hat fore-and-aft. He set off with his slow, heavy tread along the starboard side to the forecastle, his gaze flicking from the stowed hammocks to the guns, from the deck to the racks of roundshot. Lamb watched his progress with an anxious eye, his fingers firmly crossed behind his back. Slade returned by way of the larboard side and made his deliberate way up to the quarterdeck.

'Good morning, Mr Lamb. Good morning, Mr Rank.'

The two lieutenants removed their hats.

'Good morning, sir.'

Slade moved to the wheel and checked the compass course against the sailing instructions on the board. He nodded pleasantly to the master standing on the lee side of the wheel.

'I am pleased to see you up and about again, Mr Goode, but there is no need for you to resume your duties in full until you are completely fit. Isherwood can continue with the bulk of your responsibilities for a few more days; he has impressed me as a very competent young man.'

Goode gazed darkly at the captain's retreating back and muttered to himself.

'Reports, Mr Rank?' demanded Slade, standing wide-legged in the centre of the deck.

Rank repeated the morning reports of the boatswain and the carpenter. Slade nodded. 'Very good. There is a little too much rust on the roundshot in the for'ard shot garlands, Mr Lamb. Be good enough to put a few hands to work on it this forenoon.'

'Aye aye, sir.'

'Light winds again today. We will have the t'gallants, royals and stuns'ls set as soon as the hands have breakfasted.'

'Aye aye, sir.'

Midshipman Allwyn made a nervous approach, circling around so as to keep the fearsome figure of the captain on Lamb's far side as he waited for the first lieutenant to acknowledge his presence. Lamb looked down at the boy.

'Yes, Mr Allwyn?'

'Please, sir, the quarter, sir.'

'Very well. Mr Clegg! Hands to breakfast.'

The ravenous hands needed no urging. Within seconds the maindeck was clear of men as they hurtled below, eager for their burgoo and beer.

'Perhaps you would be kind enough to join me at my breakfast this morning, Mr Lamb,' said Slade, cocking an enquiring eyebrow.

Lamb was surprised. So far, the captain had issued no invitations to any of his officers to share his table for any meal and Lamb had arrived at the conclusion that his was a custom to which Slade did not subscribe. The invitation did not fill him with pleasure. The prospect of taking breakfast with a man who was a virtual stranger, who kept himself very much at a distance and who possessed a very uncertain temper was not one he viewed with delight. Refusal, of course, was out of the question.

'Delighted, sir. You are very kind.'

A round jacket and stained duck trousers were no fit clothes to grace the captain's table, Lamb decided, and as soon as Slade had left the quarterdeck he went below to forage for his second-best breeches and blue coat. He hesitated for a moment over his shirt but it had been clean on the morning before and he was loath to break his scrupulous clean-shirt schedule for a garment that apart from a little dinginess round the cuffs appeared respectable enough to present no offence.

'My, ain't we the pretty one?' said Andrews, stepping aside as Lamb made for the forward companionway. 'Breakfasting in style today, are we?'

'Yes, aft,' said Lamb, jerking his thumb upwards in that direction.

The little Scotsman made a face, whether of envy or sympathy Lamb did not enquire. The Marine at the captain's door made no face – his expression might have been carved from mahogany. Slade was affability itself, springing from his chair and guiding his guest to the table by the elbow with a warmth which Lamb found astonishing.

'I see you have taken the trouble of changing, Mr Lamb. It

was not necessary, not necessary at all but I take the complement kindly, indeed I do. Sit you down, sir, sit you down. Donovan!' This last was a muted bellow over his shoulder and Donovan came in hard on the heels of it bearing a tray. The coffee-pot was already steaming on the table and Slade poured this whilst his steward set out what Lamb took to be kedgeree and hot bacon, hot biscuits and butter still firm from its overnight storage in a water crock.

'You will be kind enough to give me your opinion of this,' said Slade, spooning a small mountain of the glutinous kedgeree on to Lamb's plate. 'It is a confection of my own devising of which I am rather proud. Salt fish, oatmeal and preserved eggs. I get my cook to make it up the night before and in these latitudes I find it cannot be beat – cold yet filling.'

Lamb tasted it gingerly. It would be somewhat improved, he thought, with the omission of the porridge and passable with the further omission of the salt fish, but catching the paternal gleam in the eye of its inventor he smacked his lips appreciatively and dug in his fork with every appearance of enthusiasm.

'Very good, is it not, Mr Lamb?' asked Slade, starting on his own heap.

'I have never tasted anything quite like it, sir,' said Lamb, with a good deal of truth. 'It has a flavour all of its own.'

Slade beamed in appreciation and the two ate in silence for a while, Lamb easing the downward passage of the sticky concoction with frequent gulps of coffee. The bacon, plain, straightforward fried bacon, was more to his liking and warm biscuits spread with butter and quince preserve even more so to his sweet tooth. Slade said little during the meal, confining himself to short remarks concerning the light winds of late, the quality of the bacon and the ineptitude of his steward, a nervous young man handsome in profile but possessed of a wicked squint full face.

Slade reached for the coffee-pot and peered inside.

'Just about a cupful left. More coffee, Mr Lamb?'

'Thank you, sir, but no,' said Lamb, sensibly.

'Well, waste not, want not.' Slade refilled his cup, leaned back in his chair, crossed his legs comfortably and produced a silver toothpick from his waistcoat pocket. He delved busily for a moment or two, examining each find with interest.

'Punishmen day today, Mr Lamb,' he said, wiping his toothpick with some fastidiousness on his sleeve before tucking it back into his pocket. 'Is it a long list?'

'Half a dozen, sir. Drunkenness mainly, except for one case of wanton damage and behaviour prejudicial to good order.'

'Wanton damage? Oh, yes, the man that pissed in Quinn's hat.' He chuckled. 'Far be it from me to condone such behaviour but I must confess I hold a sneaking regard for a man who would do that. He is clearly an individual of some spirit. Nevertheless, such activity must be discouraged, and punished he will be.' He changed tack abruptly. 'How do you find your duties, Mr Lamb? Are you quite happy? It is a formidable step, I know, from being a watch-keeping officer on a ship of the line to first lieutenant of a frigate. I remember that when it happened to me I seemed to spend a deal more time on deck than I ever did as officer of the watch and my entire day was ruled by endless lists which I had stuffed in every pocket. Mind you, I was unfortunate in that I had a perfect tyrant of a captain who made it his business to be never, ever, satisfied.'

Lamb gathered from this that he was to consider himself fortunate in having the gentle, easily satisfied Slade as his captain. 'I am perfectly content in my duties, sir, thank you, although I, too, have endless lists.'

'I am sure you have,' said Slade with a smile. 'Far be it from me to encourage complacency, Mr Lamb, but at the risk of doing so I will say that I am very satisfied with your performance to date. And with the other officers, too. So far as the hands are concerned, they all seem to have settled down remarkably well and I am particularly pleased with the gunnery. For that a large part of the credit must rest with you, Mr Lamb. You have worked hard in that area.'

Lamb smiled, pleased at this unexpected praise. 'You are very kind, sir.'

'Kind? Perhaps so, but I am also a blunt, plain-speaking man so keep up to the mark or you will hear my wrath.' He nodded at Lamb's hand. 'What happened to your finger?'

'Boarding party, sir. I lost it to a French axe.'

Slade grinned. 'Careless of you. But if you had to lose anything I daresay a little finger would be a good choice. Or a little toe. Donovan!'

Lamb took this hail to signal the end of breakfast. He pushed back his chair and ducked his head from habit as he stood, although in these spacious quarters the deck beams were well clear of his head.

'I thank you for your kindness, sir. With your permission I will attend to my duties.'

Slade smiled and flapped a large, lazy hand. 'Carry on, Mr Lamb, carry on.'

At six bells in the forenoon watch under a sky of deep, uninterrupted blue Slade mounted the quarterdeck. He took up his position in a shifting patch of shade and waited until the last bell had died away.

'Hands to witness punishment, Mr Collier.'

'Aye aye, sir. Mr Allwyn! Hands to be piped aft to witness punishment.'

'Aye aye, sir,' replied the midshipman and hurled himself down the ladder in search of the boatswain. The shrilling of the pipe was accompanied by the shouts of the boatswain's mates. 'Hands aft to witness punishment!'

The off-watch men streamed from below and joined the duty men in scrambling for the best places on the ship's boats lashed amidships and in the lee shrouds forward of the mainmast. The Marines clattered noisily up to the quarterdeck and lined up facing forward with Vaughan, his ruddy colour fully restored after his wan early days, standing stiffly resplendent at the front. Andrews and Littlefield emerged blinking from the aft companionway and took up their positions to one side of the quarterdeck ladder as the junior lieutenants and midshipmen shuffled into line at the other. Slade waited patiently for the commotion to subside, rocking backwards and forwards on toe and heel, his gaze fixed somewhere in the maintop. Lamb stood a respectful pace behind and to one side. The ship fell quiet, the wind sighing softly in the taut rigging, the sea hissing and chuckling along her sides. The captain brought his eyes down to the hushed, attentive men.

'Who is first, Mr Lamb?'

Lamb consulted his list. 'Ordinary Seaman Bean, sir. Drunk. Charged by Mr Clegg, sir.'

'Ordinary Seaman Bean!'

Bean stepped briskly forward, smart as paint, aglow with

39

virtue, shining with shaved and scrubbed cleanliness.

'Mr Clegg?

The boatswain's evidence was brief. 'Tuesday, sir, two bells of the afternoon watch. Drunk at his clew, sir.'

'What have you to say, Bean?'

'Very sorry, sir.'

'Stoppage of grog, four days. Next, Mr Lamb?'

Next was a Marine, Barrymore, also charged with drunkenness, also given four days without grog. He was quickly followed by Able Seaman Hawke, drunk; Ship's Boy Fever, drunk; Ordinary Seaman Evans, drunk; Ordinary Seaman Schmidt, drunk. All were given Slade's standard punishment for quiet, insolence-free drunkenness except for Fever who, because he was too young to have his name on the grog list, was awarded four hours extra work and a strong warning to mind his behaviour or he would be sure to grow up into a scoundrel.

'Next, Mr Lamb?'

Lamb had kept Able Seaman Hunter's hearing until last, not deliberately as the *pièce de résistance*, the top-of-the-bill act but simply because Hunter's crime was, chronologically, the last to have been committed. The assembled hands, however, who had sat quietly through the six or seven minutes devoted to the mundane business so far, now stirred themselves in anticipation of the entertainment to follow as Hunter was called forward, grinning and nodding and hugging themselves with silent glee. The seaman's crime had generated much discussion below decks and it was certain that every single man knew more of the incident than the captain was ever likely to discover. Hunter was a lively-faced young foremast topman with sparkling blue eyes and a mop of curls bleached almost white by the sun. He was neat and trim in the cleanest shirt and trousers the lower deck had been able to lay their hands on.

'Mr Quinn?'

The master-at-arms stepped forward, thrust his rattan cane beneath his arm and gave his evidence in a harsh, heavy voice, his brutal face expressionless.

'I was about my rounds at four bells of the first watch, sir, passing through the lower deck, when my hat was snatched from my head by an unseen hand, sir. I immediately demanded its return but was answered with laughter. I shone my lantern around the nearest hammocks but all the men pretended to be asleep, sir, although it was plain the miscreant had to be one of those four men. I announced that I would be back in three minutes with the ship's corporals and if my hat was not produced by then I would clear the deck and charge every man with aiding and abetting theft. When I returned with the ship's corporals, sir, there was my hat, upside down on the deck, sir, full of piss.'

A gale of delighted laughter erupted from the maindeck at these bald words. Lamb clenched his lips tight, the captain took a thoughtful pace or two round the quarterdeck with his head lowered and Vaughan's red face turned deep scarlet as he strained to control his breath. The midshipmen were openly convulsed, leaning on each others' shoulders, their hands clamped over their mouths; even the master was affected, his lips twitching as he fixed his gaze earnestly on the maintopgallant yard. Lamb mastered his lungs with an effort and stepped forward to the quarterdeck rail.

'Silence on deck there!' he roared in a carefully outraged voice. 'This is a punishment hearing on a King's ship, not a twopenny bloody playhouse! That applies to you gentlemen, too,' he added sternly, glaring down at the midshipmen as they rocked and wept beside the quarterdeck ladder. The young gentlemen froze, lips clenched, tears gleaming on their lashes, their breath held so tightly they were in danger of exploding. Lamb gave a last threatening stare at the hands' bowed heads and shaking bodies and stepped back to his place.

Slade returned from his little walk and nodded to the master-at-arms, his face rigidly solemn.

'Continue, Mr Quinn.'

Quinn jerked his head at the nearby ship's corporal who stepped forward and unrolled a scrap of sailcloth, revealing a damp, bedraggled hat which he held out at arm's length, his nose averted.

'There it is, sir,' said Quinn, 'still wet! When I demanded to know who had done this outrage nobody would admit to it, sir, all innocent and shocked, they were. But they reckoned without me, sir. I soon found out that Hunter was the culprit and I arrested him, placed him in irons and informed the first lieutenant, sir.'

Slade raised his eyebrows. 'I'm intrigued, Mr Quinn. Tell me, how did you determine it was Hunter?'

A note of pride crept into Quinn's voice. 'It was very simple, sir. I stood all eight men of that mess around a couple of buckets and gave them three minutes to piss. Only one man could not, sir, and that was Hunter. The evidence was plain, sir.'

'Or rather the lack of it!' commented Slade. 'Very ingenious, Mr Quinn – I am impressed by your initiative. Now then, Hunter, what have you to say for yourself?'

Hunter was suddenly a very worried and frightened man. So far he had been bolstered up by the admiration of his messmates and the knowledge that he was the hero of the hour but now that the moment of reckoning had arrived and the thought of the cat-o'-nine-tails loomed large his courage drained away like water through a sieve. His voice was low and hesitant.

'I didn't mean no – no disrespec', like, sir. It was a – a – a what-d'ye-call-it, a impulse, like. I'm very sorry, sir.'

Slade shook his head. His voice was cold. 'It is too late to be sorry, Hunter. This is a very serious offence – a very serious offence indeed. Wilful and deliberate damage to a superior officer's clothing, to say nothing of the affront to Mr Quinn's dignity and authority. I can find not the slightest reason for amusement in your disgusting act. You will, of course, pay for a new hat for Mr Quinn – how much would that be, Mr Quinn?'

'Thirteen shillings and sixpence, sir,' replied the master-at-arms, thoughtfully multiplying the price by a factor of two.

'Make a note of that, if you please, Mr Littlefield. Now, as to punishment. I think this is a case which calls for the punishment to fit the crime. Since you appear to be on unfamiliar terms with the heads you will clean them morning and afternoon for a week, by which time you should both be thoroughly acquainted with each other. Moreover, lest you forget why, you will wear Mr Quinn's desecrated hat each time. Pass it over to him, corporal – it can dry on his head!'

That evening after supper Lamb strolled the quiet quarterdeck with the surgeon, enjoying the peace of the hushed, sleeping ship and the clean, cool, water-washed air. A bright blanket of stars blazed coldly from a black velvet sky and the thin sliver of a moon, hard-edged and serene, brushed the dark water with silver and cast shifting patterns of black and white on the deck. Andrews, who had sailed with Slade before, was speaking of the captain's reluctance to use the cat, a fact which Lamb had already gleaned from a study of the previous voyage's entries in the punishment book.

'It was the only occasion that I ever saw the grating rigged and then his hand was forced,' said the little Scotsman as they paced slowly beside the traffrail. 'In the letter of the law – the strict letter of the law (although I suppose there is nothing else) – it was an assault, a blow, hands laid upon a superior officer, a crime that could merit a hanging. In the actuality the man merely raised his arm to ward off the bos'un's hand as he was being pushed and shoved and hustled to his place in the impatient manner that bos'uns seem to acquire with their whistles. To protect the boils on his back, the man claimed, and indeed his shoulders were a mass of inflamed pustules for which I had been treating him for some time, and gave evidence to that effect at his hearing. Even so, the man's offence was put so strongly and so adamantly by the bos'un that the captain had little choice but to accept his word. He could do little else without it appearing that the bos'un had lied (although it was clear to me, for one, that there was animosity abroad) and the man was awarded a dozen lashes. The captain was so furious with the bos'un, however, that for some time afterwards he would only speak to him by way of an officer or a midshipman, by proxy as it were. Even now, if you are in any way observant, you will notice a distinct coolness in the captain's manner to Mr Clegg.'

'So far as the cat is concerned I am totally in agreement with his way of thinking,' said Lamb. 'I believe that a very firm hand is needed in order to maintain discipline, especially with some of the out-and-out villains that find their way below decks, but to flog the flesh from a man's back does little good, I feel. It ruins the good hands and only makes the brutish ones worse. You can go too far the other way of course; if wrongdoers are treated too softly and leniently the crew will only hold the captain in contempt. No, the middle course is the best. The men will always respect a stern captain, even a hard captain, providing he is no tyrant and is a fair man.'

43

'I agree with you entirely. Captain Slade is certainly a stern man and he probably thinks of himself as a hard man but I would not say that fairness is a strong trait with him. He acts too often on anger and impulse and in those circumstances fairness is likely to go by the board. But he is not a cruel man nor a vindictive one and I have on occasion known him to explode with rage at some unfortunate officer for a trifling misdemeanour, damn and curse him to hell at the top of his voice and then later, after reflection, politely beg the officer to do some little task for him, by way of apology. For anyone with a philosophical turn of mind he is quite transparent.'

'You sound as if you hold him in some affection.'

'Affection?' Andrews shook his head. 'No, not I. I have been at the rough end of his tongue too often to hold him in any affection.'

'But you are still sailing under him, even so.'

Andrews gave a short laugh. 'Yes, I am. Well, perhaps I have a sneaking regard for the man. Or it might be a case of better the devil you know, et cetera.'

The two men fell silent, leaning on the taffrail in companionable proximity, each with a foot raised to a little truck of the six-pounder gun-carriage between them, gazing out over the dim, white wake stretching back over the water. The rounded belly of the frigate rolled in the long, gentle swell, the stern rose and fell. Forward, in the darkness of the deck, the glass was turned and the sentry sounded the bell. Four strokes – half-way through the first watch. Lamb stared unseeing over the taffrail, his mind empty, the final stroke of the bell sounding in his ears long after the last resonance had faded.

Andrews stretched and yawned. 'It is time I was seeking my pillow,' he said, in his soft, Lothian burr. 'An old man like me needs his sleep.'

Lamb smiled. The surgeon was all of thirty.

'Good night, Bones.'

'Good night, Mr Lamb.'

Thirty-two days out of Portsmouth, three days from Antigua – two, if the wind freshened – the *Adroit* had been making painfully slow progress under light winds, breezes often falling to the merest zephyr, a whisper in the slack, sullen sails. Slade had done what he could, which was little enough; he had set every stitch of canvas available – skysails, studdingsails alow and aloft, the seldom-used, light moonrakers – ordered the pumps to be played on the lower sails as far as they could reach and water manhandled aloft to wet the canvas above, edged the frigate a few miles north in the hope of finding new winds and, in the ship's quieter moments, he had tried a little surreptitious whistling as he paced the quarterdeck, gazing upwards. Several times, when the wind was at its slackest and the frigate had scarcely enough way on her to leave her galley rubbish behind, Lamb had seen him looking thoughtfully at the ship's boats, clearly considering the notion of assisting the ship's progress with muscle power. The hands, who missed nothing, became alarmed, darting dark looks at the boats and muttering beneath their breath. Their fears, as it turned out, were groundless; after each little pause for breath the wind would come sighing back, lifting the sails sufficiently to make the use of boats difficult and pointless but not enough to remove the men from their tenterhooks.

The frigate had been sailing alone in her own circle of sea for many days now; no other vessel had been sighted since two days out of Madeira and Lamb had the curious feeling, looking back and looking forward, that he had been and would be tied to the ship for ever. Within a few days of leaving harbour the face of every man on board had become so familiar to him that they might have been sailing together since time out of memory. The days merged one into the other with little to mark their passing in the unvarying routine of a man-of-war at sea except for the occasional small landmark, a bloody accident during gun-practice or Slade loudly ordering a quartermaster from the quarterdeck in outraged disgust at his involuntary fart, all quickly forgotten. Watch followed watch, four hours on and four hours off, the hands varying their night watches with a two-hour duty spell in the dog-watches in order for one watch not to suffer continually the detested middle watch. The routine of the day never varied; holystoning, breakfast, dinner, grog, quarters, grog, supper, sleep. In between came gun-practice, painting, shot-cleaning, punishment, boat drill, clothing inspections and on fine evenings dancing, singing and skylarking on the forecastle. The ship inched her way along the

flagging Trades, the capricious winds doing little to dispel the
fetid air below decks. The bilge stank, the orlop deck stank,
the beef and pork stank, the beer and water, though 'still
plentiful, grew foul. Nothing could be done about the water
but Slade ordered the beer to be replaced with Black Strap,
the Navy's rough, red wine from the Mediterranean. The men
sipped and grimaced and spat but drank it. Hatchways fore
and aft were left open and a canvas contrivance rigged to
funnel the warm air through the ship, causing some of the old
die-hards to mutter angrily about draughts and chills and the
ague. The surgeon advised that the orlop deck be washed
daily with vinegar in the water to chase away contagion and
from then on the acrid smell of acetic acid overlaid the ship's
other odours.

'At the risk of encouraging you to become lax, Mr Lamb,'
said the captain, 'I can say that I am reasonably satisfied with
today's inspection – reasonably satisfied, mark you.'

'Thank you, sir,' said Lamb gravely, touching his hat in
acknowledgement of this fulsome praise.

The two men had just emerged from the darkness of the
forward hatchway trailed by a short line of warrant officers
and petty officers, all wearing the rigidly solemn expression
befitting the occasion of the captain's weekly inspection of
their domains. The air was hot and dry and a shaft of strong
sunlight that had managed to insinuate itself between the
foremast and mainmast sails cast sharp, moving shadows on
the *Adroit*'s spotless deck as she heeled gently in the shallow
swell of the western Atlantic. Slade had been exceptionally
thorough on this Sunday, inspecting every compartment and
deck in the ship from stem to stern. Moving up and down
ladders, poking around in the galley, bread-room, spirit-room,
gunroom, cockpit, sail-locker, cable-tier and magazine, dragging a train of concerned faces behind him as he went, the
concern gradually decreasing in segments as the captain
moved out of one particular officer's area of responsibility and
passed into the next. He had prodded and pried at the
frigate's knees and futtocks, knelt and peered through the
bilge trap at the few inches of stinking water beneath,
bellowed in disgust at the sight of a dead rat on a midshipman's sea-chest (the corpse carefully positioned by a

playful colleague into a semblance of comfortable ease, on its back with its two pairs of legs crossed) and roared jovially at the patients in the surgeon's sick-bay. Lamb had listed the comments, complaints and orders that Slade had tossed to him as he moved briskly through the ship and had privately sifted those which he considered sensible and practical from those about which he had no intention of taking action. He had already learned, to his advantage, that Slade's memory concerning petty details was far from watertight.

Slade walked aft along the weather side of the maindeck, passing the seamen assembled in their separate divisions behind their lieutenants and midshipmen, their toes lined up along the seams of the deck. He moved slowly along the front row of men, casting quick up-and-down glances at the closely shaven brown faces and neat, clean rig with shining cutaway shoes or bare, horny feet. By this time he knew many of the hands by name and from time to time he would pause to criticize or exercise his wit.

'How are the piles today, Knight?' he asked one ancient seaman, his voice booming.

Knight's face flooded with colour. ''m all right, sir, thankee,' he mumbled, mortified at this public airing of his secret shame and the surgeon's report.

'Good, good. Well, try not to ride any horses in the near future,' Slade advised, chuckling and moved on, leaving amused grins behind him on the faces of Knight's neighbours. He was in his element here, full of bonhomie on the swaying, sun-dappled deck.

'What have you there, O'Toole, tobacco? Toothache! Have you seen Mr Andrews? Cowardly bugger! Put his name down for the surgeon, Mr Lamb. Get those toe-nails trimmed, Hobday – you could stab a man to death with those weapons. Look at this man, Mr Lamb; he resembles a length of wet rope. Stand up straight, man – have you no bones in your body? And how do you like being a topman, Bryant? How is he coming along, Mr Ball? Splendid, well done, Bryant.'

He stopped abruptly at the sight of a man in the rear of Collier's division and turned to Lamb with a sharp frown of disapproval on his face.

'This man is dirty, Mr Lamb. He has not shaved, his face

needs a good wash and his shirt is filthy. Take his name, the idle bugger. It is Watson, ain't it?'

'Wilson, sir,' said Lamb.

'Wilson, yes. Mr Collier!'

The fourth lieutenant hurriedly approached, a worried expression on his thin face. He touched his hat. 'Sir?'

'What the devil do you mean by allowing this man to present himself to me in this filthy condition? Could you not see his shirt – his whiskers? He is a disgrace to your division. Use a keener eye in future, Mr Collier.'

'Yes, sir. I am very sorry, sir.'

Collier cast a malevolent glance at Wilson and returned to his station, his face crimson. Lamb gave the seaman a close look as he passed by; the gleam of stubble on his chin was only too apparent in the strong sunlight and by the look of his face it had been some time since he had used soap and water.

'Sir! Sir!' grunted Wilson as Lamb moved on after the captain. Lamb swung round, astonished that a man should have the effrontery to speak uninvited on this most formal of occasions. Wilson had stepped forward out of his line, his hands held out appealingly to Lamb, tears coursing their way down the dirt and stubble of his cheeks.

'It warn't my fault, sir. They didn't tell me, sir. I would've shaved if'n they told me, sir. Please, sir, don't let 'em flog me, sir.'

Lamb was shocked, both at the display of undisciplined behaviour and the man's tearful appeal. He glanced at Collier; the lieutenant was staring rigidly to the front, obviously wanting no part in this embarrassment. 'Shut your mouth!' Lamb snapped, 'and get back into line or you will be in worse trouble.' He turned and strode off to catch up with Slade.

Wilson was one of those unfortunate men who should never have been passed as fit by the receiving-ship's doctor. He was a large, shambling figure of a man, slow and stumbling of speech with the intelligence of a small child. More of a nuisance than an asset he was easily confused by the simplest of orders and as a consequence suffered a great deal of impatient prodding and cuffing from exasperated petty officers. Lamb felt a good deal of sympathy for him; he had often seen him crouching alone on the forecastle in his off-watch hours, hugging his knees, a sad, bewildered man trying to escape the taunts and teasing of his messmates. Evidently they had thought it playful not to remind him that today was the one day in the week when a clean-shaven face and a clean shirt were demanded and, lost in his own dim world, their own preparations had been of no significance to him. Collier was at fault here; clearly, he had failed to inspect his men properly prior to the captain's inspection. Lamb resolved to have a quiet word with the captain about Wilson; certainly he would not be flogged for his offence but then any punishment would only confuse his child-like mind even further.

Lamb followed Slade up the quarterdeck ladder and took up his position to one side and a pace behind the captain as the hands were piped aft. Today Slade opted for a reading from the Bible rather than the Articles and he stood turning over the pages searching for his place as the men squatted and knelt and made themselves comfortable. His choice was Psalm 23, which he delivered in a ringing, ecclesiastical voice, his speech carefully attenuated with long, piously significant pauses. Lamb stared gravely ahead, the familiar words rising unbidden in his mind to pair with the captain's careful delivery, his eyes resting on the brown, attentive, upturned faces of the men below. They sat quietly, their expressions seemingly engrossed, but Lamb doubted if a single one of them was having his heart and mind uplifted by the ancient phrases, in spite of Slade's histrionic endeavours; more likely, he thought, their minds were more basically occupied with thoughts of dinner and the make-and-mend afternoon to follow.

Slade finished his reading, smoothed the ribbon in his Bible and reverently closed it. He raised his head, his glance caught Lamb's eye and for a moment, the briefest of instants, the expression glinting there was plain: Tiresome nonsense! He said instead, 'Dismiss the hands to their duties, Mr Lamb,' and looked on as the men scampered forward, pushing and shoving, relieved that the irksome business of remaining still and quiet was over for another week and eager for their beef, onions, peas and duff. Lamb decided that this was a good opportunity to raise the question of leniency for Wilson while the matter was still fresh in the captain's mind. He stepped forward and touched his hat.

'By your leave, sir.'

Slade looked at him and frowned. Lieutenants, even first lieutenants, were not encouraged to speak to the captain uninvited without very good reasons.

'Yes, Mr Lamb. What is it?'

'It is about Wilson, sir, the man who was put on the defaulters' list for – '

'The dirty one, yes,' said Slade impatiently. 'What about him?'

'The man is of very low intelligence, sir. In fact, not to put too fine a point on it, sir, he is close to being an idiot. With respect, sir, on the matter of the man's punishment, I feel that it would be better – '

'Mr Lamb,' interrupted Slade, with an edge to his voice. 'I am well aware of Wilson's lack of intelligence. It is his brawn I require, not his brains and if you are trying to suggest that I should grade a man's punishment according to his intelligence then let me disabuse you of the notion. All the time a man serves on a King's ship he will conform to Admiralty law and Naval custom and practice, no matter if he has the brains of a cockroach and I will not have my officers suggesting otherwise. Do you understand me, sir?' His voice had risen in volume as he spoke and his last few words were uttered in an angry bellow that carried the length of the ship. Lamb felt the warm blood rush to his face and flood his checks with bright colour.

'Yes, sir,' he said tersely.

'Good. One last word. You came dangerously close to stepping into my province then. Need I say more?'

'No, sir. It certainly was not my intention, sir.'

'I am relieved to hear it.'

Slade descended the ladder to the maindeck and turned into his quarters, banging the door shut behind him. The ship seemed suddenly very quiet. Lamb thrust his shaking hands behind his back and clasped his fingers to hide their tremble. Ball, the officer of the watch, was staring with deep interest at the empty expanse of water to larboard, young Bird was studying his shoes and the helmsmen's grave, expressionless faces were fixed firmly forward. The shame and fury of his public humiliation bubbled over and he descended to the maindeck and strode up and down in a fury beside the lee row of guns, thankful that the hands were at their dinners. Damn the man, he thought angrily, did he have to shout and bawl like a bloody Cheapside pieman? Was that the way to treat his first lieutenant, his most senior officer, bellowing at him in public as if he was a snotty-nosed midshipman? Damn, damn, damn the man and damn that blockhead Wilson, too – Slade could strip the flesh from his back for all he bloody well cared!

The vigour of Lamb's strides gradually reduced his anger if not his sense of mortification and after half a dozen or so turns along the deck the notion slowly crept up on him that perhaps he had made a fool of himself entirely at his own doing. Slade was right, of course; he had come close to overreaching himself. Punishment was the captain's sole prerogative and he had been foolish and presumptuous to make even the mildest of suggestions in that area. Even so, Slade could have checked him with a quiet, tactful word instead of exploding in that ridiculous fashion. Damn the man! Should he beg the captain's pardon? No, he was buggered if he would eat any more humble pie. Let matters stay as they are – he had been foolish, the captain had rebuked him, let that be an end to the matter. If Slade decided to be vindictive and harp on it – or even log him – that would be his affair. Lamb promised himself that he would maintain a quiet, dignified, courteous air no matter how great the provocation. Comforted by this resolution he turned as he reached the forecastle and suddenly became aware of a man matching his pace along the other side of the ship's boats nested amidships. It was Wilson, grinning at him slack-jawed as he peered over the launch. Lamb stopped short and glared.

'What the devil are you grinning at, Wilson, you ape?' he demanded.

The seaman darted around the boats and came close to Lamb, still grinning widely, his dropped jaw exposing his sparse, blackened teeth. He prodded at his chin with a finger the size of a marlin-spike.

'Look, sir, look,' he mumbled in his thick voice.

Lamb peered at him, puzzled, and then suddenly saw the

reason for the man's proud grin. He had shaved. Moreover, he had changed his shirt for one that was passably clean. Lamb shook his head and sighed wearily.

'Well done, Wilson. It was a pity you did not think to do that a little earlier. You would have saved us both a great deal of trouble.'

Wilson's smile spread large and a throaty chuckle of pleasure at these kind words rumbled from his massive chest. He dug a hairy knuckle into his forehead and shambled off towards the forecastle. Lamb shook his head again and made for the aft companionway, determined to sit at the wardroom table and eat with every appearance of normality.

Dinner in the gunroom was a curiously silent affair with the officers paying a good deal of close attention to their plates and none at all to Lamb who, in spite of his resolution, found it impossible to start any sort of conversation, certain that his words would sound forced. Only the surgeon, in happy ignorance of the reason for his colleagues' tactful silence, spoke to Lamb and even that was but once, to point out that Lamb's cuff was draped across the butter dish. Lamb chewed moodily at his tough beef, ate little and drank more wine than was his custom at this time of the day. He picked at his figgy-dowdy, debated once more whether to attempt to start a conversation, decided against it, rose and left the gunroom without a word, quite certain that his absence would lighten its atmosphere. He had probably given the strong impression that he was sulking, he thought, flinging himself on to his cot. He grinned wryly at the familiar deck-beams; well, he had been, had he not? He turned on to his side, punched his pillow and within a few seconds was asleep.

Make-and-mend was not an order to which most captains applied the strict meaning of the phrase and while some of the *Adroit*'s hands were squatting quietly at their whittling, embroidering or tailoring others were stretched out fast asleep, oblivious to the noise and activity of the younger and more energetic seamen performing handstands, turning cartwheels and generally showing off their muscles and working up a sweat. Lamb stood alone in the shade cast by the mizzentopsail and watched the acrobatics on the forecastle with a slightly jaundiced eye. An hour of deep sleep had left him with a foul mouth and a gritty-eyed feeling of exhaustion but he knew from past experience that these unpleasantnesses would disappear within a short while of walking the upper decks. He felt considerably easier in his mind now – his anger and indignation had gone while he slept – although the memory of the captain's outburst still hovered at the edge of his mind, occasionally edging in to produce a warm flush and a certain heaviness in the pit of his stomach; he did not look forward to meeting Slade again. In an effort to shake off his gloom he stepped across to Ball and spent a few minutes discussing the possibility of dipping a sail into the sea if the wind slackened further in order to make a safe pond in which the hands could splash and skylark. At the sound of the captain's door opening and shutting he and Ball moved across to the lee side where the pair of them touched their hats in salute as Slade put his foot on the quarterdeck. The captain glanced in their direction and raised a beckoning finger.

'A moment of your time, if you please, Mr Lamb.' He turned and walked to the mizzen shrouds.

Lamb set his chin as he walked across the quarterdeck. Remember, he told himself – be calm, dignified, courteous. He removed his hat as he came up to the captain.

'Yes, sir?'

Slade said nothing for a moment or two. He stared out over the side, clasped his hands behind his back and rocked to and fro on his heels for a few seconds. He cleared his throat.

'I have given a little thought to your – your remarks concerning the man Wilson.' He paused and patted his hands together behind his back. 'Far be it for me to ignore the – um – respectful suggestions of my first lieutenant, particularly so when it concerns the well-being of an unfortunate creature like Wilson; such poor brutes too rarely have anyone to speak up for them. I have given the matter some thought, as I said, and you may strike the man's name from your list. He will, however, present himself to his divisional officer before breakfast every morning for a week, clean and properly shaved. Arrange that with Mr Collier, if you will. That is all, Mr Lamb.'

'Thank you, sir,' said Lamb, grave-faced, inwardly bubbling with delight. 'You are very kind, sir.'

He turned, replaced his hat and walked back to his own side

of the quarterdeck, his step light. It had hardly been a fulsome apology but it was the closest thing to it he could expect. 'Respectful suggestions' indeed! He paced to and fro beneath the lee mizzen shrouds, humming beneath his breath.

Chapter 3

Far above the early-morning quarterdeck, with a back resting comfortably against the maintopgallant mast as it circled gently in the soft, southerly wind, Ordinary Seaman Lilley, starboard watch, removed his musing gaze from the shimmering sea to starboard and swept it slowly round to the no less shimmering sea to larboard, as he had done with dutiful regularity every sixty seconds or so ever since he had taken his post. He was not consciously and actively seeking out distant sails; uppermost in his mind was the basic and increasingly urgent desire to empty his bowels and from time to time he removed his searching eyes from the sea and turned them thoughtfully down to the bows of the ship, wherein lay the heads. Such relief as lay there, however, would not be his for at least another hour and each time he would resignedly tighten his buttocks and bring his gaze back to the sea. From long experience he knew that any object that appeared within his field of vision – a distant flash of a sail lifting on a wave, a faint plume of smoke, a slight discontinuity on the line of the horizon – would immediately register on his eye even if his mind was several thousand miles astern or concentrated more locally as it was now on his uneasily pouting sphincter. To Lilley one patch of blue sea looked remarkably like any other patch of blue sea but this particular area of ocean, the lookouts had been informed, was a stretch of sea much favoured by powerful privateers hoping to snatch up outward-bound merchantmen as they followed the parallel of their route to the West Indies. Merchantmen, the captain had told Lamb with an ill-concealed sneer, were accustomed to clinging tightly to a line of latitude for fear of losing it and the corsairs were only too happy to take full advantage of the practice, picking them off like hens from a roost. Lines of latitude meant nothing to Lilley but his orders had been plain enough and he was a conscienti-

55

ous and intelligent seaman. Something caught at his vision as his eyes swept round to larboard and his head snapped back to the direction of his sight, his eyes narrowed between his shading hands, his bowels forgotten. Yes, there it was! He caught the gleam of sunlight on bleached canvas as the distant ship hoisted her topgallants.

'Deck there!' hailed Lilley, peering down at the foreshortened figures on the tiny quarterdeck. 'Sail ahoy! Fine on the larboard bow!'

Lamb crooked his finger at Bird, the duty midshipman. 'Mr Bird, my respects to the captain and inform him – ' The sound of the captain's door banging shut stopped him short. 'Belay that. The captain is on his way.'

Slade raised his eyebrows to Lamb before he was at the top of the quarterdeck ladder. 'Did I hear a hail from the lookout, Mr Lamb?'

'Yes, sir,' said Lamb, saluting. 'I was on the point of sending Mr Bird to you, sir. A sail, fine on the larboard bow, sir.'

Slade nodded. 'Early days yet, but you may as well send up a good man with a glass.'

'With your permission, sir, I'll take a glass aloft myself,' said Lamb.

'Yes, do that, Mr Lamb.'

Lamb reached out and took his telescope from the rack. He removed his hat and handed it to the midshipman.

'Guard that with your life, Mr Bird,' he growled, with deep menace.

'Oh, I will, sir,' beamed the boy, delighted with the honour and tucked the hat securely under his arm with such a determined grip that it was crushed shapeless before Lamb had reached the mainmast shrouds.

Long legs, shoes and lack of exercise made Lamb keenly aware that to the eyes of the watching seamen his upward climb was slow and clumsy, especially so to the young topmen who would have raced up the ratlines in a twinkling and reached the maintopgallant yard long before Lamb had heaved himself into the maintop. He consoled himself, however, with the thought that his sedate pace was perfectly in keeping with his rank and climbed grimly on, to squat warm and panting beside the lookout who had courteously moved a few feet out along the yard. Lilley silently stretched out an arm in the direction of the sail. Lamb screwed up his eyes against the brilliant glare of the sea, wiped his dripping eyebrows with his sleeve and stared along the line of Lilley's pointing finger. The tiniest scrap of pale yellow bobbed and dipped amidst the shimmer.

'By God, you have keen eyes, Lilley,' he said and reached for the telescope tucked beneath his belt. The seaman gave a shy smile and rubbed his nose. Lamb pushed his back hard against the warm timber of the mast in order to anchor his body firmly against the slow dip and roll of the ship and directed his instrument across the shining waste of water. Something swam hazily into his vision; he adjusted the focal length a trifle and a brig sprang sharply into view. He grunted, seeing immediately that she was French; with the elongated shape given to her by her short yards her nationality was quite unmistakable. He attempted to count her gun-ports but the range was too far and her image too small; eighteen guns, he guessed, carronades probably, with long guns at bow and stern. The devastating little carronades had lately come much to the fore in French ships and a brig of this size could quite possibly be carrying twenty-four-pounders or even thirty-two-pounders. Was she wearing? He lowered his glass, wiped the sweat from his eyes and levelled it again. Yes, she was going about, turning into the wind. What was that astern of her? By God, another brig! – no, another two brigs! He hastily scanned the sea for more vessels. No more, thank Christ – three was more than enough. He gave a guilty start as Slade's voice floated up from the deck a hundred and thirty feet below.

'Are you quite comfortable up there or would you like a hammock sent up?'

'Coming down now, sir,' Lamb bellowed in reply and swung himself into the shrouds. He paused and looked up at Lilley. 'There are three French privateers out there, Lilley. Keep a close eye on them.'

'Aye aye, sir,' said the seaman mournfully, shifting his buttocks uncomfortably against the turbulent pressure within.

'Well, Mr Lamb?' snapped Slade with an impatient edge to his voice as his first lieutenant returned to the quarterdeck.

'Three French brigs, sir,' said Lamb, slightly breathless from his hasty descent. 'Quite unmistakable. Powerful-looking vessels, too – eighteen guns, I thought, sir; carronades, too, I shouldn't wonder. They seem none too perturbed at the sight of us.'

Slade nodded. 'Waiting there for some hapless merchant-man to wander along, no doubt. Well, we must see what we can do to blunt their ardour.' He turned his head to bark at the quartermaster. 'Luff up. Steer full and by.'

'Full and by it is, sir.'

'Man the braces! Haul sheets and tacks!'

Slade waited until the yards were braced sharp round and the frigate was settled on her new tack with the wind on her larboard bow and then nodded pleasantly to Lamb, his large, red face beaming with good humour.

'Thank God there is a bit of life in the wind today. With a little luck our gun-crews may begin to earn their pay at last. Belay that holystoning, Mr Lamb. Set the t'gallants and royals, if you please, and then stow the hammocks and send the men to breakfast. Meantime, I shall get Donovan to finish my shave – in cold water now, no doubt.'

With the frigate heading west-south-west and the wind coming almost directly from the south, she was sailing about as close to the wind as she was capable. With the wind sufficiently light to allow her to spread most of her available canvas yet brisk enough to belly her sails, the *Adroit* swooped over the long, shallow swell with singing rigging and a moderate heel. Lamb sent Isherwood up to the masthead with a telescope and went below for a hasty breakfast of burgoo, cold ham and beer. He was back on the quarterdeck in time to watch Slade mount the ladder and touch his hat to the quarterdeck with an angry scowl on his face and a small, red-stained square of paper stuck to the point of his chin.

'That bloody squint-eyed servant of mine will have to go,' he exclaimed, tenderly fingering his little piece of paper. 'It is damned unnerving seeing his eye fixed on your ear while he scrapes away at your throat. God damn it, I'm bleeding like a stuck pig!'

'A dab of seawater is what you need, sir,' suggested Lamb. 'Mr Bird! Find a hand to draw up a bucket of seawater for the captain.'

Two gallons of Atlantic Ocean were duly drawn up and

deferentially presented to the captain who solemnly dipped a corner of his handkerchief into it and applied the healing liquid to his chin. The square of paper fell away, the smear of dried blood was wiped off and the little nick oozed no more. Happy to have staunched the flow of his body's vital fluid Slade thrust his damp handkerchief back into his cuff and beamed genially upon the world.

'Your glass, if you please, Mr Rank,' he requested, holding out his hand. He scrambled up, nimbly enough, into the lee mizzen shrouds and directed the telescope at the distant group of vessels, staying unmoving for several minutes, his leg hooked through the ropes, his portly body leaning well out over the sea. Lamb took his glass and by standing on the carriage of one of the quarterdeck carronades he was by virtue of his height able to sight the telescope over the stowed hammocks and obtain a clear view of the trio of ships. Isherwood had been sending down regular reports since he was sent aloft and it had soon become clear that the privateers were neither fleeing nor advancing but were apparently content to hold the wind and await the approach of the frigate. Lamb focussed his telescope on the most leeward of the brigs and moved his glass slowly along her length before turning his attention to the other two vessels. They were all much of a muchness; large, heavy brigs with white-painted masts and narrow sails, carrying nine guns to each side; fast, well armed and agile. Lamb was puzzled; why the devil would they want to tangle with a man-of-war? He closed his telescope and stepped down to the deck as Slade lowered himself from the lee shrouds.

Slade looked at Lamb, his eyes narrowed, frowning. 'It appears as if they intend to wait for us to come up,' he remarked. 'Are they deliberately seeking action, I wonder?'

'That is the impression I gathered, sir,' said Lamb.

'Perhaps they feel there is safety in numbers. To a certain extent that is true, no doubt, but what they hope to gain by taking on a man-o'-war is beyond me. They cannot expect to find much profit in it, that's a fact; all they will get from us is a bloody nose!'

'It may be, sir, that they intend to have a little sport with us. They may feel that with three of them there is little risk and to maul a British frigate would be vastly amusing.'

'Sport?' snorted Slade. 'I'll give them more bloody sport than they bargained for. If it is entertainment they want – '

'Deck there!' Isherwood's voice filtered down from the crosstrees over the rush of wind and sea and the slap and creak of rope and timber. 'They have hoisted colours, sir. One American, one Dutch and one British, sir!'

The colour rushed to Slade's cheeks. 'By God, they are making fun of us, the insolent bastards! I'll teach them to thumb their noses at me, the impudent fucking whoresons!' He whirled round and glared at the master. 'Mr Goode, put me in reach of those bloody Frogs! Up your helm, quartermaster! Mr Lamb, beat to quarters! Clear fore and aft!'

The stentorian bellows of the petty officers and the invigorating rattle of the drum galvanized the ship into furious activity. The men ran to their guns as the boatswain's mates swarmed aloft with chains to reinforce the securings of the yards, followed less surely by the Marines assigned to the swivel-guns in the tops. The little wooden wheels of the gun-carriages squealed and rumbled on the planking as they were hauled inboard, crunching over the damp sand spread underfoot.

'More water on that screen there!' called Slade, pointing to the damp canvas draped around the main hatchway. The hatch on the deck below was also open to give access to the magazine and allow the gunner's cartridges to be passed up to the powder-boys with their little wooden boxes and Slade had no wish for sparks to find their way below.

'Those boarding nets are too tight – slacken them off!' he roared at the men draping the wide-meshed nets along the sides. 'Mr Lamb! Look to those bloody nets, if you please!'

Along the sides the gun-crews were milling about their charges, secured now to the ring-bolts amidships, the three-and-a-half-pound cloth cartridges nestling snugly between their wads at the base of the barrels, the twelve-pound roundshot, carefully selected for lack of rust and perfection of roundness, rammed hard down on top. As each gun was loaded, ready to be run out, the men placed their implements parallel to the guns on the deck and waited for their orders, three men on either side of the gun facing each other, the gun-captains with their faces turned to the quarterdeck. Lamb ran up the ladder to the quarterdeck and saluted the captain.

'All guns loaded with single shot, ready to be run out, sir.'

Slade nodded. 'Very good. We will take advantage of our greater range while we can, Mr Lamb. I do not intend to allow them free use of their carronades if I can avoid it.'

Lamb thought that Slade was being eminently sensible; at point-blank range, up to three hundred yards, the short, squat carronades could cause enormous damage with their huge shot, far more than the long-guns of the *Adroit* with an extreme range of about one mile. The frigate also carried carronades, eighteen-pounders, on her forecastle and quarterdeck, but in the eyes of the Lord of the Admiralty she was rated only by the traditional long-guns ranged each side of her single gun-deck and even if she had bristled with extra carronades from stem to stern, a thirty-six-gun frigate she would obdurately remain.

Lamb returned to the maindeck and paced up and down between the larboard guns and the ship's boats in one direction and the ship's boats and the starboard guns in the other. From time to time he peered over the starboard bow at the trio of brigs as they lay-to, as yet well out of range, the false flags snapping impudently from their mainmasts. A false flag might well be a recognized and legitimate *ruse de guerre* but for them to fly the colours of three different nations – one British! – on a squadron of privateers so unmistakably French indicated a puckish sense of humour. At last the three vessels decided to make a move and as the *Adroit* came to within four miles or so they formed a line abreast and sailed slowly and directly for the frigate under topsails and topgallantsails, their lower courses furled. Thirty minutes should see us within range, thought Lamb, and turned his attention again to his main responsibility, the long-guns.

He paced slowly along the starboard line of guns, the centre of each muzzle exactly one hundred inches from those of its neighbours on either side. The heavy monsters, loaded and waiting for the captain's order to run them out, required only a tug at the lanyards of their flint-locks to send twelve pounds of iron flying a mile over the water. This was the first ship on which he had served where flint-locks were fitted to the guns; he was more accustomed to the powder-filled quill or the traditional slow-match applied to the touch-hole. Lamb had eyed these innovations somewhat doubtfully when he first saw them. The bright, instant spark that flew from the flint on to the priming pan at the first pull of the lanyard had impressed him but even now, after many hours of gun-practice, he was not fully confident of their reliability. He had known them to fail on odd occasions; the flints broke or fell out of their holdings, the wheels jammed, the lanyards rotted and snapped. On the *Adroit*, by Slade's orders, all flints were doubled up and a slow-match, lit and coiled ready in its bucket, was placed beside each gun.

As he walked the length of the gun-deck, pausing from time to time to have a word with a gun-captain or to pass a comment to the crews, he made a point of using the names of those that he knew. It was a trifling thing but it pleased the men inordinately and a series of beams and grins and chuckles paralleled his progress along the line of guns. Bates was the oldest and most experienced gun-captain on the ship, a wrinkled, toothless giant of a man who had served a gun for more than forty years and was somewhat deaf as a result. He knuckled his forehead as Lamb stopped at his gun.

'Hello, Bates,' roared Lamb into his ear. 'Getting the hang of things, are you? If you are not quite sure what to do, I am sure Wickham can advise you.' Wickham was an ex-farm hand with rather more vigour below his chin than above it and was the bane of Bates' existence. The gun-crew thought Lamb's comment vastly amusing and Wickham beamed with delight. The old gun-captain scowled and cast Wickham a ferocious glare.

'I've forgotten more about guns 'an 'e'll ever fookin' learn,' he growled but Lamb had moved on, pretending not to hear.

He mounted the few steps leading to the forecastle to check on the bow-chasers, the six-pounder long-guns that were part of Ball's divisional responsibility. The plump lieutenant was there now, shielding his eyes as he stared at the oncoming brigs, now about two miles distant. He glanced round as Lamb approached and smiled.

'Hello, Matthew. Some warm work ahead of us, I think.'

'Yes. With luck it might sweat a few pounds off you.'

'God, I hope not. I am all skin and bone as it is. Hello, I see our gallant captain has emerged in full splendour.'

Lamb glanced at the quarterdeck. Slade had changed into his best coat, the gilt of his epaulettes winking in the sunlight, his sword-belt buckled round his waist.

'It is time I went,' said Lamb and descended to the maindeck and hurried aft along the larboard row of guns, loaded and ready to be run out but manned on this side only by the gun-captains. He took up his station forward of the mainmast and waited for Slade to give his orders. The ship was very quiet, the faces of the lieutenants, quarter-gunners and gun-captains turned towards the quarterdeck. Slade had drawn his sword and laid it across the quarterdeck rail, its point directed at the oncoming brigs, now little more than a mile away. He raised his sword high in the air, the sunlight flashing from its bright, polished steel.

'Give me of your best, my lads!' he shouted. 'There will be no profit in this but you can each earn a bucketful of glory.'

A thunderous cheer lifted from the deck and the fighting tops. Lamb smiled thinly. There will be precious little of either commodity, he thought, even if by some miracle we take all three vessels. The Admiralty took little notice of actions with licensed pirates, no matter how creditable the battle or the outcome, saving their recognitions and promotions for affairs between regular men-of-war. It was a short-sighted view, in Lamb's opinion, and led to some captains ignoring opportunities of coming to grips with privateers.

'Stand by the starboard guns!' roared Slade and then, after a two-second pause for dramatic effect, 'Open the ports! Run out the guns!'

The port lanyards had been gripped for some minutes in anticipation of this order and the gun-ports lifted on their hinges almost as one, throwing distorted rectangles of sunlight on to the long shadow cast by the hammock-topped bulwarks. The deck's five-inch planking trembled as the gun-carriages trundled their one-and-a-half tons of iron down the slight slope of the tilting deck, the black muzzles of the guns poking like a row of enormous snouts over the ship's side. At the same instant, as if they had been waiting for this unfriendly signal, the brigs separated; the nearest, weathermost vessel turned into the wind and headed across the frigate's bows, the centre vessel edged nearer to the wind and pointed her nose directly at the *Adroit*'s stem, while the leeward brig continued her course, with the obvious intention of crossing the frigate's vulnerable stern. The gun-ports on those sides of the privateers visible from the *Adroit* swung open – raggedly, Lamb was pleased to note – and the dull gleam of ill-kept brass muzzles showed as the carronades thrust their large, menacing mouths in the direction of the frigate. Eight guns to a side, twenty-four-pounders Lamb decided, staring fixedly through his telescope, with long-guns at bow and stern, six-pounders, he thought, the same as those of the *Adroit*. Slade ordered the colours to be run up and as the flag reached the mizzen-peak the flags flying brazenly from the three brigs began to jerk their way down-wards, first on the vessel to windward and then on the other two, to be immediately replaced by the French tricolour. Bloody impudence! thought Lamb, to fly their colours like regular men-of-war going into action. The weathermost brig's length foreshortened as she slanted towards the frigate, clearly intending to come up on her larboard side. The intentions of the privateers were quite plain – two would engage the frigate from either side while the third attacked her stern.

Slade's voice rang out from the quarterdeck. 'Man the larboard guns! Open the ports! Run out the guns!'

The crews from the starboard guns ran across the deck to the larboard side and clapped on to the side-tackles of the loaded guns. Slade's voice came again, over the squealing thunder of the trucks.

'Mr Lamb! Up here, if you please!'

The captain took Lamb by the arm as he reached the quarterdeck and led him to the starboard side.

'We have only a moment or two before they are in range of our guns,' he said urgently. 'You see their design, of course – to engage from both sides while the other rakes our stern. I do not intend to allow them to get close enough for that to happen – those carronades would smash us within minutes. You see the fellow to windward?' He jerked his thumb towards the larboard bow. 'I fancy he is the leader of the group; he was the first to run out his guns and the first to hoist his colours. It is my intention to concentrate on him and at the same time endeavour to keep the other two at a distance. As soon as we are within range I shall luff, bring the starboard guns to bear and attempt to get to

64

windward. Make the most of the opportunity, Mr Lamb. Fire the instant we bear and keep on firing. If we can batter that one into submission we will have shortened the odds to a reasonable level. Now get to your guns and stand by.'

Lamb saluted, ran down to the maindeck and passed on Slade's intentions to Rank and Collier, who quickly spread the word amongst the gun-crews. The seamen grinned, hitched up their trousers, spat on their hands and bent their knees, ready to hurl themselves at their guns the instant they were fired. Lamb looked over the larboard bow at the privateer; she was now well within range of the long-guns, he thought, and glanced about the deck. The sail handlers were at their places, ready to haul on the yards as the helmsmen spun the wheel.

'Stand by the starboard guns!' bellowed Slade, leaning over the quarterdeck rail, his large, red face glowing with heat and excitement. God! he must be close to melting in that heavy broadcloth, thought Lamb, his own back wet with sweat beneath his little round jacket, aware of the familiar tightness in his chest and the faint feeling of nausea that always gripped him before action. It would disappear, he knew, with the first firing of the guns. He kept his eye firmly on the brig to windward, noting at the edge of his vision the other brig at a similar distance to leeward, her bow pointing directly at the frigate.

Slade's voice sounded from the quarterdeck. 'Luff up! Mains'l haul! Luff, luff! Ease her a shade. Steady!'

The deck heeled as the frigate tacked sharply and came close to the wind, her topsails rippling, her yards braced sharp, her starboard guns suddenly brought to bear on the southernmost brig. The gun-captains crouched over their flint-locks, lanyards in hand, feet splayed well clear of the line of recoil, their free hands patting the air as they called for tiny adjustments to the lay of the guns.

'Another inch, Joe. An inch, I said, you cunt! Bring her back, Sam – steady, steady, leave her!'

The gun muzzles dipped towards the sea as the ship rolled. Lamb, tense, waited the long second for the muzzles to rise again.

'Fire!'

Lanyards jerked in unison. The tremendous smash of sound

slapped at Lamb's ears as all the starboard guns erupted in one huge, stunning roar. As the guns hurtled backwards to the limit of their breechings clouds of dirty yellow, grey and black smoke billowed into the air and were swept away over the quarter-deck, the bitter, gritty taste and smell of it filling the decks. The gun-crews flung themselves at their charges, worming, swabbing, reloading, running out. Lamb stared through the last wisps of gunsmoke, endeavouring to see the fall of shot. The sea around the privateer suddenly shot little geysers into the air and a small section of her low, forward bulwark was blasted away. Long streamers of ragged canvas appeared at the leeward edge of her foresail as it was split by flying splinters or a random roundshot.

'Well done, my lads!' shouted Lamb, his voice going almost unheard in the general pandemonium of the activity at the guns. 'You have hit her fair and square!'

A small, orange flash winked from the bow of the brig as she fired her small bow-chaser but it was merely a defiant gesture and the shot fell unseen into the sea well clear of the frigate. As her gun was fired she tacked to windward, endeavouring to close the gap and present her larboard carronades to the *Adroit*, at the same time maintaining her weather advantage. Lamb spared a glance behind him for the other privateers. They had swung in pursuit but from this range and angle of sailing they were of little danger to the frigate, restricted as they were to the use of their light bow-chasers.

The starboard guns rumbled back to their gun-ports and the men on the handspikes heaved and grunted as they trained the guns to the satisfaction of the gun-captains. Lamb glanced along the line, forward and aft. All the guns were ready. He waited for the upward roll of the deck and screamed the order.

'Fire!'

The frigate and the privateer were now little more than half a mile apart, the brig crossing the T of the *Adroit*'s line. The starboard guns had been man-handled to point as far forward as the opening of the gun-ports would allow and Lamb feared that the sharp angle would affect the aim of the gun-captains. The many hours of gun-practice now paid dividends, however, and to his delight he saw the privateer hit heavily. Splinters flew from her side, the shards visible even at this range and he gave a great shout of excitement as a lucky shot severed the bowsprit close to the cap, causing her three jibsails to sag and dangle uselessly in a mass of flapping canvas, suspended by the stays attached to the foremast. Lamb could only guess at the damage done to her crew; if the privateer was typical of her kind her deck would be crowded with men, possibly as many as a hundred and fifty, with little protection on her low-sided flush deck.

The stern-chasers barked from the quarterdeck as the furious work of swabbing and re-loading began. Lamb presumed, concentrating his attention on the starboard guns, that they were fired in the optimistic hope of keeping the other privateers at arm's length while the business of hammering away at their lone companion continued.

Slade's voice rose in a bellow from the quarterdeck. 'Double-shot the guns! Roundshot and grape! The next time with canister!'

So, we are going to close her, thought Lamb as he strode along the line of guns. He was not surprised. The cool business of picking off the privateers one by one from outside the range of their carronades would be a long and probably inconclusive affair and one that did not suit the impatient and aggressive nature of the captain.

'Close-quarter work, then, Matthew,' remarked Rank as Lamb passed him.

'Yes, but a few minutes' hot work will soon put paid to that Frenchman,' said Lamb loudly for the benefit of the men's ears. The comment raised some hearty nods from the men within earshot, confirming as it did their opinion that one British tar was worth at least three Frenchmen any day. Lamb grinned and walked on, eyeing the business of loading grape on top of roundshot. The mass of two-pound iron balls sewn into canvas cylinders was capable of cutting through chain at close range and a lucky shot or two might sever enough stays and standing rigging to bring down a mast. Canister, murderous on an enemy's deck at close quarters, was not intended to be used at a distance of more than a cable or so – the tightly-packed lead bullets would otherwise disperse too widely and lose too much velocity. If Slade was using canister then he must be intending to get very close, thought Lamb, and this conclusion was reinforced a moment or two later when he saw one of the gunner's mates kneel to unlock a weapons locker – Slade was evidently ready to take his ship right alongside.

Flames and smoke erupted from the privateer's guns as she fired her massive broadside at last. The range was long for her short guns but even so the hull shook to the strike of a twenty-four-pound ball somewhere near the mizzen chains and hammocks spewed on to the deck from their netting on the forward bulwarks. Plumes of water from the remainder of the broadside pockmarked the sea around the frigate's starboard side, the extreme elevation of the carronades spreading the fall of shot over a wide area.

The guns were ready again; the brig was now almost within musket-range.

'Fire!'

This time the guns were fired on the downward roll of the ship and the privateer was hit very hard; Lamb doubted if a single gun missed its target.

The twelve-pound balls smashed into her upper side, enlarging her gun-ports and sending great shards of timber whirring murderously across her deck. Her lateen-rigged driver collapsed untidily across her starboard quarter, the gaff shot through close to the mainmast. Simultaneously, dozens of holes and rents appeared in the sails above her furled courses and several stays and braces dangled from her masts and yards. A delighted cheer erupted from the gun-crews.

'Silence on deck!' roared Lamb, with a ferocity he was far from feeling. 'Save your breath for your work and keep your bloody eyes inboard!'

The men bent to their guns, silent but still grinning. The powder-boys scuttled along the deck, clutching their wooden boxes close to their bodies. With the guns now hot and the range very short the charges were much reduced.

'We'll see the splinters fly now, boys!' grunted Bates from the gun at Lamb's side. Lamb knew that the old gun-captain was referring to the widely held theory amongst gunners that if just sufficient powder was used to make the shot barely penetrate the enemy's timbers the resultant shaking and rending of the woodwork would produce the most lethal and damaging splinters. Lamb had no idea if there was any truth in it. The stern-chasers were still sounding regularly from the quarter-deck, the light guns firing at a faster rate than the heavier guns at the side and from time to time, in the brief intervals of silence, he had heard the distant replies from the bow-guns of the privateers astern. It was going to be a close-run thing, he thought, as he watched the canisters of case shot being loaded; if we close and the brig turns out to be stubborn then in a very short time we will have his two compatriots to deal with as well.

The privateer's broadside sounded for the second time, very ragged now, her shattered bulwark bearing testimony to the havoc wreaked on her line of guns. Even so, hesitant and incomplete as the broadside was, the huge roundshot smashed with a tremendous force into the *Adroit*'s timbers, the ship shuddering under the impact. A long section of the forward bulwark, already damaged by the brig's previous broadside, flew into the air in an explosion of timber, hammocks and men. Two of the guns there were also hit, one hurled on to its side with men beneath it and the other driven backwards across the midline of the deck, its breechings snapped like string, the mouth of its barrel opened up like a grotesque metal flower. The maintopmast yard and the mainmast chains were hit, the starboard half of the yard swinging down to tangle in the shrouds, dangling at the end of the lacerated topsail still attached to the broken spar. Lamb ignored the shrill screams and the carnage in the forward division. Collier could deal with that. He cast rapid glances fore and aft along the broken line of guns, scanning the upraised arms of the gun-captains signifying their readiness. He waited for the ship to begin her roll to starboard.

'Fire!'

At a range of less than a cable the heavy masses of canister shot scythed their wicked way across the deck of the privateer, cutting bloody swathes through the press of men crouching low in the scanty shelter of her torn bulwarks. The roundshot, fired on the downward roll, added to the slaughter as jagged pieces of timber thrummed through the air, ripped from her shattered ports to expose the slewed and overturned carronades. The *Adroit*'s own carronades now began to sound their angry thunder from the quarterdeck and forecastle. Aimed low, at the bottom of the frigate's starboard heel, the powerful, short-barrelled guns sent their huge shot smashing through the timbers at the brig's waterline. From the fighting tops the little swivel-guns were savagely barking, and overlaying the deep note of the large guns was the high-pitched crack and rattle of the Marines' muskets.

Hopping with excitement, Lamb was unaware of little Bird standing beside him, his head on a level with Lamb's belt buckle, calling his name in a piping treble. Desperate, greatly daring, the midshipman plucked at Lamb's sleeve.

'Sir! Sir! Mr Lamb, sir!'

Lamb glanced down. The boy was white-faced with the shock and horror of the action. Behind him a man was being dragged to the hatchway, blood pumping from the stump of his leg, a crimson trail on the white-scrubbed planks.

'Yes, Mr Bird, what can I do for you?'

'Beg your pardon, sir, but can you man the larboard guns, the captain said, sir?'

'Very well, Mr Bird.'

The midshipman touched his hat and scampered off back to the quarterdeck. Lamb cupped his hands to his mouth and bellowed, turning his head fore and aft.

'Stand by the larboard guns! Stand by the larboard guns!'

The frigate was already wearing as the men at the guns dropped their implements and ran across the deck. The brig was low in the water, the sea pouring into her through the ragged holes in her side. Goode brought the frigate sharply round her stern.

'Stand by!' yelled Lamb to the gunners.

'Belay that, Mr Lamb,' boomed Slade from the quarterdeck. 'She is not worth the powder. Save it for the other two.'

The frigate tacked again, putting the wind on her larboard quarter and pointing her bow towards the other brigs. Lamb ordered the men back to the starboard guns to complete their reloading and cast a quick glance behind him. The privateer's larboard rail had dipped into the sea, exposing the copper sheathing on her bottom planks and hiding from his view the confusion on her steeply canted deck as men and guns slid into the water. Her copper was very clean, Lamb noted with professional interest; she must have had a scrape very recently. He turned his gaze and attention to the remaining brigs, putting the vessel's death-struggles from his mind.

The others were evidently in no mood to continue their sport; they had come about and were now running before the wind, one a few points west of north, the other heading to the north-east. Slade flung out an arm at the nearest, about half a mile distant.

'Give her a crack, Mr Lamb. I shall bring the ship round a trifle.'

The frigate's bows swung a few points to the west, allowing her starboard guns to bear. The gun-crews sweated and grunted to train the muzzles sharply forward while Lamb paced impatiently up and down eyeing the fleeing privateer.

'Fire as you bear!' he ordered, looking with mounting frustration at the widening gap between the *Adroit* and the brig. The frigate was not at her most comfortable point of sailing with the wind directly astern, and the useless maintopsail combined with a small divergence from the brig's track had allowed the gap to increase to about a mile. The gun-handlers stepped clear of the trucks and the guns began to fire, near enough together to give a long, rolling broadside. Lamb had his telescope to his eye and observed with angry disappointment the fall of shot. He saw a great deal of damage done to the surface of the sea in and about the brig's wake but so far as he could tell none at all to the vessel itself. Slade also had his glass to his eye and what he saw caused him to stride to the quarterdeck rail angrily brandishing his telescope at the distant privateer.

'What kind of bloody gunnery d'you call that, Mr Lamb? God damn me, my squint-eyed steward could have done better! Stand fast the guns!'

Lamb tightened his lip, stung by the unfairness of the rebuke. Much of the fault lay with Slade, he thought hotly. If he had stopped to give a thought to the wind for a second instead of putting the ship impulsively on the larboard tack things might have gone better. A tack to starboard to allow the larboard guns to bear would have put the wind on her quarter, her best point of sailing. The extra knot or two gained would have been sufficient to keep the brig within range. Even as these thoughts ran through his mind the order came to man the braces and the frigate came round to the opposite tack. Better late than never, he thought savagely, and tersely ordered the gun-crews to stand by the larboard guns. He moved to the side and stared astern. The first brig had disappeared beneath the water, leaving a mass of rubbish on the surface. He levelled his glass. Broken timber, hammocks, corpses and struggling men washed up and down on the gently heaving water. One man, sprawled on a grating, reached out a hand to another man in the water. Lamb shrugged. They were both as good as dead.

Within the hour, even with the maintopsail set (untidily, to a hasty lashing), it became clear that the Frenchman more than had the edge on the frigate, but Slade persisted with the chase until the brig was hull down. He levelled his telescope at the privateer for the last time and turned to the master.

'Bring her back on course, Mr Goode,' he ordered and descending to the maindeck he paced slowly along the starboard side. He paused for a thoughtful moment at the damaged bulwark and the ruined gun and then moved on, turning at the forecastle to make his way down the larboard side. He halted beside Lamb and gazed pensively out to sea for a moment, rocking backwards and forwards on his heels and toes in his habitual manner. Lamb waited edgily for him to speak.

'Secure the guns, Mr Lamb,' said Slade mildly. 'The hands can have their dinner and grog and then we will see to the maintopmast yard.'

'Aye aye, sir,' said Lamb with a touch of his hat.

Slade turned towards the quarterdeck and then swung back to look directly at Lamb, his large, fleshy face lightened by the merest touch of a smile.

'We did quite well this morning, Mr Lamb, quite well.'

'Thank you, sir.'

The smile vanished as Slade nodded his head in the direction of the barely visible topgallant royals of the vanishing privateer. His voice was cold. 'But we should have done better. That last firing did you little credit, Mr Lamb.'

Lamb gazed at his retreating back in a fury. 'Insufferable bastard!' he muttered silently.

Chapter 4

'Haul away!' roared Clegg. The line of men stepped out briskly in the direction of the forecastle taking with them the stout rope that ran through a huge block attached to a ring-bolt amidships, continued up to a similar block seventy feet above the deck and ran down again to the replacement maintopmast yard at the foot of the mainmast. Other men tagged on to the end of the line as it moved forward and by the time the leading man had reached the forecastle, released his hold on the halyard and trotted back to join the endless circle of men, the forty-seven-foot spar had travelled, almost without effort, some thirty feet into the air. Lamb stood beside the boatswain and watched the yard rising quickly and smoothly up beside the mast.

Until today the spar had nestled snugly between the mizzen shrouds and the bulwark on the larboard quarter and the memory of that bitterly cold morning in Portsmouth Harbour when he had attempted to warm himself by assisting his men to stow it brought a smile to Lamb's lips as a bead of sweat rolled down his forehead. Ice and frost belonged to another world now. He craned his neck to keep his eyes on the yard, now nearing the men waiting to receive it.

'Handsomely, now,' growled Clegg in his deep rumble and the line of men slowed their pace to a crawl. The yard inched its way up the last few feet until an arm was urgently waved from aloft and a shout of 'Hold her there!' came faintly down. The boatswain's whistle shrilled close to Lamb's ear, 'Belay!' Lamb watched the halyard safely lashed to a belaying pin and then gave a satisfied nod to the boatswain.

'Bend the new canvas on it as soon as it is secured, Mr Clegg.'

'Aye aye, sir,' rumbled Clegg and hoisted himself into the shrouds to climb aloft and assure himself that the blockheads above were securing the new yard in a safe and seamanlike way, the probability of which, to judge from his expression, he deemed to be low. The boatswain was a very short, square-built man, almost as wide as he was tall and burdened with a huge pair of ears that stuck out at right-angles to his hairless head. 'Juggy' was the lower deck's very secret name for him; it had, on occasion, been suggested that if he was nailed to the forepeak the frigate could well dispense with her foresail but such wits had taken care not to moot the idea within his not inconsiderable earshot. He was an invaluable man, an officer of vast experience and indefatigable energy whose hold over the lower deck had much in common with the relationship of the stoat to the rabbit.

Lamb moved aft to the quarterdeck, passing as he did so the canvas-shrouded bodies of the two men killed in the exchange with the brig. One had been crushed by the dismounted gun and the other pierced through the head by a sliver of flying timber. Below, in the cockpit, the surgeon was still busy at his bloody work repairing the wounded. Slade lifted his head enquiringly as Lamb approached and saluted.

'The maintopmast yard is secured, sir,' Lamb reported formally, well aware that the captain had followed the progress of the yard every inch of its journey aloft.

'Very good. As soon as the tops'l is set we will heave-to for the burial service. Prepare for that if you would, Mr Lamb.'

'Aye aye, sir.'

Jno. Brett, ordinary seaman, discharged dead and Jno. Whitfield, ordinary seaman, discharged dead, sank to their final resting places on the sea floor some two hundred miles north-east of Antigua, their nostrils pierced by the sailmaker's final stitch in their sailcloth shrouds and their feet resting comfortably on the rusted, poorly cast roundshot carefully selected as fitting for this use by the gunner's mate. The *Adroit* sailed on to the noise of hammering as the carpenter made good the damaged bulwark and his mates repaired the torn and splintered deck planks. By dusk the following day the frigate was creeping towards the black mass of Antigua under shortened sail, her canvas sewn and patched, rigging spliced and tarred, deck scrubbed clean of blood and the ship smelling strongly of fresh paint. As she rounded the lee of Green Island the sun winked its last and vanished behind the dark heights to the west. The prospect of picking his way through the darkness to the narrow entrance of English Harbour was not one that Slade viewed with pleasure and in the happy knowledge that twelve hours here or there would not be considered amiss he gave orders to back the topsails and anchor just south of the little island. The night was almost windless; what little breeze there was came gently from the north-east, barely rocking the frigate as she squatted at her sheltered anchorage.

'Keep a close watch on our holding, Mr Collier,' ordered Slade as he moved towards the quarterdeck ladder.

'Aye aye, sir,' responded the saturnine lieutenant, his voice, as always, almost as morose as his expression. Lamb cocked a thoughtful eye in Collier's direction as he, too, descended the ladder to make his way to the gunroom and the supper his growling stomach demanded. An odd bird, Collier, he reflected, as he made his way down the darkness of the aft companionway; quietly competent and reliable in all matters of shipboard routine, as was to be expected in a master's mate who had made his way to the quarterdeck, he was also a secretive and withdrawn man, even in the easy atmosphere of the gunroom. A certain spark of enthusiasm seemed to be missing in the man – his acknowledgement of Slade's parting order lacked, to Lamb's ears, the normal crispness of a junior officer anxious to impress his captain with his alert dependability. Lamb gave a slight shake of his head; strange, dour fellow – perhaps he had been crossed in love, he thought, smiling. He pushed open the door of the gunroom and entered the noisy atmosphere of the officers at supper.

'Matthew! The very fellow,' cried the surgeon above the loud cross-talk of his table companions. 'We need an independent arbiter here, before these fellows come to blows – a man of wisdom, erudition and unparalleled knowledge. You will do, though, at a pinch. Come, sit you down and let us pick your brains.'

Lamb seated himself at his chair at the head of the table and gave the ebullient Scotsman a weary grin.

'Curb your exuberance for a moment, Bones, while I snatch a mouthful or two, there's a good fellow. We savants do not perform well on an empty stomach.' He turned to the steward hovering at his elbow. 'Have these gannets left anything for me to eat, Sykes?'

'I can probably find you a little something, sir. 'Ow about a nice bit of beef, some choice biscuits and a nice bit o' cheese, not too 'igh?'

'That all sounds drearily familiar. I will not be sorry to see fresh stores come aboard tomorrow. Very well, Sykes. Is there any coffee left?'

'I'll make some fresh directly, sir.'

Lamb worked on his cask beef for some minutes with the skill of long practice, cutting away the more obvious obnoxiousness and manfully swallowing the rest before turning his attention to the simpler problems of the biscuits and cheese. He gathered from the heated voices around the table that the officers had been discussing Sir Richard Grenville's last fight in the *Revenge* against the Spanish fleet off the Azores but had now got bogged down in dissent over details of the ship's armament. Lamb tapped his biscuits and munched his interesting cheese as he listened with some amusement to the earnest arguments put forward as to why, without the shadow of a doubt, the *Revenge* carried eighteen guns, twenty-eight guns or even, in the Marine lieutenant's opinion, forty-four guns, an assertion greeted with hoots of scornful laughter from Rank and Ball. The weight of her roundshot was no less contentious, ranging from a confident six to an assertive twenty-four pounds.

Lamb drained his cup and pushed his plate to one side. Andrews immediately seized on him. 'Come, oh Great Solomon, let us hear your opinions, dropping like pearls before this swinish gathering.'

Lamb smiled and ran the back of his hand over his mouth in lieu of a napkin. 'As it happens, I am in a position to give the definitive answers to both questions. Allow me to put all your minds at rest. Sykes!'

The steward, called from his struggles with dirty china and glass in his tiny pantry, thrust his head through the hatch with a harassed 'What now?' expression on his perspiring face.

'Sir?' he enquired politely.

'Cut along to my cabin, there's a good fellow. You'll find a book on the shelf, *Exploits of British Seamen*. Bring it to me, would you?'

'*Exploits of British Seamen*, sir,' repeated Sykes, slowly.

'That's right, Sykes.'

Sykes nodded doubtfully and removed his head from the hatchway, only to reappear a second later.

'Would that be a big, black book, sir?'

Lamb laughed in sudden understanding. 'No, Sykes. A small green book with gilt lettering on the spine.'

The steward's head vanished again and appeared at the door of the gunroom complete with body a few moments later. Sykes advanced on Lamb holding the book with all the reverence of a man carrying the Holy Grail.

''ere y'are, sir. Spotted it right off.'

'Thank you, Sykes,' said Lamb taking the slim volume, a present from his father on the day he joined his first ship as a midshipman. 'Thank God you are not colour-blind.'

He began to turn the pages but was stopped by an urgent shout from Vaughan. 'Wait, wait! I see the opportunity of a small wager here – a little bet. What do you say, gentlemen?'

A chorus of assenting voices came from around the table.

'Bloody good notion – I can risk sixpence.'

'Sixpence? Miserly cur! I'll have a guinea on it.'

'Ten shillings.'

'Croesus!'

Lamb raised his hand and waited for the din to subside.

'How about this? A guinea each into the pool, the winner to take half, the remainder to be set aside for Mr Vaughan to spend on wine – for the wardroom, that is, not for his own selfish indulgence.'

'Capital notion!' cried the Marine who had few duties on board apart from looking after the wardroom's purchase of victuals.

Doubt showed on one or two faces. A guinea was quite a sum, more than four days' pay for most of them and the meagre return for the winner did not seem a high sum for the outlay of so much capital. Having given their enthusiastic support in principle, however, none of them wished to appear so tight-pocketed as to quibble over the stake and Lamb accepted the majority shouts of agreement with a nod.

'Sykes! Pen and paper in here, if you please, toot sweet. Right, gentlemen, let me see the colour of your money. Now then, it was the Marine's idea, let the Marines be first into the breach. Number of guns, Mr Vaughan?'

'Forty-four!'

'Weight of shot?'

'Twenty-four pound!'

Vaughan settled back in his chair with a wide beam of confidence, not in the least put out by the pitying headshakes of the two junior lieutenants.

'Mr Rank?'

'Thirty-four and twelve.'

'Mr Ball?'

'Twenty-four and six. Shall I take my winnings now to save time or do we have to plough on to the bitter end?'

'We plough on. Mr Andrews?'

The surgeon spread his hands. 'Now what do I know of ships and guns of two centuries ago? What do I know of them today, come to that? I am at a disadvantage here amongst you experts; I could as well ask for your opinions of the effective treatment for the black vomit. Put me down for eighteen and nine, Matthew. No, no, wait. Make that eighteen and six – I prefer the mathematical resonance of those figures. Yes, eighteen and six, if you please. A wild stab but who knows?'

'Mr Goode?'

The master scratched his nose thoughtfully with his good hand. 'There were no very big ships in those days, of that I'm sure, but I have the idea they were heavily gunned, in spite of their size. Put me down for thirty-four twelve-pounders.'

'Ha, ha, you are too late!' shouted Rank. 'Those are my selections.'

'Thirty-four nine-pounders then, blast your eyes.'

'And Mr Littlefield?'

'Wait, wait,' murmured the purser, busily scribbling on a scrap of paper. He sucked the end of his new, steel-barrelled, half-crown pen and studied his figures.

'Come on, Littlefield,' urged Ball, impatiently. 'You were very firm on your twenty-four nine-pounders a moment ago. Why are you dithering now?'

'Can't a fellow change his mind before the off? Can't a fellow study the field?'

'And can't a fellow keep the rest of us waiting!'

The purser waved his hand in the air. 'Patience, patience. You know, a little study of these figures could well pay dividends. I see here in the "Number of guns" column that the figure thirty-four appears twice and in the "Weight of shot" column the figure six also appears twice. But – ' here he raised his finger in a significant gesture ' – no one name has both those figures against it. So, on the basis of frequency of occurrence, I shall enter myself for those two figures. Thirty-four and six, if you please, Mr Lamb.'

'Very clever,' muttered Ball darkly, 'and I am not too sure of the legality of it. It smacks of downright deviousness to me.'

'Deviousness? I heard no rules against – '

'Right, gentlemen,' said Lamb hastily, rapping his knuckles on the table. 'Now that all the bets are in it is time for us to consult the oracle.'

He opened his book but was again stopped by the Marine.

'Wait a moment. Supposing none of us has the correct answers? What happens then?'

Lamb gave a broad smile. 'Well, in that case of course, nobody wins – apart from the wine ledger, that is. Naturally you will all be free to try again, for the same modest outlay.' He chuckled at the suddenly solemn faces. 'Courage, gentlemen! The situation might not arise.' He already knew, in fact, that it would not. *Exploits of British Seamen* had been a close companion on his every ship and after several years he was familiar with almost every word.

'Now let me see. Chapter three, I think it is. Yes, "Sir Richard Grenville's Gallant Last Stand". Hm. Well, it seems the *Revenge* carried thirty-four guns, so some of you are half right, at least.'

Rank gave a triumphant clap of his hands and the master and purser grinned widely. The others shook their heads in disgust.

'Now for the size of her guns.' Lamb pushed the open book across to the surgeon, his finger pointing to a line. 'Would you care to read that, Bones?'

Andrews pushed the book away to arm's length in order to accommodate his long-sightedness. ' – murderers, swivel-guns and – '

'No, no, the line above that.'

The surgeon grunted and moved his finger-nail up a fraction. 'In addition to her thirty-four nine-pounders, she also carried—'

A volley of hand-claps cut the surgeon short, none more enthusiastic than those of the master who applauded his own success by smacking his free hand loudly on the table before stretching it out to receive his winnings.

'Well done, Ralph,' said Lamb, adding his own hand-claps. 'I think the wine account can now afford an extra bottle or three. We must toast both Ralph's good luck and a safe landfall. Sykes!'

The hatch to the steward's pantry opened with a petulant slam.

'Yes, sir?'

'Have we any of the white left?'

'You know full well we ain't sir. It's long gorn. Can find you some more Black Strap, sir.'

'Half a dozen of your best then, Sykes, suitably chilled of course.'

'Oh, o' course, sir, naturally,' said Sykes, lifting his eyes to the deck beams.

The wine arrived, red, rough and far from chilled but eagerly downed for all that. With the formality of the toasts over the officers loosened their clothing and relaxed, chairs pushed back to make room for comfortably sprawled legs, the bottles passing freely from hand to hand.

'Come, Ralph, give us a song,' said Lamb.

'Yes, yes, a song!' cried Vaughan. 'Make the bloody beams ring!'

The master, with the best part of a bottle of Black Strap inside him, needed no further persuasion and draining his glass he pulled his chair close to the table and sat stiffly upright for want of being able to stand erect under the low beams. Fixing his gaze sternly on the facing bulkhead he filled his lungs and began to sing in a fine, rich, Welsh baritone.

'Oh, cruel were my parents to tear my love from me,
And cruel were the press-gang that took him off to sea,
And cruel was the little boat that rowed him from the
    strand,
And cruel was the great big ship that sailed from the land.'

His audience listened with rapt attention to the maiden's sad words coming from the master's weathered, whiskered face and sat, quiet as mice, until the tragic little tale was finished.

'Well sung, Ralph!'

'Superb!'

'Give us another, Ralph – a jolly one, this time.'

Goode obliged again with a well-tried favourite, the officers bellowing the familiar words of the chorus, making up with enthusiasm what they lacked in tunefulness, pounding the table and rattling the glassware.

> 'Then sling the flowing bowl –
> Fond hopes arise –
> The girls we prize
> Shall bless each jovial soul.
> The can, boys, bring –
> We'll drink and sing
> While foaming billows roll.'

'Enough, enough! No more!' panted Goode as he mopped his streaming face with a spotted handkerchief almost large enough to cover the table. 'No, no, you forget, I'm an old man. Such exertions in this heat will be the death of me.'

With the master adamant and the bottles empty, the officers slipped away one by one to their duties or their cots, leaving Lamb, Ball and the surgeon sprawled at ease in their chairs. Andrews gave an enormous yawn, stretched his legs under the table and thrust his hand beneath his wig to scratch vigorously at his black stubble. He yawned again, closed his eyes and began instantly to snore. Lamb gave a discreet belch and began to discuss with himself the probability of his finding the energy to rise from his chair and make his nightly round before turning in.

Bell interrupted his cogitations. 'Has the captain let drop any hints about our duties in the West Indies?' he asked, emboldened by wine and the easy atmosphere.

'None at all,' answered Lamb, rousing himself. 'My own opinion, for what it's worth, is that we'll be on convoy duties.'

Bell groaned and pulled a glum face. There was little to be expected in the way of prize money or promotion in shepherding merchantmen along the trade routes, only a tedious crawl in the company of dull ships, akin to a greyhound safeguarding the slow, homeward plod of fat dairy cows.

'An exciting prospect,' he said, his plump face downcast. He was a young man of easy temperament, popular with the men, who recognized his occasional ferocious tongue as a mere squall passing quickly through an otherwise clear sky, soon gone and soon forgotten.

Lamb smiled at Ball's expression. 'It's a task that has to be done. Our merchant ships have to be safeguarded. Do you know much of the situation in the Caribbean?'

'Not as much as I should, I fear.'

'That means next to nothing, I take it.'

Lamb was not surprised at Ball's ignorance. Politics and naval and military strategy were subjects that by and large failed to excite any sparks in the minds of young officers below post rank – and too often in the minds of those above it, from what Lamb had heard. Young lieutenants considered the more immediate interests of action, prize money and the promotion that came with them to be paramount, saving only their stomachs, sex and the present conflict with France, which they hoped would go on for ever. Lamb shared their priorities to some extent but as he also had an insatiable lust for newsprint his grasp of the Navy's extensive commitments was, by Ball's standard, excellent.

'You have never been this far west, have you, Roger?'

Ball shook his head. 'No'.

'Neither have I, but at least we are both quite familiar with the charts of the area, are we not?'

Ball grinned.

Lamb dipped his finger in his wine-glass and traced the outline of the Caribbean in Black Strap on the polished surface of the table.

'Here to the south we have the Spanish Main and Trinidad – then, stretching north, the Lesser Antilles, with Barbados here and Antigua here. Now, we swing westward – mind your elbow, there's a good fellow – and we find Puerto Rico, Hispaniola, Cuba and just here, Jamaica. There – the Caribbean drawn to make a cartographer sick with envy! Now, some of these islands are in our hands – Barbados, Jamaica and Antigua, for instance – and some are under French or Spanish rule. As I understand it, we are not likely to come across many of their men-o'-war because they haven't the ships to spare for these waters, but the area is swarming with privateers and letters-of-marque ships, some of them very powerful, too, like those brigs yesterday. Cuba, in particular, is a hotbed of them. The West Indies squadron has the task of safeguarding our possessions, protecting the spice-and-sugar ships through the Mona Passage here, east of Hispaniola and the Windward Passage, west of it, and also keeping the numbers of the privateers down.'

Ball glanced up from the damp table, an optimistic gleam in his eye. 'Perhaps that is what the Admiral has in mind for us – an independent cruise searching out privateers would be just the thing, wouldn't it?'

Lamb shook his head. 'Not much profit in that. In any case, we won't be that lucky. Last come, worst served. It will be convoy duties for us, young Ball, so you may as well get used to the idea.' He stretched and yawned. 'Ho hum! It is time I did my evening round before I fall asleep in my chair like Andrews.'

'And almost time I relieved Collier. He gives me such a dark look if I am five seconds late.'

'Five seconds is five seconds too much. I always made a point of relieving the watch five minutes early when I was a watch-keeping officer,' lied Lamb.

'Oh,' said Ball and rising hastily from his chair he began to fasten the buttons of his waistcoat over his comfortable stomach.

Sykes, lightly dozing curled up on the tiny deckspace of the little pantry, heard the bang of the gunroom door and the receding sound of footsteps climbing the aft companionway. He struggled sleepily to his feet. Bloody officers, he thought angrily, bloody yarning away half the bloody night without a thought for the poor, overworked sod waiting to clear up after them. He picked up his tray and a selection of rags and entered the gunroom. The sight of the sleeping surgeon brought a curl to his lip and advancing to the table he noisily clattered the dirty glasses on to his tray. The empty bottles were each carefully inspected in turn. Gawd! Not a fucking drop left in any of them, the thirsty bleeders, not a single half-decent bloody heel-tap. Thank Christ he had his own little supply – he would die of thirst if it was left to this lot. The surgeon stirred in his sleep, smacking his lips and rolling his head. His wig fell to the deck as he began to snore again, his head tilted back, his mouth open. Yes, you've had your bloody share, ain't you? thought Sykes in angry envy. He wiped the surface of the table with wide sweeps of his cloth, muttering to himself. The sight of the spidery loops and whirls of Black Strap that Lamb had deposited on the table brought a sharp frown to his face. Messy buggers! Not a thought to the bloody polish! He dabbed at the stains with his cloth but stopped short as an idea suddenly struck him. Picking up the surgeon's wig he balled it in his hand and vigorously polished off the damp smears, spitting on to the wig in order to bring up a gloss. Stepping back, he gave the surface an admiring glance and shaking the creases from the wig placed it gently atop the surgeon's head, back to front. He collected his tray and crept quietly from the gunroom, chuckling inanely.

Chapter 5

A slight mist clung closely to the surface of the water as the
Adroit broke her anchor free from the sea bed and turned her
stern to Green Island, a mist that would vanish within minutes
of the sun's appearance in the pale, green-washed skies to the
east. Under topsails and driver the frigate coasted easily under
a light north-easterly along the serrated green flanks of
Antigua's eastern coastline and rounded Half-Moon Bay as the
sun frowned redly over the invisible rim of the horizon. Skirting
the wide mouth of Willoughby Bay the ship crept along well
clear of the low, rocky cliffs fringed with white water that led to
the harbour entrance. Mr Goode was the only quarterdeck
officer to have visited the island and he now stood by the wheel
directing the helmsmen, growling his orders in a deep rumble
that carried the length of the ship. Slade and Lamb, separated
by a dozen yards, adopted the same posture, feet wide apart,
hands clasped behind their backs, their heads thrown back as
they stared up at Shirley Heights and the massive fort brooding
watchfully over the near-landlocked harbour beneath.

'Down helm.'

'Down helm it is, sir.'

'Steady as she goes.'

'Steady as she goes, sir.'

The ship was very quiet. The maindeck was crowded with
the men of both watches, gazing silently at the dark-green hills
and the blue, distant heights. For nearly all of them this was
their first glimpse of a tropical island and like most seamen they
had only the dimmest knowledge of global geography; indeed,
many of the pressed men had no idea whether the ship had been
sailing east or west for the past weeks. They had all heard of
island paradises, however; memories of the tales of Captain
Cook's legendary sojourn amongst Tahiti's uninhibited people
rose warmly in their minds, heated still further by the

86

mischievous lies of two or three of their more knowledgeable shipmates. Waves of silent lust emanated strongly from the maindeck like heat from a brazier. The harbour entrance, a dark break in the line of low cliffs, came into sight a mile or two ahead.

Slade stirred himself. 'We must make a proper entrance here, Mr Lamb, a frigate's entrance, not creep in like a nervous dago. Plenty of speed and dash! Forecourse and t'gallants, if you please. Look to the helm, Mr Goode and when the time comes I want her stopped on a sixpence.'

'Aye aye, sir,' rumbled the master with deep misgiving, thinking of the narrow entrance and the sharp turn into the inner harbour.

The ship picked up her heels with a surge as the wind caught the added canvas and as Lamb descended to the maindeck a few minutes later the deck heeled sharply and the frigate set her bow at the harbour's outer mouth. Low, scrub-covered cliffs shot by on either side and the ship entered the circular seaward harbour, quite empty of shipping. Then as Goode brought her head round on to the larboard tack the inner harbour was revealed, showing the bare masts and spars of a large two-decker and several smaller vessels at anchor. There came a few minutes of crackling orders and furious activity as the spread of canvas was reduced and the *Adroit* entered the harbour at a swift but much safer pace. The captain had his glass to his eye studying the fourth-rate and the flag hanging limply at her stern.

'It will be eleven guns, Mr Lamb,' he boomed.

'Eleven guns, aye aye, sir.'

Lamb turned and advanced to the gunner, Mr Winter, whose ancient ears were not what they used to be.

'Eleven guns, Mr Winter!'

'Eleven it is, sir,' mumbled the gunner and hurried off to start his pacing along the line of guns.

'Commence the salute!' shouted Slade.

Lamb spun on his heel and raised his hand to Winter.

'Fire one!' piped the gunner in his thin, worn-out voice.

The long, rolling salute to the rear-admiral's flag sent the birds squawking and protesting high into the air and echoed around the little harbour. The thunder crossed the narrow isthmus and the larger stretch of water behind, reverberated off Monk's Hill and died in a distant grumble beyond as the master raised his own, lesser thunder from the quarterdeck. The ship came smartly round into the early-morning island breeze, slowed as her topsails were backed and lay-to, rocking on the still water as the two-decker sounded her reply. That was smartly done, thought Lamb as the best bower plunged and dug its flukes into the sandy bottom – plenty of speed and dash there! He hoped the Admiral was an early riser; it would be a pity for that impressive display of sail handling to have been admired only by the flagship's watch-keeping warrant officers.

Signal flags, plain to the unaided eye, rose smoothly aloft on the two-decker, identified now as the *Hengist* by several of the older hands within Lamb's earshot. Little Bird, gazing determinedly through an unnecessary telescope almost as long as he was tall, read off the flag numbers and leafed hastily through the signals book.

'"Captain to repair on board," sir,' he piped in his clear treble.

'Pass the word for the captain's cox'n,' called Lamb along the maindeck but there was no need. Leyton had already anticipated the flagship's order and the gig was in the water while Slade was still buttoning his best heavy broadcloth in his cabin.

The early sun was hot on his face as Lamb watched the captain's gig pulling swiftly across the placid water to the *Hengist*. He filled his lungs with the warm, golden air and smiled as the thought of the Channel in winter came into his mind, the damp, freezing, sunless dawns and the grey, treacherous waters of the French coast where the Channel Fleet kept constant vigil on its ports. Lamb had spent many miserable months as a midshipman on cold and unrewarding duty and as he narrowed his eyes against the glare and felt the first trickle of sweat roll down his spine he reflected on the misery of the men of the Channel Fleet without the slightest twinge of compassion. Poor bastards! he thought with a silent chuckle. The gig, he saw, had hooked on to the flagship's chains; there was time for a pint or so of Sykes' abominable coffee before Slade returned. First, though, he must give orders for the *Adroit*'s empty water casks to be brought up from below;

whatever instructions Slade received from the flagship, replenishing water would be his first priority.

The captain of the *Hengist* had put up his epaulette several years before Slade had arrived at that glorious moment but the memory of a long year of subservience to Slade's volatile temper in the wardroom of a third-rate on the American station had dimmed but little since the two men had last seen each other. Thus, with positions of seniority now reversed, it was with a great deal of honest pleasure that Captain Mortimer was able to say brutally: 'Hello, Slade. I was pleased to hear that you were made post – eventually.'

The two men extended reluctant hands and exchanged the briefest of handshakes. Slade, sweating in his heavy coat from the effort of hauling himself up the pipe-clayed man-ropes, glanced at his erstwhile junior with dislike and grunted. His manners had not improved at all, he thought; still the same sarcastic, arrogant little bastard he was years ago.

'Thank you, Mortimer,' he said coldly. He glanced about him at the perfect orderliness of the ship, the snowy, spotless deck, the carefully Flemished ropes, the gleam of brass, fresh paint and shining guns. 'Very nice, very pretty, under the circumstances. Obtaining enough paint to do a proper job is always a problem, ain't it?'

'So I saw through my glass,' said Mortimer neatly, nodding in the direction of the frigate. 'Shall we go aft?'

'I was expecting to see Dillforth's flag here,' said Slade as they left the boatswain's mates and the side-boys and the rigid rows of Marines and headed towards the quarterdeck.

'Oh, Sir John keeps himself at Kingston, in the main; he rarely comes this way nowadays. You will be meeting his second-in-command, Sir Sydney Upton, based here at Antigua. Do you know him, at all?'

'No, never had the pleasure. He was on the China station some years ago, was he not?'

'Yes, until last year; made himself a fortune several times over, I believe. He is a talkative old stick but pleasant enough. Spends all his time on board – refuses to take up his residence ashore; too many damned mosquitoes for him, he says.'

They ascended in silence to the quarterdeck and walked to the break of the poop where stood a stout young officer who smiled nervously and removed his hat as the two captains approached.

'This is Bowers, the Admiral's flag lieutenant; he will look after you,' said Mortimer dismissively and turning on his heel strode back along the quarterdeck, leaving Slade looking at his retreating back with the uncomfortable feeling that he had been well and truly put in his place.

'It is very hot today, sir, is it not?' smiled the flag lieutenant pleasantly.

Slade turned and gave him a cold stare. 'Of course it is, standing here in this fucking sun.'

Bowers gave a nervous titter. 'Oh, excuse me, sir. Sir Sydney said to show you in directly, sir.'

'Then why are we standing here frying, blast your useless eyes?'

Rear-Admiral Sir Sydney Upton was at his breakfast when Bowers ushered Slade into the huge cabin that stretched across the width of the quarterdeck. Sunlight streamed in through the open stern-windows, directing its beams at the papers and breakfast dishes spread in untidy confusion over the wide surface of the enormous table.

'Come in, captain, come in!' cried the admiral, waving the crusty remains of a slice of toast at Slade. 'Don't stand on ceremony, sir – sit you down, sit you down. Slade, is it? That fool Bowers will mumble so. You look very warm, Slade – let me give you some lemon water, made fresh this morning. No? Some coffee then – I'm sure you drink coffee. Pascoe! Pascoe! Where has that bloody man – ah, a cup for Captain Slade, Pascoe. What have you there, captain, your reports? Put them on the table, I shall read them later – mind the bloody butter, man! Thank you, Pascoe. No, no, leave all that – you can clear away later. Here, Slade, drink it while it is hot; there is nothing worse than cold coffee. I much prefer tea in the mornings but it has all gone now, I'm afraid; that idiot Pascoe let it go mildew.'

Upton folded his piece of toast into two and popped it into his mouth, effectively damming his wordy flow. He leaned back in his chair and chewed busily, beaming warmly at Slade sipping at his unwanted coffee. The admiral was a tiny, bald-headed man, pushing hard at seventy in Slade's estimation. His face was creased and lined, the colour of old parchment, but his blue eyes were bright and clear and shrewd as they examined Slade.

'You didn't have an entirely uneventful voyage out, did you, Slade, judging from your bulwarks and your canvas?'

'I had a brush with three privateer brigs yesterday, sir,' said Slade, edging his cup on to the table between the butter dish and his reports. 'Sunk one but lost my maintopmast yard in the doing. The other two got clean away, I'm afraid. It is all in my report, sir.'

'That's a pity,' said Upton, placing his own cup on the table a yard or so from its saucer. Slade was uncertain from this remark whether the admiral was referring to the lost yard, the escaped brigs or his report. Upton did not bother to elucidate further.

'Your orders are to report to the Commander-in-Chief, I take it, Captain Slade?' he asked, suddenly brisk.

'Yes, sir, either here or at Kingston.'

'Yes. Well, strictly speaking, of course, I should send you on your way without further delay, but I have urgent need of a frigate just now. You would not object, I take it, to delaying your arrival in Port Royal for a few days?'

'Of course not, sir,' said Slade, giving the only answer that he could.

'Splendid. I have a little task for you, a very urgent one. To be candid, I was delighted to see your ship enter the harbour just now because I had been seriously considering taking this weed-encrusted hulk away from her bed of beef-bones but your provident arrival has solved my problem. Did you see the extent of my squadron out there?' he asked, waving his arm at the stern-windows. 'Two cutters and an armed lugger are all I have, apart from a brig-sloop not due back from Jamaica for another week. What wouldn't I give for another two or three sloops and a couple of frigates! Dillforth keeps me woefully short of ships, the – ' He pulled himself up, dangerously near to openly criticizing his Commander-in-Chief in front of a captain about whom he knew little. 'Well, never mind my little problems. Let us concentrate on yours.'

He rose from his chair and walked across to his chart table. 'Come over here, Slade, if you please.'

Upton ran a yellow finger along the curving chain of the Leeward and Windward Islands and halted it with a decisive jab at a small island between Dominica and Martinique. 'San Paulo. Captured by us in fifty-nine but in French hands these many years now. There is a man being held on that island. I want you to bring him here to Antigua.'

Slade peered at the chart, frowning. 'Is he a Frenchman, sir?'

'Far from it. He is an Englishman – from Jersey, to be more precise – and a post-captain into the bargain. So far as you are concerned his name is Black – the French Republicans on San Paulo knew him by another name, rather more Gallic. Suffice to say that he was concerned with the work of certain Royalist factions on the island and that is all that you need to know. He failed to make his rendezvous with one of my cutters last week and yesterday I learned from sources in Guadaloupe that he is in Republican hands, being held in Fort St Pierre on the south-west of the island here. I also learned that certain officials from Guadaloupe are on their way to question him even now, no doubt in their usual, gentle, Republican fashion.' He looked up from the chart and fixed Slade with his penetrating old eyes. 'Captain Black is very highly thought of in Admiralty and Government circles; he has done sterling work, dangerous work, for us for many years. If he is still alive, captain, get him out and bring him here.'

'I shall do my best, sir.'

'I cannot ask for more than that.' Upton searched beneath the charts and papers on the chart table. 'I had Bowers draw up a sketch-map of the island. Now where –? Ah!' He walked back to his jumbled table and put his hand unerringly on a sheet of paper beneath the toast-rack. 'Here it is!'

The two men bent over the sketch-map, the little admiral stabbing with his finger.

'To the south-west here is Fort St Pierre. Bowers has a plan of that. As you can see it is about a mile inland, built on flat land where the hills level out to the sugar-cane plantations. There are high cliffs along this stretch of the coast but just here there is a little bay where Black used to meet the cutter once a month. I would suggest that as your landing site. Six miles along the coast here is the island's main harbour, Pointe Rouge. A very nasty place this, from your point of view – see the narrow entrance? And it has thirty-two-pounders set up on the heights on either side. A bad place to try and get into and just as bad to get out again. I would not advise you to attempt to enter.'

He paused and looked up at Slade with an expectant expression on his worn face. Slade gathered that it was time for him to make a contribution.

'You have a diversionary attack in mind, sir? A feint at the harbour to hold their attention and possibly draw the soldiers from the fort?'

'Well, that is what *I* had in mind when I was thinking of taking this old tub out but of course you are at liberty to make your own plans. Now, I can let you have an armed cutter and forty Marines to bolster your landing party. I would press on you once again, captain, the need for urgency. If Captain Black is to be brought out alive every minute is vital.'

'I understand, sir. However, I do need to take on water and if I am to make a diversionary attack on the harbour I shall need more powder. Yesterday's skirmish left me a – '

Upton smiled and clapped him on the back. 'You will have your water and powder within the hour and your Marines within two. I will send your written orders across very shortly, together with all the information I have on San Paulo. Try and bring your ship back in one piece, Slade – Sir John will be displeased enough as it is that I have delayed one of his precious frigates from taking up her proper duties.'

'I will bear it very much in mind, sir.'

Upton chuckled. 'I am sure you will.' He took Slade by the arm and walked with him to the door. 'I will not detain you any longer. You will have things to do, water, Marines, so forth, but no doubt you will be ready to sail by – noon, shall we say?'

Chapter 6

Lamb uttered a soft curse as his foot struck one of the heavy iron ring-bolts amidships. It's blacker than a witch's quim, he thought, as he edged his way past the mainmast, the line of armed seamen waiting at the side evident only by the stench of stale rum and long-chewed tobacco. Slade had ordered almost every light in the ship to be extinguished while the frigate and the cutter were still several miles from the island and the lean moon and heavy cloud made the familiar walk of the deck a blind stumble littered with obstacles. Feeling his way forward Lamb's ears picked up the shuffle of leather soles and the faint clinking of brass buckles and musket-sling swivels.

'Mr Vaughan?' he called softly.

'Beside you,' came the quiet voice of the Marine lieutenant close to his ear.

Lamb reached out and gripped Vaughan's arm, substituting touch for vision. 'We should be embarking in a few minutes, Harry. Are your men all ready?'

'As ready as they will ever be, though how the devil the boats will find the shore in this darkness, let alone that little bay, is beyond me.'

Lamb grinned in the darkness. 'Have no fear, little soldier man; we simple seamen have our mysterious ways. And to put your mind completely at rest, I am in charge of the leading boat!'

'Should I take comfort from that?' wondered the Marine aloud to Lamb's unseen back as he made his way along the dark deck to the quarterdeck.

Light-hearted as his remarks to Vaughan had been, the imminent boat journey was a source of worry that had nagged at him for the past hour or so. He had not expected the darkness to be so utterly complete and the prospect of leading the boats over a pitch-black sea to a narrow cove without benefit of a

94

shaded lantern by which to check his compass was daunting. Slade had been unsympathetic and quite adamant – the only hope, in his view, of an undisturbed landing lay with a silent and unseen approach.

'Far be it from me to tell you how to navigate a boat at this late stage in your career, Mr Lamb,' he had said stiffly. 'In any case, you will have less than a mile to pull and the sea is almost flat calm. But remember – wait off-shore until you hear the sound of the harbour's guns. Then pull for the shore for all you are worth. I shall not be able to entertain those French gunners indefinitely.'

Lamb made his way up the quarterdeck ladder and touched his hat punctiliously to the dark bulk standing by the rail as he reported the men and Marines ready and the boats at their falls.

'Very good,' said Slade and turned to the master standing behind the wheel. 'How much longer, Mr Goode?'

The master bent to peer at the watch beside the dim light of the binnacle. 'Just over two minutes, I make it, sir.'

Lamb fervently hoped that Goode's reckoning was accurate. Slade had instructed the master to take the frigate to one mile off the shore, where he would drop the boats before continuing on to Pointe Rouge, but Goode was a cautious man, bound to err on the side of safety and Slade's mile would be rather shorter than the master's mile. If Goode was a minute or two out in his reckoning into the bargain, then Slade's promise of a one-mile pull for the boats might well turn out to be twice that distance or more. The commander of the cutter, Lieutenant England, had suggested, with cheerful innocence, that as he knew these waters well the *Adroit* should latch on to his stern and follow him in. Slade had listened with a cold stare and then flatly refused, adding the comment that the suggestion smacked of impertinence. The twelve-gun cutter, all jibs and fore-and-aft mainsail, was now following sedately astern, her captain no doubt grateful for the dim light showing through the frigate's stern window, thoughtfully arranged by a considerate Slade. Lamb would have been only too happy for Slade to have fallen in with England's suggestion. Goode was without doubt an excellent navigator but he knew little of these waters. The landing place was a narrow, sandy bay between high, rocky headlands and a few hundred yards in either direction would bring the boats to steep cliffs that plunged straight down into deep water. The thought of leading a chain of boats crammed with men into that horrible situation made him go cold.

'I'll get to the launch, sir,' he said.

'Very well,' said Slade absently.

And good luck to you, too, sir, thought Lamb as he descended to the maindeck. He made his careful way to the waist and the launch hanging from its falls at the starboard side. Slade's voice sounded in a deep growl from the quarterdeck. 'Haul tops'l sheets and clew lines. Helm a-lee.'

The frigate came round into the wind and immediately began to lose way, ghosting quietly along on the black water.

'Into the launch!' hissed Lamb to the group of dark figures at the side. 'Quietly, now.'

He turned his back on the men's dark jostlings and muttered curses and made a quick round of the deck. Besides the launch, the *Adroit* carried the captain's gig, two cutters, a pinnace and a jolly boat, and they were all to be used tonight by the landing party. Satisfied that each boat was preparing to be lowered, he had a hasty, last minute word with the boat commanders and returned to the starboard waist. The slack fall-ropes told him that the launch was in the water and clambering upon the side he hitched his sword into the small of his back and lowered himself hand over hand down the ropes.

'Stand clear below,' he muttered and searched with his feet for a thwart. An unseen hand gripped his shin and guided his foot to a clear space on the thwart. He released his hold on the ropes just as the boat rocked to a small swell and he landed heavily, one foot on the thwart and the other on the bottom boards, his shin smartly protesting at the loss of several inches of skin. Swearing savagely beneath his breath he squeezed his way between the tight-packed men to the stern of the launch and settled himself at the tiller.

'Shove off,' he gritted between clenched teeth. 'Out oars. Give way together.'

Fifty yards from the ship he ordered the men to rest on their oars and turning on his seat, searched anxiously in the darkness for the rest of the flotilla. He heard their oars before he saw the dim, white splashes of their blades and called softly. One by one they lined up astern; the cutter's gig, containing twenty of the additional Marines, crossed oars with those of the *Adroit*'s gig. The resulting clash and the muted snarls of cursing brought forth a furious hiss from Lamb.

'Hold your fucking tongues back there!'

A line was passed from the launch to the boat immediately astern and was passed on in turn before being finally secured to the bow of the last in line. Lamb sat and waited with his hand on the smooth timber of the tiller bar until he received the message relayed from the last boat.

'Line secured, sir. Five boats in line astern of us, sir.'

Relieved that so far none of his flotilla had gone astray Lamb ordered the launch to give way and the men dug in their oars and pulled for the distant, invisible shore. The line astern lifted and pulled tight, bringing a temporary check to the progress of the launch before it slackened as the the boat astern picked up the pace.

'We ain't got to tow that fucking lot, have we?' whispered a wag in the centre of the launch, raising a soft chuckle from the other men and an immediate warning snarl from Lamb.

The black water was calm, with just a gentle swell to give a slight rise and fall to the stern of the launch as Lamb gripped the tiller and strained his ears to catch the hiss of the sea washing the shore. Mercifully, after rowing half a mile or so the clouds thinned long enough for a brief glimpse of the moon's meagre light to shine through and Lamb thankfully checked his compass. They were ten degrees off course. He eased the tiller over to bring the launch round in a gentle curve, grateful for the line stretching astern. There could be no excuse for any of the boats losing touch with their leader.

'Cliffs ahead, sir.' This was from Isherwood, leaning well out over the stem in order to give his eyes an extra yard of vision.

'Can you see the cove?' Lamb whispered anxiously, peering ahead at the dark, low mass that had loomed up ahead, dimly visible against the charcoal clouds. There was silence for a second or two as Isherwood scanned the line of cliffs.

'No cove, sir.' The tone was definite.

Shit! They must have been off course for a considerable time before he had discovered the error – perhaps since they had left the ship – and his correction had been insufficient. He pushed the tiller away from him, bringing the launch parallel with the shoreline.

'Keep your eyes skinned, Isherwood,' he called in a low voice.

'Aye aye, sir,' came the soft reply.

Lamb eased his watch from the tight confines of his waistcoat pocket and opening the case he held it in his lap hoping for another glimpse of moonlight. It came almost immediately and he brought the timepiece close to his eye. The hands showed a solid vertical line. Midnight – the *Adroit*'s guns should be sounding any minute now, he thought, holding his watch to his ear in order to listen to its reassuring little heart-beat. He scanned the black, undulating line of cliff-top to his left as the launch moved southwards to a medley of creaking rowlocks, softly-splashing oars and heavily-breathing men. The sickening thought suddenly came to him that he had made a dreadful error. Had he turned the wrong way? Were they, in fact, pulling away from the bay instead of towards it? He felt the sweat break out on his brow. Any moment now and the frigate's guns would sound, the French would answer and instead of dashing for the beach they would be floundering about like –

'The cove is in sight, sir,' reported Isherwood quietly.

Thank Christ for that! Lamb wiped his sleeve across his forehead and pulled the tiller towards him slightly, edging the boat over to the shore. Two more minutes of hard pulling and the little bay was directly abeam, visible only as a gap in the skyline between steeply rising headlands. Lamb pointed the bow at the bay and when a glance behind him showed the dim bulk of the *Adroit*'s cutter directly astern he called a low-voiced order over his shoulder and directed his own men to back their oars and hold the water. The launch lost way and sat gently rising and falling on the black silk of the water. The clouds thinned again and Lamb snatched a glance at his watch. Twelve minutes past the hour. The *Adroit*'s guns were overdue.

'It will be midnight, give or take a few minutes,' Slade had stated at the briefing of his officers. 'By the time your boats have reached position I should be off Pointe Rouge. Captain England and I will be dodging about a great deal and our gunfire will necessarily be erratic but at the first sound of the harbour's thirty-two-pounders you will head for the shore.

From then on, do not waste a minute.'

Twelve-fifteen. Well, there was no great need for haste yet. All being well, once they landed the thing should all be over in two hours and they would be back in their boats heading out to meet the *Adroit* well before sunrise. A curious sound came to his ear from within the launch; he leaned forward, frowning in puzzlement. Jesus Christ, someone was snoring!

'Wake that idle bugger up,' he hissed.

There was a low titter of stifled laughter from the men and the dull thump of a hard hand on the sleeper's head. The snoring stopped abruptly and the boat rocked as the indignant seaman turned to glare behind him.

'Who the fuck – ?'

'Shut your mouth,' growled Isherwood from the bow.

A tiny flash of yellow light suddenly showed to the south, followed long seconds later by the faint, flat bark of light guns – three or four pounders. So Slade had allowed Lieutenant England the dubious glory of inviting the first retaliation from the French guns? Slade was no fool, Lamb decided. There was a long silence as they waited for the sound of the harbour's heavy guns. The cutter's guns fired again – bang! bang! Her four-pound bow-chasers by the sound of it, thought Lamb. The silence came again, deep and heavy. Were the French asleep? A yellow flash lit up the sky to the south. Ah! He waited, counting the long seconds. It came at last, the deep, unmistakable grumble of a big gun, followed straightaway by the sound of another. The French had woken up at last.

'Give way together! Pull hard, lads!'

The men bent their backs with a will, pleased to have done with the long, silent wait. This time there was no tightening of the line stretching astern – the sound of the heavy guns had been as plain a signal to the other boat commanders as it had been to Lamb. The headlands hugging the sides of the little bay opened out to receive the launch and the keel dug into the soft sand a dozen yards from the line of gently hissing surf. The men pulled in their oars and sprang over the side to hold the boat steady as Lamb picked his way forward and stepped into the warm, shallow water.

'Get the boat well up the beach,' he ordered as he splashed ashore. 'Smartly, now! the others are very nearly on top of you.

Mr Allwyn, see to the unloading. I'm going to climb the slope yonder for a look round.'

Leaving the men struggling with the launch Lamb turned his back to the sea and ploughed his way up the steep, grassy slope that backed the tiny cove. He could see the dark silhouette of trees at the top. The sound of a heavy gun grumbled in the distance, followed immediately by the lighter note of the *Adroit*'s long-guns and then the heavy guns again, one, two, three, a pause and then twice again; the French gunners had finally got the sleep out of their eyes, he thought grimly. He set himself at the steep rise at a run, crouching forward against the slope, his toes digging into the sandy soil beneath the thin turf, the smell of crushed grass and damp earth in his nostrils. The short confines of a frigate's deck provided little space in which to exercise leg muscles and long before Lamb reached the trees at the top of the rise he had slowed to a walk, his calves aching abominably and his panting breath loud in his ears. The slope levelled out to a small plateau in front of the trees and here he halted, panting and sweating. The quarter-moon suddenly found a ragged hole in the clouds and the scene below him was bathed in hard, silver light.

Lamb swore softly. 'Stay dark, stay dark,' he muttered, thinking of the *Adroit* and the little cutter exposed to the eyes of the French gunners. He glanced quickly around him. The rocky headlands on either side of the little cove curved inwards as they retreated from the sea and merged into the tree-clad knoll behind him. Below, the boats had been pulled high up the beach into the shadow of the enclosing cliff and he could see Vaughan and the two sergeants marshalling the Marines into two long files at the foot of the slope, their red coats showing black in the moonlight. The seamen, in the unmilitary but no less disciplined manner of seamen everywhere, were bunched into groups beside their divisional officers, their sections of scaling ladders, barrels of powder, coils of rope and muskets piled into untidy heaps on the sand. The *Adroit*'s guns sounded again, four of five separate reports in as many seconds and Lamb turned and headed for the trees. The spinney was no more than fifty or sixty yards deep and he was able to follow an ancient path of soil and rock through the sparse undergrowth. The path came out in the cleared, cultivated land that stretched to as far as he could see in the dim light, planted with straight rows of young sugar canes as high as his knee. Keeping in the shadow of the trees he held his breath and listened, turning his head from side to side. He heard nothing apart from the rustle of the young canes in the light wind and he turned and plunged back into the trees, emerging at the top of the rise as the moon vanished again. The French guns were sounding in the distance as he returned at a headlong run, his coat-tails flying and his sword jumping on his hip, revelling in the unaccustomed pleasure of stretching his legs at speed and his effortless strides downhill on the soft turf.

Vaughan, standing in front of his men at the foot of the slope, turned in alarm at the sound of Lamb's thudding feet and made a grab at his sword hilt.

'What the devil – ?' he snapped as Lamb came to an unsteady halt beside him, breathing hard.

'Forgive me, Harry, I did not mean to alarm. I came down a shade faster than I intended.'

Vaughan slammed his half-drawn sword back into its scabbard and turned away with an annoyed click of his tongue. Lamb felt his ears grow warm, aware that his precipitate descent had been foolish. He tugged his watch from his pocket and peered closely at its face. Twelve-forty. He made some silent calculations. With a little over a mile to march, albeit in strange country, the Marines should be at the fort in thirty minutes or less. Give them another fifteen minutes to get into position and set their bomb, that takes it up to forty-five, add on five minutes for set-backs, say half-past one.

'Are you and your men all ready for off?' he asked the Marine.

'Yes, and have been these past five minutes,' said Vaughan shortly, clearly not intending to forgive Lamb for alarming him in a hurry.

'Off you go, then. You have fifty minutes. At half-past one precisely I shall expect to hear your powder go up. Good luck, Harry.'

He held out his hand. The Marine gripped it briefly. 'And to you. Sergeant O'Keefe! Get them moving!'

The red-coated files moved off and began to climb the slope, two of the Marines carrying a barrel of the gunner's second-best gunpowder slung between them. At their rear trailed a single disconsolate seaman, Little, second gun-captain on number-eight gun. His pockets were stuffed with lengths of slow-match, tallow and other accoutrements of his art. It would be Little's task to set off the bomb and he plainly had no liking to be taken from his mates and put with the bullocks. The moon had started to play hide-and-seek with the earth, peeping and retreating from little breaks in the clouds and enabling Lamb to watch the Marines disappear over the brow of the slope. He made his way to the waiting seamen.

Slade had retained Rank, the second lieutenant, to help him work the ship and had sent Ball and Collier with the landing party. The cutter could ill afford to send any men at all and her gig had been crewed by men from the *Adroit* with the ungainly Midshipman Hopper in charge.

'Right, Mr Ball,' said Lamb, briskly formal. 'It is time you were on your way. We have forty-five minutes before Vaughan's bomb goes off so keep up a smart pace. Mr Collier, follow on behind and don't lose touch with the leading division. The same goes for you, Mr Hopper.' He turned to face the waiting seamen and raised his voice. 'Remember what you were told, you men. Silence is absolutely vital during the march. If I hear any man jawing I shall personally slice off his tongue and stuff it up his arse – let him see how it wags there! Lead on, Mr Ball.'

The men bent for their loads, grinning at Lamb's coarseness and the imagery it evoked. Lamb watched them plough through the sand in single file, laden with coils of rope, grapnels, sections of ladders, muskets and cutlasses. As Ball's men began to climb the slope he turned and made his way to Hopper's division, scanning the dim figures as they passed him.

'Mr Quinn? Where is Mr Quinn?'

A bulky figure plodded from the line of men towards him. 'Here, sir.'

'You are bringing up the rear-guard, are you not, Mr Quinn? We have not a great deal of time so don't let the men straggle – keep them moving at a smart pace. And don't forget, any injured men are to be left and collected on the way back. And don't lose touch with Mr Hopper. Right, off you go, Mr Quinn.'

The stone-faced sergeant-at-arms touched his forehead in

salute and set off to take his place at the rear of the column. There would be few seamen inclined to hang back, knowing that Quinn was treading on their heels, thought Lamb, himself never entirely easy in the presence of that menacing personality. He gave a last quick look around the little beach, cursed as he saw a coil of rope left behind by an absent-minded or crafty seaman and snatching it up hurried off after the trudging line of men.

'Here, Mr Quinn, find a man to take this,' he said as he caught up with the master-at-arms, passing him the coil of rope without breaking his stride. The grassy slope seemed steeper and longer the second time up and Lamb was drenched with sweat and breathing heavily by the time he drew level with Ball at the head of the long column just entering the trees. He matched the stout lieutenant's pace and the two of them strode on together in silence, Lamb content to allow Ball to navigate while he went over the details of the plan for the attack on the fort.

Within the broader framework of the admiral's proposals, the assault had been worked out by Slade and tactfully amended by Vaughan and Lamb, the captain grudgingly allowing that the Marine might have a little expertise in this field. Fort St Pierre, according to the information Slade had gleaned from Upton's flag lieutenant, was not so massive as Fort St Louis in Martinique which the men of HMS *Zebra* had scaled recently but it was, nevertheless, a substantial and heavily manned stronghold. Its walls were over twenty feet high, topped with three-pounder guns, unbroken except for one great gate. Slade's diversion at Pointe Rouge would, it was hoped, entice many of the men and their officers away from the fort, either with thoughts of assisting in the defence of the harbour or of viewing the entertainment. Vaughan staked his life that the ruse would work; no soldier worth his salt, not even the French, would skulk in safety while foreign forces threatened to destroy the town a scant few miles away. Slade had the most difficult task, that of convincing the harbour's defenders for an hour or so that he meant business while at the same time endeavouring not to get the *Adroit* and the cutter blown out of the water. The darkness would help; by constantly dodging about and firing the guns from different positions it was hoped that the French would not realize that there was but one ship and a cutter intent on destroying their harbour.

The task of the Marines was to create a second, smaller diversion at the entrance to the fort. Hopefully, the destruction of the gate by the bomb and the Marines' musket-fire from without would convince the defenders that a frontal attack through the gate was about to take place and while the French soldiers were occupied there, Lamb and his men would scale the wall at the rear. It all seemed straightforward enough, reflected Lamb, if one disregards the ifs and the buts. What if the fort commander is suspicious or indifferent or simply drunk and refuses to allow his men to leave the fort to go off to the harbour? What if Vaughan and his men are surprised on the road and get pinned down – or lose their way? What if the gate withstands the blast from Little's bomb? What if the scaling ladders are too short? Well, thought Lamb philosophically, what will be, will be; we will either succeed or we will not. Two hours will tell, by which time we should be back in the boats pulling for the *Adroit* – if she has not been blown out of the water by then. He grinned at himself and his thoughts – he was fast becoming a prophet of doom.

Ball halted the column at the edge of the trees beside the plantation and he and Lamb peered across the neat rows of young canes. Lamb pictured the sketch-map in his mind; skirting the far side of the field and backed by steeply rising ground was the road which ran along the western flank of the island, connecting the settlement in the north to Point Rouge in the south, passing Fort St Pierre on the way. The fort lay in the elbow of the road as it swung south-east, at the foot of the hills which climbed to a high range along the spine of the island. The column must cross the road and climb the slope beyond for several hundred feet before turning south and rounding the hill in order to approach the fort from the rear. There was a little more light here than there had been among the trees but even so Lamb had to bring his watch close to his face to make out the position of the hands. Very nearly one o'clock, with half-a-mile of rough ground yet to cover.

He tapped Ball on the shoulder. 'We must make haste. Send out the for'ard party.'

Ball turned and hissed his orders. The half-dozen men

scurried off into the canes at a low crouch, their feet almost noiseless in the tilled soil. Lamb sank to one knee to await the return of the messenger and felt a heart-jerking shock as an enormous explosion from the direction of the harbour smashed the silence of the night air and the sky to the south was momentarily lit by a baleful orange glare. The two officers stared at one another as the rumbling echoes died away, the same unspoken question on their lips. The *Adroit*? They waited in frozen silence for long seconds and then gave simultaneous grins of relief as the distant growl of the frigate's twelve-pounders sounded, one, two, three, four, five. Whatever the source of that mighty explosion might have been, it was certainly not the *Adroit*. If it had been the cutter's magazine blowing up that was unfortunate but hardly a loss on the same scale. As if in defiance of this slur, the cutter's guns barked, once, twice, followed by the deep grumble of the harbour's thirty-two-pounders. Things were still busy around Pointe Rouge.

A dark figure came into view, running hard, about twenty yards to their left and halted in front of the trees, his head turning to left and right. Lamb called him with a low whistle.

'Sorry, sir,' said the man, coming up. 'You was too well hid. Mr Allwyn sends his respec's, sir, and it's all clear at the road.'

'Very good, Minter. We'll be on our way directly. Run back and inform Mr Allwyn so.'

Lamb was very conscious of the passing minutes. Slade and England could not keep up their game of tip-and-run for much longer – sooner or later they would run out of luck and a roundshot fired from the two-hundred-foot heights above the harbour could plunge through each of the *Adroit*'s decks and still have sufficient force to punch its way through her bottom. Slade's task was almost done – Lamb's part had barely begun. He and his men had to be at the fort and ready in less than thirty minutes; the thought of blundering about a dark hillside and hearing Vaughan start his commotion in the distance did not bear thinking about.

He tapped Ball on the shoulder. 'Right, Roger, off you go. Time is pressing – keep up a smart pace.' He peered over his shoulder at the little midshipman squatting behind him. 'Mr Bird, stay here and keep the men moving at a run. Tag on at the end and collect Mr Allwyn's men as you pass them.'

Lamb's long legs caught up with Ball's short ones half-way across the plantation and together they pounded through the canes until they reached Allwyn and his men crouched at the side of the road, its pale, dusty surface stretching left and right against the darker background of the cultivated ground. Ball went across at a run and plunged into the dense vegetation of the steep slope beyond as Lamb paused to have a few hasty, breathless words with Allwyn. The road was hard and rutted and Lamb crossed it in three long strides. The thick under-growth and low shrubs that covered the hill's lower slope slowed him down considerably as he made his own path beside the slower column of men, his heart pounding madly and perspiration bursting from every pore. Ball glanced at him as he came alongside but, too breathless to speak, Lamb merely gestured ahead and scrambled on. At a point he judged to be about three hundred feet above the road he halted, winded, his lungs on fire and his legs trembling, while Ball and his long tail of straggling men struggled up to meet him.

'Post a man here, Roger. He can act as a pivot for the column. If we continue around the hill we should see the fort below us.'

Ball wiped his streaming brow with his sleeve and nodded, panting hard. Lamb grinned, comforted by the knowledge that the plump lieutenant was in no better shape than he and moved on, keeping the dim road below on his right hand. The realization suddenly came to him that he had not heard gunfire for some minutes. Slade must have called an end to his game – or had it called for him. The action now rested entirely with him and his party, he thought, pushing forward at a fast pace through the clinging, scratching scrub, sliding and cursing as he struggled to keep upright on the steep, awkward slope and forced to make frequent little detours for outcrops of rock, large shrubs and trees. Five or six minutes of hard, panting work brought the fort into sudden view below, illuminated by a timely gleam of thin moonlight.

The fort was much as Slade had described it, square and squat, the sandstone blocks rising straight from the ground with strengthening columns at intervals throwing dark shad-ows into their angles. Atop each wide column guns were sited, the muzzles just projecting beyond the line of the wall; three-pounders by the look of them, thought Lamb, dismissing them. He could see no signs of activity on top of the wall although Slade had informed him that it was permanently patrolled by sentries, and he turned his attention to the three or four hundred feet of clear ground between the foot of the slope and the fort. A thin shadow meandered across the level ground and he followed it back with his eyes to where it disappeared into the scrub off to his left. He nodded thoughtfully. It was the course of a small stream, one of the many running down the hills from the craggy heights above and at this time of the year it would almost certainly be dry. The fort commander had probably considered the task of filling and diverting the stream not worth the trouble and effort, if he had considered it at all. Splendid! thought Lamb; if we can get there under cover of darkness it will provide an excellent staging place while we wait for Vaughan to start his little sideshow. He turned his head and passed his instructions to Ball in a forceful whisper. Ball nodded wearily, licking his dry lips, his face a mask of dirt and sweat.

Lamb made a careful descent to the foot of the hill and knelt at the edge of the scrub, wincing at the noise the men made as they crashed and cracked and slithered their way down to join him. The din seemed so horribly loud that he tensed expectantly, certain that a challenge from the fort was inevitable. None came and he breathed a few words of thanks upwards as the last man came to a halt behind him. By chance, it was the master-at-arms and Lamb took the opportunity to put a quiet question.

'Yes, sir,' came Quinn's hoarse whisper in reply. 'All present and correct, sir.'

Lamb felt a warm glow of pride and gratitude at the performance of his men. In spite of being out of their element, loaded down with heavy equipment and forced to run and climb in this stifling heat, not one of them had fallen behind and apart from one or two involuntary curses all of them had kept miraculously wordless. He eased his watch from his pocket. Barely three minutes left, by God! There was no time to wait for the moon to hide itself; they must take the risk and move now. He stood upright.

'Run for the stream in front of you,' he called softly. 'Lively now!'

Men were rising to their feet on each side as he left the cover of the shrub and hurled himself at a flat run across the coarse, tuffety grass, gripping his sword to keep it clear of his legs. He dropped into the dry bed of the stream and threw himself at the far bank, peering through the long grass at its edge; there was still no sign of life from the fort. Unencumbered by equipment and blessed with the longest legs in the party, he had a wait of eight or ten long seconds before the others began to arrive. He crouched on the stones of the little watercourse and watched the dark shapes of his men loom up and leap down with a thud of feet and the rattle of pebbles, ladders, muskets and cutlasses. The fort remained quiet.

Lamb moved along the bottom of the ditch at a crouch, his voice a husky whisper. 'Any moment now, lads. Get your breath back and prepare yourselves.' He moved on, repeating his message and then returned to take up his position in the centre of the long, crouching line. He waited, his eyes fixed on the fort, for Vaughan's bomb to rip apart the quiet night. The use of the bomb was a risk, the danger being that it would alert the soldiers at the harbour. Slade had taken the decision to use it; without it the fort gate would remain shut and the Marines' diversion with their muskets would lose much of its usefulness. It was hoped, however, that by the use of sandbags the sound of the explosion would be muffled to a large extent.

The seconds dragged on. It must be half-past one by now, thought Lamb, anxiously. Perhaps Little had been unable to plant his bomb? Had he given Vaughan enough time to reach the fort and position his men? The Marines' journey had been the longer, travelling in a curving march in order to approach the fort from the south but they had moved over flat, cultivated ground and had set out five minutes earlier. Yes, they must be in position now; if they had run into trouble earlier, he would have heard their musket-fire. The wait seemed interminable. He wiped the sweat from his sword-hilt on his coat-tail and rubbed his hands dry, feeling the usual faint nausea and thudding heart-beat while waiting for action. As a younger, green lieutenant, he had attributed such feelings to his apprehension over the coming battle, both in the way he would conduct himself and to the fear of having his skin punctured. Now, after experiencing battle and woundings, he no longer had any doubts as to his conduct but his fear for his flesh was as strong as ever.

A yellow flash lit the sky at the far side of the fort, the sound of the dull explosion reaching Lamb's ears a bare instant later. He was on his feet and running for the fort in the same second, the dark shapes of his men extending in a ragged line on either side, the sharp crack, crack, crack of musket-fire from Vaughan's men urging on his flying feet. Well done, Harry, smack on the minute! he thought exultantly. A dozen yards from the fort he halted and turned to wave the men on and direct the placing of the ladders. He glanced over his shoulder at the top of the wall – no movement there yet, thank God. The men in charge of the ladders were working frantically to put the sections together, surrounded by groups of milling seamen. Lamb was pleased to note that the men with the muskets had remembered their orders and were kneeling in an extended line, their weapons levelled at the parapet. The sight brought to mind his own firearms and he fumbled at his belt, clicking back the hammers on his pistols.

The ladders were being flung up against the wall, their tops projecting above the parapet, Lamb saw with relief. He ran to the nearest, holding his sword high, intent on leading the way, but as he lifted his foot to place it on the bottom rung he was elbowed aside with scant deference by a seaman, who ran up the ladder with as much ease as if it had been a staircase complete with banister rails. Insolent bastard! thought Lamb indignantly – I'll have his balls for that. He gripped the ladder again with his free hand as the seaman's head came level with the parapet. A cry of alarm came from above and a dark shape rose up behind the topmost rung of the ladder. There was a quick movement of gleaming metal and the seaman gave a choking scream. He fell sideways, landing with a bone-crunching thud beside Lamb's foot. The ladder shook as the Frenchman attempted to push it away from the wall against the pressure of the men holding it below. More shadowy figures now appeared along the parapet and immediately there came the sharp bangs and bright flashes of musket-fire from above, speedily answered by the kneeling seamen below.

'Up! Up! Before they reload!' screamed Lamb and flung himself at the rungs, his sword tucked beneath his arm and one hand scrabbling for the pistol at his belt. The ladder rocked and bounced beneath his scrambling feet and he sensed, rather than saw, the musket levelled at him from above. He swayed violently to one side as the piece fired, the ladder shaking alarmingly, his ears numbed and singing from the shattering report so close to his head. Without conscious thought he levelled his pistol at the bulking head and shoulders looming over him and pulled the trigger. The man gave a loud grunt and vanished from sight. Lamb attempted to stuff his pistol back into his belt, cursed as it slipped from his hand and took a firm grip on his sword-hilt. He took the last few rungs and vaulted over the parapet on to the walkway behind, nearly falling as he landed on the crumpled figure of the Frenchman. For a few seconds he was left unchallenged, his arrival unnoticed. To left and right of him men were leaning out over the wall, shouting and pointing, stabbing down with their bayonets, pushing at the ladders. In the lantern-lit courtyard below he could see Frenchmen with muskets streaming towards the stone steps at each end of the four walls; at the far end soldiers were kneeling and firing through the shattered gate into the darkness beyond, from where came pin-pricks of orange light as Vaughan's men plied their muskets. Suddenly Frenchmen were running at him from both sides, their mouths agape, roaring, screaming, their muskets outstretched, the long bayonets gleaming murderously. Lamb gave a back-handed slash with his sword, felt the jolt of his strike and whirled in time to knock aside the thrust of a bayonet. He stepped back and set his back against the wall, striking left and right at the men crowding in from both sides. A figure leaped from the parapet and landed lightly beside him, his cutlass whirling and hacking.

'Come on, you bastards, come on!' he snarled.

It was Isherwood, the master's mate, normally a pleasant and polite young man but now a cursing, grinning madman. Another seaman dropped down from the parapet and immediately added his own rich language to that of the master's mate as he cut and slashed. From Lamb's right, running cat-like along the top of the wall and aiming sly downward blows with his cutlass as he came, was another of the *Adroit*'s men. A bayonet lunged at Lamb from his left and he parried the blow with his arm, the point scoring his flesh from wrist to elbow.

'Bastard!' he gritted, the sharp pain flaring. He took a quick half-pace forward and struck heavily at the soldier's face with the edge of his sword. The man screamed, dropped his musket and fell to his knees, his hands clasped to his eyes. Suddenly seamen were all around, hacking, yelling, cursing; swarming on to the parapet along the length of the wall, cutting viciously at the heads beneath them. The soldiers began to fall back in disorder, struggling to reach the steps leading down to the courtyard. The Frenchmen below, unlike their colleagues above, still had loaded muskets and the lead balls suddenly began to take their toll, dropping Frenchmen and Englishmen alike as the soldiers fired indiscriminately into the milling crowd above. Stone-dust stung Lamb's cheek as a bullet glanced off the parapet close beside him and nearby a seaman dropped his cutlass and clutched his shoulder as a heavy ball knocked him backwards against the wall. A louder, more ordered volley sounded below and Isherwood gave an exultant shout into Lamb's ear.

'The Marines, sir! The Marines are in!'

The French resistance, already on the ebb, vanished completely with the inrush of Vaughan's men. Muskets clattered to the stone flags as the soldiers raised their hands in surrender, a gesture a dozen seamen chose to ignore as they pursued a handful of Frenchmen along the righthand walkway, hacking at their retreating backs. Lamb, furious at this flagrant breach of convention, screamed at them to stop, his voice thin in his dry throat.

'Stand fast, you men! Stand fast, I say!'

It was Ball and Isherwood who stopped them, beating at their shoulders with the flat of their blades and hauling them back from their victims by brute force. The seamen leaned their backs against the wall, fierce-eyed and panting hard, clearly indignant at having their sport so rudely brought to an end. Ball stayed to harangue them and Isherwood returned to Lamb, wiping his streaming face with his sleeve.

'It's difficult to stop some of them once they've got their blood-lust up, sir,' he said in an apologetic tone.

Lamb nodded wearily. He was sweat-soaked and exhausted,

his throat so dry he could scarcely swallow. Ball finished his finger-shaking lecture and strode back along the walkway, his deep frown of disapproval vanishing the instant he turned his back on the seamen, to be replaced by a broad grin of triumph as he caught Lamb's eye. From the other direction came Hopper, equally happy, with blood dripping from a gash across his knuckles, a wound he was proud to ignore.

Lamb wasted no time in mutual back-slapping. 'Assemble the men in the courtyard, Mr Ball,' he ordered, reverting to quarterdeck formality now that the intimacy of shared danger was over. 'They can assist the Marines in rounding up the prisoners. Mr Hopper, take a couple of useful men and spike every gun on the walls. You will find all you need in the blacksmith's forge, I should imagine. Where is Mr Collier, by the way? Was he hit? Have either of you seen him lately?'

'He's still below, outside the wall. Sprained ankle, he said,' said Ball shortly.

Lamb raised his eyebrows slightly at Ball's tone. Was he suggesting that Collier had been shy? He moved towards the steps leading down to the courtyard, dismissing Collier from his mind – time enough for that later.

The French officers had deserted the fort, leaving, as a quick count of the French dead and living revealed, about a hundred and forty soldiers to guard the stronghold. Fair enough odds! thought Lamb, thinking of his own one hundred and eight men. Small parties of seamen and Marines were sent off to search the buildings around the inner walls of the fort and a larger group of Marines under Sergeant O'Keefe sent trotting south a hundred yards to keep watch on the road from Pointe Rouge. The prisoners squatted in a sullen mass under the muskets and bayonets of a dozen Marines; an unkempt, dirty, unshaven lot, thought Lamb, as Ball bound his none-too-clean handkerchief around the gash in his forearm, and he sipped gratefully at a pint of cool, earthy-tasting water drawn from the deep well in a corner of the courtyard. Vaughan returned from his tour of the fort, with two of his men escorting a huge bear of a man wearing the chevrons of a *sous-officier*.

'Well, if Captain Black is in the fort I don't know where they have hidden him,' he said. 'There are a couple of soldiers in the guardroom cells but apart from those there are no signs of any other prisoners.' His uniform was dark with sweat and the fine white dust of the road coated his damp face. Lamb dipped his beaker into the bucket of well-water and handed it to the Marine.

'They must have a place here for their civilian prisoners,' he said. 'Either in one of these buildings or else underground.'

'Well, it is not in any of the buildings, I can swear to that. We did find something very interesting, though – a dozen whores, ensconced in rooms above the officers' mess. Some fine pieces among them, too – one yellow-haired wench in particular set my –'

'Yes, I'm sure,' said Lamb impatiently. He nodded at the giant Frenchman. 'Who is this?'

'The senior warrant-officer, I believe, according to his badge of rank. I thought you might want to question him.'

'I see. How is your French?'

'Execrable,' grinned Vaughan proudly.

Lamb looked at Ball. 'And yours?'

'Worse!'

Lamb grunted and studied the warrant-officer. The man stared back at him, defiance showing in every line of his dark-eyed, dark-bristled face.

'*Où sont les prisonniers?*' asked Lamb, enunciating slowly.

The man lifted his lip. '*Cochon!*' he sneered.

Vaughan brought the flat of his sword heavily across the man's shoulders. 'Manners!' he cautioned.

A Marine corporal came running from the squat building set beside the gate and halted beside Vaughan, his arm flashing up in a salute.

'Yes, corporal?'

'We've found a trap-door at the back of the guardroom, sir, padlocked. I've left two men breaking it open, sir.'

'This could be what we are looking for,' said Lamb and strode off in the direction of the guard-house.

The trap-door was leaning back against its hinges, the huge lock dangling open from its hasp.

'You found the key, then?' enquired Lamb of the two Marines.

'No, sir,' said one of them proudly. 'Morgan here can do

113

wonders with a two-inch nail, sir.'

Lamb regarded Morgan thoughtfully; there were a good many locks on the *Adroit*, including two on the spirit-room door. He reached for a lantern hanging from a wall-bracket and held it over the opening. Stone steps led down into darkness. He descended cautiously with Vaughan and Ball hard on his heels, the air hot and humid, the stench of human waste thick in his nostrils. A stone-flagged passage ran forward from the bottom step with doorless openings along one side. Lamb held the lantern in at the first. A black man, shackled to the wall, rolled wary, bloodshot eyes at him. Lamb moved on to the next cell. It was empty. The next contained a swarthy Creole who at the sight of Lamb clasped his hands with a rattle of chains and let loose a torrent of pleading Spanish. Lamb shook his head and moved on.

'Jesus Christ, the stink!' exclaimed Ball, spitting in disgust. Lamb made no answer; he was peering closely at a man, filthy but unmistakably white, manacled by his ankle to the wall of his cell. No, he decided, after a brief examination, this was not Black; the man was too old and cadaverous. The man nodded and chuckled and proffered his drinking bowl with a courteous dip of his head and a courtly sweep of his hand. Lamb glanced at the bowl and grimaced; it contained a large, human turd. He moved quickly along to the last cell to the accompaniment of a burst of maniacal laughter.

'He's here,' said Lamb quietly, over his shoulder. 'Can one of you go back and find that lock-picking Marine? And bring water and a blanket back with you.'

He placed the lantern on the floor and knelt beside the last prisoner's ruined body. He heard Vaughan give an indrawn hiss of breath at the sight of the ugly mess at the man's groin.

'Are you sure it is he?' asked the Marine in a low voice.

Lamb pointed to the man's exposed ear. Only the lower half and the lobe remained; it was an old wound. 'That is what I was told to look for.' He shook Black gently by the shoulder. 'Mr Black! Captain Black! Wake up, sir.'

The man rolled his head and muttered, his eyes flickering, showing the whites. His head fell limply to one side again. Lamb shook him more vigorously.

'Captain Black, sir! Wake up, sir! We have come to take you away from here.'

Black opened his eyes and immediately brought his hand up to cover his face. '*Non, non, ne plus,*' he protested in a faint voice.

'It's all right, sir,' said Lamb, patting Black's shoulder. 'We are friends – the Navy, sir. Can you hear me, sir?'

Black slowly rolled his head away from the wall and peered at Lamb with swollen, red-rimmed eyes.

'Who are you?' he breathed.

'Lieutenant Lamb, sir. HMS *Adroit.*'

Black nodded his head slightly, as if this was in the natural order of things. Amazingly, a tiny smile lifted the corners of his cracked lips.

'I think perhaps it would have been better had you come sooner, Mr Lamb,' he whispered and closed his eyes again.

Lamb snapped shut his watch. They had been in the fort nine minutes short of the hour and it was high time they were gone. The Frenchmen had been herded into the guardroom and the door nailed fast with half a dozen heavy spikes. The British dead, three seamen, had been laid together in a corner of the fort and decently covered with a blanket, a little tidying-up ceremony wholly for the benefit of their shipmates. Captain Black had recovered consciousness again long enough to take a little water before he slipped back into a death-like sleep and was now wrapped in a blanket at the feet of the four seamen told off to carry him.

Vaughan and Ball completed their roll-calls and reported to Lamb.

'Royal Marines all present and correct, sir,' said Vaughan, standing stiffly erect and saluting.

'Collier says he has two men adrift in his division,' said Ball, rather less formally. 'Lyall and Bentley.'

'I know where they are,' exclaimed the Marine. 'I'd forgotten all about them. I left them to watch over the whores' quarters – I didn't think it right that they should be left unguarded with all our randy men running about.'

'Hell's teeth!' said Lamb. 'It would have been safer to put a fox in a chicken-run! Mr Ball, get the men moving along the road at as smart a pace as they can manage. Harry, show me

115

where this bloody love-nest is.'

The two men ran across the courtyard to a wide, two-storey building built into a corner of the fort, a building distinguished from the other plain structures by its shrubs and flowers planted in wooden tubs along its walls and lace curtains at the windows. The wide, double doors at the top of the steps were open and Lamb followed Vaughan as he ran through the wide lobby and up the stairs. The Marine halted as he reached the top and turned to Lamb with a grin on his face and a finger raised to his lips. Lamb cocked his ear at the sound of an English voice coming from a room at the end of the corridor.

'That's it, my son, go to it hearty! Bang it home, bang it home, she can take plenty more 'an you can give her!'

The two officers strode quietly along the carpeted floor and peered in through the open doorway. A small number of young women, ranging in colour from milk-white to coal-black and apparently as unconcerned by the recent conflict outside their room as the present set-to within it, sat in a group at one side of the room busy with needles and scissors and curling-tongs. The two seamen had their backs to the door, one sitting astride a chair with a bottle in one hand and a cutlass in the other which he was flourishing to and fro in time with the rhythmical exertions of his shipmate, and the other, his trousers in folds around his ankles, gripping the naked hips of a woman whose petticoats were draped over her back as she bent forward over the back of a chaise-longue. Her head was bent low and from between her supporting arms she caught sight of the two officers in the doorway. She gave a wide, upside-down smile, not in the least abashed at being caught at her work and sang out something in patois to her workmates. The seaman's muscular buttocks clenched and lifted as he thrust, his face turned towards the ceiling, a groan beginning to grow in his throat.

Lamb's lips tightened. He took a pace into the room.

'Stop that at once!' he snapped.

The seated seaman leaped to his feet as if a powder barrel had exploded beneath him. His mate, surprised on the upthrust, became rigidly still, the girl's hips pulled tight against him. He made no attempt to turn round – placed as he was it would have been difficult. The girl said something in a droll voice and tittered into her hand while her colleagues stayed their needles and stared at the newcomers, amused and curious. For a long second the little tableau of seamen, officers and girl remained stock-still, frozen into their respective attitudes. The absurdity of the situation suddenly struck Lamb and he struggled to contain the laughter that bubbled up from his stomach. He jerked his head at the stony-faced, unattached seaman.

'Lyall, outside. Wait in the courtyard.'

The man sidled past and thudded along the corridor.

'Bentley – '

Vaughan gripped Lamb by the elbow. 'For God's sake let the man finish what he's doing. To stop him now would be brute cruelty.'

Lamb considered for a brief second. 'Right, Bentley, you have one minute. We shall wait outside the door.'

Bentley's head drooped. His voice was abjectly forlorn. 'It don't matter, sir. It wouldn't do me no good now, sir.'

He stepped back a few inches, hauled up his trousers, snatched up his cutlass from the floor and took off after Lyall like a whippet after a hare. The girl remained as she was, yellow hair cascading down, her head shaking from side to side in silent amusement, her shameless buttocks poised invitingly at the two officers, drawing their eyes like needles to a lodestone.

Vaughan's tongue flickered around his lips. 'What say we – er – ?'

For a brief moment lust struggled with duty in Lamb's mind.

'No, certainly not,' he said firmly. 'Are you mad?'

He pushed Vaughan's reluctant body through the doorway and closed it behind them with a decisive slam, cutting off the rising feminine laughter within.

The two seamen were waiting beside the steps, nervous and fidgety, as Lamb and Vaughan hurried from the building.

'Well, you are in deep trouble, you two,' said Lamb sternly. 'Negligence of duty, abandoning your post – did you pay for your pleasures, by the way?'

Lyall pointed to the small hole in his ear. 'A gold earring, sir, more than enough for us two.'

Lamb grunted. 'You have not heard the last of this little

matter. Fall in with the Marines outside the gate.'

Vaughan watched the two men haring across the empty courtyard and sighed. 'Idiots! Of all times and places.' He eased his tight breeches around his crutch.

'Harry,' said Lamb, giving him a keen look, 'if I had not been here just then would you – ?' He jerked his head in the direction of the upstair rooms.

'No, of course not!' said Vaughan valiantly. 'The very idea! I have some sense of duty, you know.'

Lamb grinned. 'Come on, you ram. Your Marines are waiting.'

The Marines were lined up in the road outside, with Lyall and Bentley trying to hide themselves at the rear. Sergeant O'Keefe was pacing up and down beside his men with every sign of impatience that he could decently exhibit.

'Are the men from the outpost all here, sergeant?' called Vaughan.

'Yes, sir. Been here for some minutes, sir.'

'Right. Let's get moving then.'

The rounding up of Lyall and Bentley had cost them nearly five minutes and as the Marines started off along the road Lamb calculated that Ball's party, with their slower pace, should be about a quarter of a mile ahead. He had a quick word with Vaughan and set off after the seamen at a rapid trot. A warm, southerly breeze was now blowing from the sea, pushing the cloud cover before it and leaving large breaks through which the moon made increasingly frequent appearances. Lamb kept to the centre of the narrow road to avoid the deep ruts at the sides, his feet kicking up puffs of white dust. He smiled as he ran; a feeling of elation which had begun to simmer quietly as Black's broken body was carried from the dungeon now boiled over and he laughed aloud – they had done it! No matter that Black was near to death; no matter that the bodies of three seamen lay under a blanket in a foreign fort; no matter that a dozen or so wounded men were now limping painfully towards the beach; he had carried out his orders to the letter and by so doing had cut another little step in the long climb to a captain's epaulette. All that remained now was to get his men back to the boats and on to the *Adroit*.

The main party came in sight as he rounded the elbow of the road, no more than a couple of hundred yards ahead, a long, straggling column, their pace slow to accommodate that of the wounded and ease the journey of Captain Black, slung between the four corners of a blanket. Lamb caught up with the rear of the column, tailed by the watchful Quinn, and moved into the ruts at the side of the road, calling out words of encouragement as he made his way to the front of the lines of men.

'Well done, my brave lads! Keep moving, keep moving! Not far to go now. We'll soon be at the boats. Step out, now! Keep moving!'

Bird's voice sang out as he drew alongside Collier's division. 'Did you find Bentley and Lyall, sir?'

'Yes,' called Lamb, slowing his pace, 'and not a moment too soon. They were in danger of losing their innocence.'

A loud rumble of laughter rose from the miscreants' shipmates and Lamb moved on, pleased that the men still had the energy and inclination to laugh after the exertions of the night, even at his weak sally. Collier, at the head of his men, was limping badly and he gave Lamb a nervous smile as he drew level.

'Wretched luck, your ankle, Mr Collier,' said Lamb loudly, 'but these things can happen to the best of us. Try not to let it slow you down.'

That should stop the mutterings among Collier's men, he thought, as he drew near the head of the column. He had no idea whether the lieutenant's injury was genuine or not. Collier's failure to make the ascent of the wall would not have gone unnoticed by his men and the plea of a badly wrenched ankle was bound to be treated with some scepticism. A reputation for shyness in battle, no matter how undeserved, could kill Collier's prospects stone dead. Lamb resolved to have a quiet word with the surgeon later and ask him to run his eye over Collier's ankle. If his injury had been faked, then, so far as Lamb was concerned, Collier was finished. In the meantime, he would give him the benefit of the doubt.

Ball's stout figure was bent over Black's body, the lieutenant walking awkwardly crabwise to keep up with the blanket bearers as Lamb panted level.

'How is he?' called Lamb.

Ball joined him at the edge of the road. 'He's not good. He is burning hot and muttering nonsense – some sort of fever, I suppose. I've just sponged his face with the last of the water.'

'Well, there is little else we can do until we reach the ship,' said Lamb, peering ahead. 'We should be nearing the point where we turn off the road. Did you mark it?'

'Yes. There is an uprooted tree with its branches caught in another, fifty feet up the hill, right opposite. We should be seeing it at any moment.'

A hundred yards further on the column swung left off the road on to the plantation. Lamb let Ball take the lead again and stood in the centre of the road to act as a turning point, chivvying the men on. He watched them pass, some limping, some wearing blood-stained rags, some, apparently, still fresh and jaunty. One seaman dragged himself along supported by two of his mates, his face twisted with agony from a bullet in his leg. Lamb's eye rested thoughtfully on Collier as that officer limped by and with some amusement on the French shakoes sported triumphantly by a few of Hopper's men.

'How is Captain Black, sir?' asked Hopper as he drew level.

'Still with us, Mr Hopper. Keep up with those in front, if you please. Step out now, you men.'

He pondered a little on Black's ghastly wounds as he tagged on to the end of the column beside the master-at-arms. Several of his fingers were quite obviously broken and he was missing a few toe-nails but the worst savagery inflicted on him had been the crude butchery done on his private parts, leaving him with a mere stub and no scrotum, the wounds cobbled together with rough stitches. Lamb winced at the thought of the agony the man had endured and the further agony of mind the future held for him if he survived. He felt the stub of his own little finger; its ghost could still make itself felt with an occasional itch and in cold weather the non-existent knuckles would ache with the chill. If a mere stub of a finger could retain the memory of its whole, could the same – ? He was jerked abruptly from this line of thought by the sound of Vaughan's voice roaring at his men some little distance behind. The drumming of hoof-beats suddenly registered on his ears, followed a half-second later by the sharp rattle of musket-fire.

'Step out smartly now!' Lamb shouted, directing his voice along the column. 'Quick as you can, straight for the beach. Lively now – move, move!'

The men picked up their feet and broke into a trot. Lamb could hear the voices of Ball and Collier urging their men on as he began to run in the opposite direction.

A party of Marines with Sergeant O'Keefe at the rear approached him at a run. There was no sign of Vaughan. Lamb held out his hand to halt the sergeant as he came level.

'Where is Mr Vaughan?'

'He's holding the road, sir, with a dozen men. Told me to make a stand at the edge of the trees, sir.'

Lamb waved him on and ran for the road. Vaughan had placed his men in two ranks across the road, facing the direction of the fort. As Lamb came near he could see the dim shapes of horsemen milling about along the road and a bright, yellow flash as a horse-pistol was fired.

Vaughan's voice rang out. 'Front rank – fire!'

The muskets of the kneeling Marines sparked and banged and jerked, with no visible results that Lamb could see. The two lines of Marines exchanged places without further orders, the front rank kneeling and aiming their muskets, the men now at the rear busy with powder, ramrods, ball and wads. Lamb hurried up to Vaughan, standing at the rear of his men.

'You cannot stay here,' he said urgently. 'They'll cut across the field and separate us from the column. Pull your men back to the trees – they can hold them off there until the boats are launched.'

'Those are the orders I gave Sergeant O'Keefe,' replied Vaughan. 'But you are right – it's time we moved. I'll give 'em a last volley. Front rank – fire!'

The muskets banged and a horse reared and screamed.

'Break off!' roared Vaughan. 'At the double, make for the trees and regroup.'

They were none too soon. As Lamb pounded along with Vaughan at the head of the small party, the sound of hooves, muted by the soft soil, and the shrill shouts of angry Frenchmen came from their left.

'Marines, halt!' barked Vaughan. 'Horsemen on the left, kneel, aim – fire!'

The dozen or so horsemen that had suddenly loomed up out of the darkness broke apart in disorder at the rattle of the muskets, wheeling left and right, some mounts rearing and a couple dashing off with empty saddles.

'Run for the trees!' screamed Vaughan with commendable brevity and the last seventy or eighty yards were covered in a headlong, breathless rush. The sergeant had deployed his men in a single line at the fringe of the wood and Vaughan's men passed through them into the shelter of the trees. The lieutenant wasted no time in gathering his breath. He ordered O'Keefe to withdraw at once to the beach.

'Corporal Hardy, Fitt, Leinster, stay with me. Grab an extra musket apiece.' He turned to Lamb. 'I'll stay here until the boats are in the water,' he said, in a tone that was in no way one of suggestion. 'When you are ready, fire a single shot – we'll come running.'

Lamb assented with a nod. Leaving Vaughan and his three men, he and the remainder of the Marines pushed on rapidly through the darkness of the little copse and emerged at the top of the steep, grassy slope leading to the beach. This time there was none of the exuberant leaping and running of his earlier descent – his legs, leaden and aching, protested painfully enough at this slow, stumping, downward progress. The boats, he was pleased to see, were in the water, held steady by seamen standing thigh-deep just beyond the surf. Ball's rotund shape advanced to meet Lamb at the foot of slope.

'The boats are in the water, sir,' he reported formally.

'Good man. Put half a dozen of these Marines into the launch and the rest among the other boats. Leave the launch and take the others well out. There might well be – '

He stopped as the crack, crack of musket-fire sounded from the heights behind him.

'That's Vaughan! Take those boats out, quick as you can. Sergeant O'Keefe! Fire one shot into the air. Into the boats, you men – smartly now!'

Lamb waited, clinging to the bow of the bobbing launch, the water swirling between knees and waist, his gaze fixed anxiously on the dark blur of the rise at the back of the beach. Suddenly, the thin crescent of the moon slid coyly out from behind a bank of cloud and gently illuminated the boats, the beach and the slope in silver and black shadow.

'Shit!' said Lamb tersely. Vaughan and his men were starkly visible half-way down the slope, leaping and sliding, bent-legged, encumbered with their extra muskets. Behind them, swarming over the knoll, was a group of about two dozen Frenchmen carrying muskets, pistols and naked sabres. This is cutting things a bit bloody fine! thought Lamb and threw a hasty glance behind him. The nearest boat was a couple of hundred yards out and pulling hard – safe enough, he decided. He called to the men in the launch.

'Those men with muskets, kneel and cover our men ashore. Don't fire until I give the word. The rest of you keep your heads down!'

The four men were thirty yards from the surf when a single musket-shot sounded from behind them. Vaughan was knocked violently sideways and fell headlong on to the sand, his tall hat rolling away down the beach. Two of the Marines immediately turned back and taking an arm each dragged him, his toes furrowing the sand, headfirst into the surf. The third Marine, not to be outdone in the way of gallantry, chased after his commander's hat and brought it, grinning, to the launch.

'Bloody fool!' snapped Lamb, furious at this time-wasting display of bravado. 'Get in!'

More shots sounded from the beach as Lamb swung himself inboard and crouched beside the wet, slumped figure on the bottom boards. A lead ball hummed menacingly past his ear and another thudded into the bow. The group of musketeers knelt forty yards from the launch, their weapons levelled.

'Give way together! Fire your muskets, you men!' shouted Lamb in an odd mixture of seamanlike command and unmilitary order. The rolling, dipping launch was no steady platform from which to aim muskets and the little fusilade of lead balls left the Frenchmen unscathed; they, too, panting and trembling from their chase, were no better marksmen and the reply they sent after the launch did no more than send splinters flying harmlessly from the starboard strakes. Mercifully, the moon slipped back behind its curtain of cloud while the soldiers were reloading and their last volley was sent over a dark sea, leaving the launch and its occupants untouched.

Chapter 7

Lamb kept the boats together a mile from the shore and there, as the sky began to pale in the east, England's cutter found them, flashing a signal to the *Adroit* a mile to windward as she tacked to meet them. The frigate immediately came round into the wind and backed her topsails, sitting on the water and holding the wind as Lamb ordered his tired men to ply their oars again. He sat in the stern of the launch, his hand resting on the tiller, bone-weary; it was an effort to raise an arm in response to England's cheerful wave from the deck of the cutter where he stood awaiting the arrival of his gig and his share of the Marines. The boats crept like snails towards the frigate; Lamb made no attempt to quicken their pace – the fact that the men had enough energy and strength to row at all was, from his standpoint, surprising. He glanced at Vaughan sitting on the bottom boards, his back resting against a thwart, his torn and bloody shirt draped over his shoulders. He was fortunate, thought Lamb, who had examined him and placed a rough dressing of part of Vaughan's shirt, dampened with sea-water, over his wound. The bullet had been deflected by a rib, cutting a deep groove beneath his armpit and biting a lump of muscle from his upper arm as it glanced off. Providing he kept infection at bay he would suffer no more than a cracked rib and a sore arm for a week or so. Lamb had a great deal of faith in the curative and cleansing properties of sea-water. Vaughan's conduct during the night had surprised Lamb somewhat; until now, judging him only by his speech and manner in the gunroom, he had placed him as a pleasant, idle fellow with a loud laugh and too little in the way of shipboard duties to occupy himself. The night's events, however, had revealed him as a capable, decisive officer. The white-faced lieutenant opened his eyes and peered groggily at Lamb.

'How are you feeling?' asked Lamb.

Vaughan gave a wan grin. 'Never better!'

The frigate seemed to be undamaged as the launch approached but as it pulled round her starboard side Lamb saw a gaping wound in her forward bulwark, the timbers below scarred and splintered as though a giant axe had swung down and clipped her side from her rail to near the waterline. He needed no telling what had been the cause; it was clear enough – an enormous roundshot falling from a great height. A foot or so more travel or with the frigate heeling the other way and the results would have been vastly more unfortunate.

Slade and the surgeon were bending over the unconscious body of Captain Black on the deck as Lamb dragged himself wearily over the side. He called to a nearby boatswain's mate.

'Send down a chair for Mr Vaughan, Hopgood. Hoist him slow and easy.'

Slade turned at the sound of Lamb's voice and strode across the deck to meet him.

'Well, Mr Lamb?' he asked, his heavy eyebrows lifted.

Lamb had no hat to remove; that had vanished in the desperate dash to the fort. He touched his forehead instead and said simply, 'Three seamen dead, eleven wounded, sir, not counting Captain Black.'

Slade grunted. In spite of his activities of the night he looked spruce and clean, his large, red face freshly shaven. He nodded at the sodden rag around Lamb's forearm. 'And do you include yourself among that number?'

'No, sir, it is but a scratch.'

'So, three men dead, a dozen wounded and my ship damn near sunk. A heavy price to pay for a near corpse, Mr Lamb; hardly a bargain, would you say?'

Lamb's lips tightened. A retort concerning the value of hindsight hovered on his tongue but caution prevailed. 'Perhaps not, sir,' he contented himself with saying.

'Well, it cannot be helped.' Slade smiled and gripped Lamb warmly by the arm. 'I have no criticism of your actions, Mr Lamb. You did all that was expected of you and I shall underline your efforts in my report to the Admiral. You had better turn in for an hour or two – you look all in. I shall not need your written report until noon.'

'You are most kind, sir,' said Lamb, careful to keep any trace of irony from his voice. He nodded in the direction of the damaged bulwark. 'I see you had a close shave there, sir.'

'Yes, too damned close! I misjudged their range at the outset and that was from their very first shot. Pure luck on their part, of course, because it was as black as Newgate's knocker at the time. Did you hear one almighty bang later?'

'Yes, sir. We thought for one awful moment that the *Adroit* had blown up.'

'So did I for a second! No, from the size of the explosion it was a magazine, on the right-hand side of the harbour. A little carelessness on someone's part, I imagine. At any rate, it put paid to their capers for quite some time, I'm glad to say.'

The surgeon approached, fastidiously wiping his hands on his coat-tails. His long-jawed Scots face was dour.

'Well, Mr Andrews, what are his chances?'

'Not very high, in my humble opinion, sir. Those Republican butchers cobbled him together with a few sutures – an untidy job they made of it, too! – but he has lost a good deal of blood, I fear, and what he has left is almost certainly poisoned. He is weak and in high fever. I shall give him infusions of bark with a little antimony as a tartar-emetic and see how he responds but I am not at all sanguine, sir. The shock of castration is often a mortal blow in a full-grown man, sir.'

'Yes, I can quite imagine,' said Slade, shifting his hips uneasily. 'Put him in my spare sleeping-cabin – he will be more comfortable there. Strive to keep him alive, Mr Andrews, at least until we get to Antigua. If we can deliver him alive, we can consider our mission to have been successful – even if we did leave his balls behind, eh, Mr Lamb, ha, ha, ha!'

'Quite, sir,' said Lamb, somewhat taken aback by Slade's brutal levity. 'Unless you have further need of me, sir, I'll – '

Slade flapped a casual hand. 'Yes, yes, off you go, Mr Lamb.'

Lamb's elevation to the position of first lieutenant carried few extra privileges and a great many more responsibilities but the one advantage he prized most was his freedom from watch-keeping. Although he now spent most of his daylight hours on deck (and much of his night) he had the privilege of leaving it whenever he wished, within reason. Now, as he went below without a thought for the unfortunate Ball who had gone straight from the ship's side to the quarterdeck to take up what was left of his morning watch, his immediate priorities were coffee, a wash, breakfast and sleep, in that order. His written report to Slade would take him at least two hours, he thought, and with luck he could squeeze in two or three hours' sleep first. Breakfast was not due to be served for an hour or more yet but he had no intention of waiting that long.

'Sykes! Sykes!' he bellowed as he ducked his head and entered the empty gunroom. The pantry hatch slid open with a bad-tempered bang and Sykes thrust through his frowsty head.

'Yes, sir?' he snapped, with barely a hint of a snarl.

'Coffee, Sykes, if you please, strong, hot and immediate.'

'Strong, no, sir. Today's the day for yesterday's grounds. 'Ot, sir, yes, perwiding you don't 'ave it immediate. I can't make 'ot coffee wi' cold water, sir.'

The hatch slid shut, cutting off Lamb's exasperated curse. 'Insolent bastard!' He shook his fist at the unresponsive hatch and retreated scowling to his cabin for a cold-water wash and a change of linen. A shave, he decided, rubbing his chin, could wait until he had slept. The wound on his arm, though long, was not very deep and had started to scab over nicely. He had taken the precaution of trailing his arm in the sea while in the launch and was now confident that he would have little trouble from his gash.

The coffee, when Sykes eventually produced it, was hot and satisfyingly strong.

'This was not made from yesterday's beans, Sykes, I'm sure,' said Lamb, sipping appreciatively.

'No, sir, I thought I'd give you a little treat this morning, sir, seeing as 'ow you've 'ad a 'ard night of it, scaling forts and rescuing people left, right and centre, sir.'

'Most thoughtful of you, Sykes. It's warming for us heroes to know that we are appreciated.'

'Oh, you are, sir,' said Sykes with a leer. 'Us what was left on board, with not much to do 'cept four men's work apiece while we tacked and wore, firing the guns all night, with bloody great roundshot dropping on our 'eads, we really –'

'Watch your tongue, Sykes!'

'Yes, sir. Ready for your breakfast now, sir?'

When Lamb emerged on to the maindeck after three hours of

fitful sleep and a dream of intense eroticism concerning a shameless woman with yellow hair, the ship was rolling heavily over a lumpy sea beneath fast-moving, dark clouds. He could see no sign of the cutter – presumably the *Adroit*'s course did not suit Lieutenant England and he had taken his own, less conventional route home. He cast a quick glance aloft. The topsails were unreefed and full-bellied and the studdingsails stretched iron-hard from their booms. The press of wind, coming strongly over the starboard quarter, was pushing the frigate's head down so that she butted through the waves, bringing a white curtain of spray hissing over the forecastle. Lamb mounted the quarterdeck and frowned at Rank and Goode, standing companionably together beneath the weather mizzen shrouds.

'Have you not noticed the ship's head is being pushed down, Mr Rank?' he enquired testily. 'Why have you not sent down for permission to shorten sail?'

Rank's thin lips twisted in the faintest of righteous smiles. 'The captain gave firm orders that he was not to be disturbed before noon, except for fire, a sail, or a visit from God. He was quite definite on that.'

The master looked smug and said nothing, happy in the knowledge that such matters were the responsibility of the officer of the watch. He lifted his square, Welsh chin and hummed a little tune, shooting the glowering Lamb a sly smile.

Lamb's short sleep had left him feeling irritable. 'That is no excuse. You should have damn well sent for me. We'll have the stuns'ls taken in, the mizzen tops'l handed and the forecourse clewed up, if you please.'

'Aye aye, sir,' said Rank formally and strode forward to bellow over the quarterdeck rail. 'Rouse yourselves, the watch! Hands to shorten sail! Topmen aloft! Man the fore-clew garnets!'

Goode gave Lamb an approving nod. 'And not before time, sir,' he commented, glancing at Rank's back with a traitorous frown. 'We should have shortened sail half an hour back.'

Lamb was in no mood for the master's hypocrisy. 'Then why didn't you?' he asked shortly.

Goode smiled. 'Ah, now, it weren't up to me, else I should have called you.'

Lamb gave a disbelieving grunt and stood and watched as the canvas was taken in. Satisfied that the frigate was riding higher forward and was making easier progress, he gave orders that he was to be called if the weather worsened and went below to write his report.

As he descended the dark companionway a figure stood aside at the bottom to let him pass. It was Collier.

'How is the ankle, Jack?' asked Lamb, suddenly remembering that he had failed to have a word with the surgeon on the matter.

'A little painful still, thank you, sir, but more comfortable now that the surgeon has strapped it up for me.'

'Oh, you have seen the surgeon?' remarked Lamb, a trifle surprised. He was pleased to learn that Collier's injury had been genuine but thought it a little odd that he should have bothered Andrews with such a comparatively trivial complaint when the surgeon had so many wounded men on his hands.

'Yes, sir,' said Collier, his dark eyes fixed intently on Lamb's face. 'Not so much for the sake of my ankle as for my reputation.'

'Ah!' said Lamb. 'Well, I am sure there was no need to worry about that. The thought that your injury was anything other than genuine had certainly never entered my head, at least.'

He clapped Collier on the shoulder and walked on, hoping that his words had put some cheer into the man's heart. An odd fellow, he reflected, as he ducked into his cabin; he dwells too much on himself. He sat down at his little writing shelf and busied himself trimming the point of his quill as he composed the opening line of his report, Collier and his problems forgotten.

Ninety minutes later he had finished, two full pages closely written on both sides, with just enough space left for him to squeeze his signature in at the bottom, if he wrote small. He carefully blotted dry the last page and sat back in his chair to read the report through but was interrupted in the first paragraph by a rap at the door and the appearance of Midshipman Allwyn's tousled head.

'Mr Rank's respects, sir, and the wind's got up,' the boy gabbled and immediately disappeared.

Lost in the throes of composition Lamb had failed to register the increasing motion of the ship and as he stood and staggered to a heavy roll he swore loudly at Rank's intransigence. On deck he saw at once that the morning light had diminished considerably since he went below. The wind was sounding a warning in the rigging and the bow was plunging heavily. Rank was moving along the larboard line of guns checking their lashings and as Lamb climbed to the quarterdeck the master, his heavy belly resting comfortably on the forward rail, nodded pleasantly at him.

'Looks like there's a bit of shit coming our way,' he said, jerking his head at the starboard quarter.

'So I see. I think we are in for a nasty blow very shortly.'

'Yes,' agreed Goode cheerfully.

Lamb hooked a finger at Allwyn, who was attempting to relieve the boredom of quarterdeck duty by trying to stretch out his tongue far enough to touch the tip of his nose, going cross-eyed in the process.

'Mr Allwyn!'

The midshipman's ugly grimace vanished. 'Sir?'

'My compliments to the captain and there is some nasty weather building up from the south-east.'

'Nasty weather building up from the south-east, ay aye, sir,' repeated Allwyn and made a dash for the quarterdeck ladder.

Lamb halted him with a shout. 'Mr Allwyn! Remember – wake but don't shake.'

'Wake but don't shake, aye aye, sir.'

Lamb's warning, lightly given, had good reason behind it. To lay hands on one's captain, no matter how innocently, could be construed as an assault and this crime carried the ultimate punishment. Lamb doubted if Slade would interpret a waking shake from a young midshipman as an assault upon his person but it was safer to steer clear of such a risk. He knew of one proud captain who had such a horror of contact with lesser mortals that he had ordered his coat to be scrubbed after being brushed by a passing seaman.

He turned to the master. 'In the meantime, Mr Goode, I think we should prepare for the worst and make the ship nice and snug.' He raised his hand and beckoned to Rank who had just climbed the quarterdeck ladder. 'Mr Rank, kindly rouse out the gunner, the bosun and the carpenter and get them to make all fast on deck. Extra lashings on the boats, double-breechings on the guns, tarpaulins and battens for the hatches.'

'We could be in for a hurricane,' remarked Goode as Rank strode along the maindeck, bellowing.

'The thought had crossed my mind.'

'Nasty things, hurricanes – especially when you are short of sea-room.'

Slade arrived on the quarterdeck, dressed in shirt and breeches with scarlet slippers on his feet.

'It looks none too sweet out there, Mr Lamb.'

'No, sir. Mr Rank is making all fast on deck, sir, just in case. Hurricane waters, these, sir.'

Slade frowned. 'Don't be impertinent, Mr Lamb. I was sailing these waters long before you were a gleam in your father's eye. I am well aware of the sort of weather to expect in this part of the world.' The words were characteristic but the tone was abstracted, his attention fixed on the black storm-clouds racing up from the south-east and spreading ominously overhead. 'Right, Mr Lamb,' he said, suddenly brisk. 'We'll have the main and mizzen courses furled and the t'gallantmasts struck down. Close-reef the tops'ls and make all secure with spare gaskets. Make sure the booms are spanned and there are good, rolling tackles on the yards. Bend on the foul mizzen stays'l – we may well need it later. Mr Goode, keep her running free for the time being and put two extra hands on the wheel.'

Lamb made his way down the skittish ladder to the maindeck and cupped his hands to his mouth. 'All hands! All hands! Prepare to strike t'gallants and shorten sail! Look alive! Stir them up, Mr Clegg!'

The three divisions of topmen raced up their respective, rolling masts. Lamb craned his neck and watched anxiously as the topgallantmasts were loosed from their shrouds, unstepped and lowered swiftly through the tops – too swiftly for Lamb's peace of mind.

'Handsomely now!' he roared up at the maintop. 'I want that mast on the deck, not in the bloody bilge.'

Faint chuckles floated down to him over the noise of the wind but the descent of the mast slowed fractionally and the butt of its twenty-one-foot length came to rest on the deck with not enough of a bump to crack an egg. Lamb left it to the boatswain to supervise its lashing and made a round of the deck, conferring with the gunner who had just completed double-breeching the guns, and checking the security of the boats and hatch-covers. He made his way back to the quarterdeck and as he reported to the captain the first drops of rain began to fall from the dark sky and spot the white deckboards.

'Very good,' said Slade and over his shoulder he called, 'Quartermaster, steer nor'west by north.'

The *Adroit* had been running before the wind and was now about seven miles off the western coast of Dominica. Lamb pictured in his mind's eye the Leeward and Virgin Islands stretching across the frigate's bows, not so many miles to the north. The swing to larboard would now point the *Adroit*'s head at Puerto Rico but that huge island was some three hundred miles distant and hardly likely to be a dangerous factor for at least another twenty-four hours.

Slade made his way across the wet, heeling deck to the forward rail and ran his eyes over the deck below and the masts and spars and sparse canvas above. Satisfied that the ship was tight and snug he gave orders for the duty watch to join the off-duty men below and descended to his quarters. Lamb crooked a finger at Allwyn and sent him to fetch his tarpaulins from his cabin but before the midshipman had reached the aft companionway the rain began to sheet down in earnest and within seconds Lamb was soaked to his very skin. With the rain came an increase in the wind and the heel of the deck became more marked, forcing him to hold on to the mizzen shrouds. The ship's bell sounded the hour of noon but there would be no sextants taken from their cases today to determine the time at which the sun was at its maximum altitude. He could hear the cook's mates bellowing for the mess cooks to come running with their kettles. At this moment the purser's steward and a quartermaster would be mixing the grog for the midday issue. Lamb could picture the comfortable, domestic scene below, the clatter of ladles and containers, the rich, warm smell of boiled pease-pudding as it gushed from the cauldron, the richer, warmer smell of stirring rum and water and the eager, smiling lines of seamen smacking their lips in anticipation. He huddled deeper into his damp collar.

Ball, his stout figure draped in voluminous tarpaulins,

placed his foot with exquisite timing on the quarterdeck just as the bell sounded the final chime. He and Rank huddled together for a few seconds, their heads bent close as Rank raised his voice against the din of wind, rain, sea and creaking timbers. The second lieutenant dashed thankfully below and Ball advanced on Lamb with an amused grin at his senior's saturated shirt and breeches, clinging to him like a second skin.

'What is the matter with Collier?' asked Lamb. 'This is his watch.'

'Oh, the poor bugger can barely put his foot to the deck,' said Ball. 'I suggested that he put his foot up for a few hours while I did his afternoon watch, on condition that he does both dog-watches.'

Lamb nodded; it mattered little to him who did which duty. The officers were perfectly free to arrange their watches between them as it suited them although generally they kept strictly to their regular turns of duty. Ball's gesture, off-handedly though he had put it, was typical of his good nature although Lamb was not so sure that Collier would have done the same had the positions been reversed.

Ball continued to grin widely at Lamb's wet condition. He shook his head in mock admiration. 'Oh, I do so admire you brave stoics, laughing at wind and rain in your shirt-sleeves, standing there, smiling, four-square to the – '

'Be so good as to check the for'ard guns, Mr Ball,' said Lamb coldly and turned away. He turned back a moment later and chuckled wickedly at the sight of Ball making his careful way forward, head bent against the driving rain. Let him find some humour in that, he thought, eyeing the spray bursting high over the forepeak. Allwyn arrived a moment later with his tarpaulins and went off watch with a mammoth flea in his ear for his tardiness. Lamb struggled damply into his waterproofs, the unco-operative material flapping wildly in the stiff wind and calling for a great deal of selective cursing before he was warm and perspiring beneath them. Ball fought his way back to the quarterdeck and reported the forecastle guns secure, his voice formal and his former high humour completely quenched.

The wind was beginning to sound a dangerous note in the rigging and the rolling, plunging, lurching motion of the ship was becoming more severe by the minute. Lamb made his way to the taffrail and clung to the mizzenmast backstay, gazing out at the waste of turbulent grey water astern. If Slade chose to continue running before the wind it was from here that the most dangerous seas were likely to come; if Goode was right and a hurricane, or the edge of one, was about to envelop them, the mountainous waves built up by the terrible wind would rear up from behind and call for delicate, knife-edged steering in order to avoid being rolled beam ends over. He felt the tension in the backstay beneath his hand; it was iron-hard but thrummed and vibrated in his fingers like a live thing from the trembling of the rolling spar above. It might have been better, he reflected, had Slade ordered the doubling of the stays earlier, while he had the opportunity; it was too late now – to send men aloft in this wind and sea would be akin to murder.

It seemed to him that the wind had increased in strength even in the few minutes he had been at the taffrail and he turned and made his cautious way forward, clinging to the shrouds and the bulwark, his tarpaulin coat flapping and banging like an unsheeted sail and his sou'wester flying before him at the end of its tethering cord. The master, he noted, had returned from his dinner and was now standing wide-legged beside the four helmsmen at the wheel, his head turned aft, looking at the waves astern. Lamb halted beside Ball and the two stood in silence for a few moments, staring at the rearing and plunging bowsprit.

'We had weather very similar to this the last time I was at my father's farm,' said Ball conversationally, his good humour evidently restored. 'It absolutely ruined the hay, quite knocked it flat.'

He was being modest. Lieutenant the Honourable Roger Cathcart Ball's father was a baron by tenure and his farm consisted of a great stretch of Shropshire and included half a dozen villages. Nevertheless, wealthy and influential as his father was and lofty as his own prospects might be, here on the *Adroit* he was merely the third lieutenant and if he had ever dared let slip pretensions of grandeur in the wardroom he would have been instantly hooted down from all sides. As it was, he was an amiable, pleasant, lazy young man without an ounce of conceit in his body.

'Really?' responded Lamb. 'Well, you probably know more about farming than you do about navigation, that's for sure.'

Ball guffawed at this barb, quite without shame. Lamb's grasp of mathematics was far from secure but compared to Ball he was an absolute Newton. Had it not been for his aristocratic background Ball would still be a midshipman.

Lamb moved over the deck to the wheel, glanced at the compass in the binnacle and took up his stand on the heaving quarterdeck beside the master, one hand clinging tightly to the mizzen shrouds. Presently Slade arrived, sou'wester pulled low, bulkier than ever in his tarpaulins. He moved with care over the wet, heeling deck to the weather rail and hooked an arm through the ratlines, allowing his body to sway with the motion of the ship. Goode glanced up at Lamb from beneath the dripping brim of his shapeless hat.

'It's time we came about,' he said shortly.

Lamb had been thinking much the same for some little time. The afternoon light had diminished to an eerie, dusk-like quality which, coupled with the hard-driving rain, reduced the visibility to little more than the length of the ship. Green water was now regularly surging over the forecastle with each dip of the bows and occasionally washing over the lee bulwarks along the waist. The note of the wind had risen to an alarming pitch as it shrieked through the taut rigging, whipping the tops off the waves and lifting the heavy pigtails of the men at the wheel.

'There is the captain,' said Lamb, with a jerk of his head at the weather shrouds. 'Tell him so!'

Goode ignored the suggestion. 'When I was a youngster, a master's mate, I was sailing these very waters in a fourth-rate, the old *Nobleman*.' His head was close to Lamb's, his voice raised to make his words heard. 'Terrible winds sprang up, hurricane winds – oh, it was a fearful time we had! We lost our mainmast and foretopmast and ended up on a lee shore off a little island in the Virgins, broached-to. I thought for sure we were all dead men but some of us managed to creep along the mizzenmast to the rocks off-shore. We clung there for two days and two nights, the sea reaching up and plucking men off like plums from a tree. A little brigantine took us off, the thirty that were left, half-dead and near crazed with thirst. Oh, it was a bad time, a wicked time. The thought of a lee shore on a foul, black night still makes me shudder.'

'Well, there is little chance of that happening to us,' roared Lamb. 'Not with three hundred miles of sea ahead of us.'

'Three thousand'd make me happier. They can blow you anywhere, these hurricanes. I can remember – '

'Mr Lamb!' Slade's voice boomed out of the noise of the weather. 'Rouse the hands. We shall come about. Look to the helm, Mr Goode.'

Lamb plunged dangerously down the wet steps of the cavorting ladder.

'All hands! All hands! Stand by to go about! Man the braces! Look alive! Rouse yourselves!'

The hands came running from the forward hatchway, bent low against the thrust of the wind as they scuttled along the weather side, urged on by the shouts of the boatswain and his mates. As they settled into their lines and gripped their ropes, Lamb fixed his eyes on the quarterdeck and the helm, ready to reinforce the master's order the instant he gave the word. Goode was darting quick, appraising glances abeam and astern, choosing his moment with care, while Slade clung to the mainmast backstay, content to leave the manoeuvre to the master.

'Ready about!' cried Goode. 'About ship!'

'Mainsail haul!' roared Lamb over the noise of the wind.

The helmsmen rapidly turned the great double-wheel and the hands on deck leaned back on their ropes, cracking their muscles as they pulled against the enormous pressure of the wind on the topsails.

'Haul, haul!' screamed Clegg. 'Dig those bloody heels in and haul, you idle whoresons! Haul!'

Lamb switched his anxious gaze from aloft to the sea and back to the topsails as the frigate's head began to swing to larboard and the yards edged closer to the wind. This was the moment of extreme danger, the few seconds when the ship was thinly balanced between the thrust of the rudder and the pressure of wind and waves, with the sails in no position to assist the swing of the bow across the fine dividing line. A moment of poor co-ordination, a little unfortunate timing or an errant wave and the ship would be in irons, wallowing vulnerably beam-on to the rollers and unable to move to larboard or starboard, liable to be rolled over in the twinkling of an eye. The yards swung, the ship shivered and hesitated for a heart-beat and then she was coming firmly round, the topsails gripping the wind and the forepeak rising and falling across the lines of oncoming waves.

'Meet her, meet her!' yelled Goode and the helmsmen rapidly spun the wheel in the reverse direction to counteract the swing of the ship's head.

'Loose the mizzen stays'l!' shouted Slade through his cupped hands. 'Haul jibs fore and aft!'

With the frigate heading bravely into the wind Lamb felt considerably easier in his mind and turned his attention to his stomach. It was almost four bells in the afternoon watch and his chances of obtaining anything hot were long past but cheese, cold ham and pickles would fill a large hole and with luck he could bully Sykes into producing a pot of coffee. He descended the dark, swaying companionway, suddenly famished and desperate for coffee, promising himself that if Sykes produced his usual crop of whining excuses about the shortage of coffee beans and the lack of hot water he would kill him on the spot. Twenty-five minutes later he returned to the maindeck, leaving an unscathed Sykes below and burping pickle fumes into the damp air. The rain had ceased but the wind, saturated with salt water, was scarcely any less damp and was noticeably stronger, sounding a deep, baleful note in the rigging and blowing horizontal steaks of foam off the grey, heaving wave-tops. The afternoon light now had a strange yellow tinge to it, a threatening, oppressive dimness, as if something huge and menacing hovered blackly overhead. Lamb made his careful way to the quarterdeck against an almost solid wind, noting that lifelines had been rigged between forecastle and quarterdeck. The motion of the ship was now savage as the steep waves rolled beneath her, sending the stern high as the bow plunged, and then towering over the taffrail as the jib-boom climbed, the stern falling into the trough with a jarring crash. This fore-and-aft movement was combined with a sideways motion as the frigate rolled her fat, rounded sides from larboard to starboard and back again, so that her mast-tops performed a vast, erratic, circular dance in the air. The foul-weather mizzen staysail boomed and cracked and the constant creaks and groans of the spars and timbers were overlaid by the thunder of the sea and the menacing roar of the wind.

The captain and Ball had their heads close together, their sou'westers almost touching, as Lamb reached the quarterdeck. Slade glanced up at Lamb's approach and beckoned him nearer.

'Mr Ball has just made his round of the deck and tells me – yes, Mr Armstrong, make your report.'

The carpenter had arrived hard on Lamb's heels. He touched his bedraggled fur cap. 'I've made my rounds, sir. The timbers are working just a little but she's keeping fairly dry. There's some water in the cockpit and the pusser's stores, sir. Mr Littlefield is in his store, cussing and complaining, sir, but it's not so bad. There's maybe half a foot of water extra in the bilge – I've rigged the pump-chains, just in case, sir.'

'Very good, Mr Armstrong. Keep me informed.' Slade turned his attention back to Lamb. 'Where was I? Yes, Mr Ball informs me that some of the guns need their lashings and wedges attended to. Be so kind as to seek out the gunner and look after that.'

'Aye aye, sir.'

The maindeck was deserted as Lamb descended the quarterdeck ladder; even the lookouts had long since been dismissed below with the duty watch, who were now, no doubt, crouched snugly in their favourite corners, backs to the bulkheads, sleeping or yarning or singing to themselves. The boatswain, scourge of the lower deck and the iron link between the quarterdeck and the forecastle, was no fool and he, too, had removed himself to a comfortable little nook but somehow, as Lamb began to fight his way forward, his presence on the deck was transmitted to Mr Clegg through at least five inches of deck planking and he emerged from the forward hatchway with two of his mates. They dashed along the weather side of the skittish deck and joined Lamb as he paused at the first gun. Lamb made no comment and asked no questions; the boatswain's infallible powers of divinity were a byword throughout the ship. The guns, however, were not Clegg's responsibility and Lamb asked the boatswain to send for the gunner.

'He won't be no good to you, sir,' roared Clegg. 'He's cracked his head open and the surgeon has put him to bed. I'll go round the guns with you, sir.'

Lamb nodded, pleased at the suggestion, much preferring the solid help of the boatswain to the frail presence of the ancient Mr Winter.

Clegg put his head close to Lamb as they crouched over the first gun's breechings. 'Wind's picking up a mite, sir,' he bellowed.

Lamb ignored the boatswain's attempt at levity. 'We shall make the most of this inspection, Mr Clegg,' he roared into a hairy, projecting ear. 'Things will get worse shortly, I feel. Pay particular attention to the tackles and breechings – I want no slack at all. Make sure the guns are snubbed up tight and snug and the wedges rammed well home.'

Jerking at the tension of the doubled breechings, tugging at the ring-bolt lashings and hammering at the wedges beneath the trucks, the little party made their slow way forward along the line of guns. Midway along the starboard side one of the boatswain's mates raised an arm as he moved on to the next gun, his shout carried away by the wind. Lamb and Clegg hurried forward; the side-tackles had slackened sufficiently to allow the carriage enough motion to loosen its wedges and the gun was now snubbing violently at its ropes. The men needed no instructions from Lamb; the lashings at the ring-bolts were cast free and as the gun-carriage rolled forward with the heel of the deck the side-tackles were hauled bar-tight and quickly re-secured.

'We'll have another lashing on the breechings,' shouted Lamb, pointing. The boatswain nodded his shining head, unable to hear the words but comprehending the gesture. The breeching, a stout rope of best hemp that ran through a thimble on the pomelion of the gun, had its two ends led forward and clinched to ring-bolts on either side of the gun-port; its purpose was to limit the inboard travel of the gun during recoil. When not in action the two halves of the breeching were lashed together to take up the slack and Clegg now quickly whipped another lashing round them to prevent any further play. With a final tap at the wheels' wedges the party moved on to the next gun.

The motion of the deck increased as the men approached the

forecastle. Each time the bow plunged into a trough, flinging spray to the height of the foretop and bringing green water roiling inboard, the angry water towered high over the beakhead, threatening to smash down and crush the ship; each time, slowly and stubbornly, the bows would shoulder the water aside and climb the menacing slope, the jib-boom almost vertical, before plunging down its far side to begin the struggle again. As Lamb and his party crossed the deck to the larboard guns a huge sea burst inboard, sending a smother of white water boiling waist-high over the forward part of the maindeck. Lamb's legs were knocked from under him and he fell, completely submerged, rolling and bumping, clutching frantic-ally for a handhold, wondering vaguely whether he was on the ship or in the sea. A hard object crashed painfully into his ribs and simultaneously an agonizing pain shot through his scalp as his head was jerked above the water. He opened his eyes to see the several yellow and brown teeth still remaining to Clegg bared in a grin above him as he held tightly to Lamb's hair. Lamb struggled to his feet, coughing out salt water and wincing from the pain in his side, gained, apparently, from contact with the gun-carriage beside him.

'Thank you, Mr Clegg,' he panted, clutching at the boat-swain's massive shoulder for support as he wheezed and spluttered.

'Pleased to be of service, sir,' roared Clegg, making no effort to hide the sardonic amusement on his leathery, white-bristled face.

Lamb continued to spit out and cough up a considerable amount of the Caribbean Sea as he tailed the boatswain and his mates along the larboard guns, the men pausing here and there to make little adjustments to breechings and wedges and making a short detour to tug at the doubled lashings of the ship's boats amidships. Arriving back at the break of the quarterdeck, he wiped the last of the salty mucous from his upper lip and dismissed Clegg and his men, satisfied that everything on the maindeck had been made as snug and secure as possible. He climbed the ladder and reported as much to the captain.

'Very good.' Slade made a rare essay at humour. 'I saw you take a ducking for'ard. I thought we had lost you for good, then, and I was busy rearranging the watch-bill in my mind when I saw Clegg haul you up by the hair.'

'Your grief and concern touch me deeply, sir,' said Lamb, dryly.

Slade chuckled. 'I overflow with the milk of human kindness, Mr Lamb.'

The weather gradually worsened as the afternoon watch crept by. When Collier made his limping and precarious dash to the quarterdeck to relieve Ball at the start of the first dog-watch the day was as dark as night, the light blotted out by solid, inky clouds racing unseen overhead. The four helmsmen gratefully relinquished their posts, stepping back one at a time to hand over their share of the spokes. The master, brooding and watchful, maintained his position abaft the helm, staring steadily ahead at the dark turmoil of rearing water. Little Bird, the duty midshipman, was sent back to the cockpit with a growl from Slade before he reached the top of the quarterdeck ladder, the captain evidently fearing that a strong gust would lift his tiny frame over the side.

Collier took up his station beside Lamb, each gripping tightly to the lee mizzen shrouds as the deck dipped and rolled and rose. Lamb cocked a thoughtful eye at the fourth lieutenant; he knew he could expect little in the way of conversation or comment from him, even if the two had been sharing the quietest, balmiest of watches. Collier had proved in the past he was quite capable of passing four hours without uttering a single word more than those needed to carry out his duties. Well, he thought, if Collier had ever needed an excuse not to talk, there was none needed today; in this weather, conversation would only be possible by bellowing in each other's ears.

'Mr Lamb!'

Lamb turned his head at the faint shout from Slade, some fifteen feet away, the wind snatching at the efforts of his powerful lungs. The captain motioned impatiently with his free arm. Lamb released his hold on the shrouds, dashed across the deck and grabbed another beside Slade. The two men leaned their heads towards each other.

'I want you to –' Slade stopped abruptly. The howling of the wind had dropped, sharply and suddenly, as if a huge curtain had been pulled across it. Both their heads turned towards the bow as Goode's voice rang out in the sudden, comparative stillness.

'Hold tight, for God's sake!'

Lamb's blood went cold. Racing down on the ship, looming black and enormous, was the highest wave he had ever seen or dreamed of seeing. It towered over the frigate, its curling peak visible above the foremast as it seemed to draw itself up to strike. Lamb wrapped his arms tightly around the rigging, his mind numbed by the menacing hugeness of the thing. Out of the corner of his eye he saw Goode leap to the wheel to add his weight to that of the helmsmen. Astonishingly, he heard a throaty chuckle from Slade.

'Another ducking for you, Mr Lamb!'

By an effort of will, Lamb kept his eyes open as the massive wall of water leaned over the forecastle and the bows suddenly reared. This is the end, he thought, his mind cold. Up, up she climbed until she appeared to be standing on her rudder and then everything was blotted out as the wave's crest fell on the ship. For the second time that afternoon Lamb's legs were struck from beneath him and he clung grimly to the ropes, his body flailing and twisting as an almost solid body of water swept the length of the ship. The noise of the breaking crest was like the thunder of a hundred guns in his ears. The ship's timbers creaked and cracked and groaned as if she had been struck a death blow. Gasping, he shook the water from his face as his feet swung down to the deck and he concentrated his gaze on the frigate's bows beyond the drowned waist. Amazed, his heart lifting, he saw the bow rise shudderingly from the water, bravely shouldering aside tons of green water as the wave rolled beneath the ship. Her bow dipped again and she plunged, heavy and tired, into the trough that followed. The jib-boom had gone, he saw, and the foretopmast was leaning wearily to starboard. Beside him Slade cried hoarsely, 'See to the wheel!'

Lamb flung himself at the helm. Moments before there had been four men at the helm; now there were just two, desperately turning the spokes to meet the next wave. He added his weight to the turning of the wheel, wondering vaguely why Slade still stood clinging to the ratlines. The ship was heavy with the weight of water she had taken on board and her head moved sluggishly in response to the movement of the rudder. Mercifully, the next rolling crest was considerably lower and the frigate crabbed her way over it, the deck canting at so steep an angle that Lamb thought she would never recover. Recover she did, slowly and hesitantly, the water draining from her waist through the gaping hole in her bulwark where the carpenter's temporary repair had been swept away. Slade was shouting something indistinguishable and turning his head Lamb saw him, still gripping the shrouds with both hands, jerking his head in the direction of the taffrail. He shouted again and this time Lamb caught his faint words.

'Get him!'

Lamb glanced behind him. The crumpled figure of the master was sliding to and fro beside the taffrail, face down in the water that sloshed about the quarterdeck. The ship's head was now once again facing the line of oncoming waves and with a shout of 'Keep her so!' to the men at the wheel he turned and dashed for the taffrail.

Goode's eyes were shut and an ugly swelling blossomed on his right brow. Lamb dragged him to the mizzenmast, set his back against it and lashed him there with the length of cord the master had tied around his tarpaulin coat. As he gave the knot a final jerk Goode opened his eyes and spat blood from a gashed tongue.

'Jesus, Mary and fucking Joseph!' he muttered and turned his head to vomit a pint or so of sea-water over Lamb's shoes. Lamb left him there and ran to the helm but as he reached it Slade shouted again.

'Bring a knife here, Mr Lamb.'

Lamb snatched the blunt-pointed seaman's knife hanging from around the neck of one of the helmsmen and hurried over to the captain. He saw almost immediately why Slade had not moved from his spot. Somehow, during his kicking and flailing as the wave had lifted him from his feet, a ratline had looped itself around Slade's wrist and now held it tightly and immovably against the unyielding shroud.

'Go gently with that wrist,' boomed Slade as Lamb reached up with the knife. 'I think the damned thing is broken.'

Lamb sliced through the ratline and Slade lowered his arm, supporting his wrist with his other hand, his good arm hooked around the shroud for support.

'Thank you, Mr. Lamb. Leave me and see to the ship.'

The men at the wheel seemed to be coping well; both were strong and experienced helmsmen and Lamb turned his attention to the maindeck. The guns, thanks to the careful doubling and checking of the tackles and breeches, still squatted sullenly in their precisely spaced positions; the main hatch-grating and its canvas cover, however, had been shifted askew from its seating and undoubtedly many tons of water had overflowed the coaming and poured below. Caught up in the starboard fore-rigging was one of the ship's cutters, its side showing splintered strakes and entangled in the lower foremast shrouds was the remains of the other. The foretopmast leaned untidily to starboard, held precariously by its remaining stays and whipping to and fro in the wind; Lamb could not tell, in the uncertain light, whether it had snapped above the foremast or had been wrenched from its seating. The foretopsail, closely-reefed as it had been, was in shreds, long streamers of canvas snapping loudly and raggedly astern.

Suddenly, men were pouring from below, swarming over the maindeck and up the quarterdeck ladder. Rank and Ball were first up, closely followed by the carpenter, the boatswain and half a dozen senior hands. Within seconds, four fresh men were at the wheel and a dozen men were busy replacing and relashing the shifted hatch-cover. Clutching his injured wrist, Slade issued a stream of orders.

'Mr Clegg, would you look to the foretopmast? If you can lower the yard, lash the mast and double the stays; we might yet save it. Yes, Mr Armstrong? Three feet of water? Well, it could be worse. Turn the off-watch men below – they can lend a hand with the chain-pumps and we'll have the head-pumps manned, too. Mr Ball, be so good as to check the guns and Mr Hopper, kindly assist the master below – he may well need the attention of the surgeon. Are you aware that we have lost Collier, Mr Rank? Yes, quite. Mr Hopper can take his place on the watch list but in the meantime I would be obliged if you took over as officer-of-the-watch. Send a few hands to remove that wreckage from the fore-rigging and the foremast shrouds before it does a mischief. And send for young Isherwood – he can take over the master's duties until he is fit again.'

Lamb had not realized, until Slade had mentioned it, that

Collier had gone and he glanced across at the vacant lee shrouds with a feeling close to guilt. The unhappy man had made little mark on the ship's company and now he had gone without a cry, making as little impact in death as he had in life. The thought came to him that if the captain had not called him across to the weather shrouds he, too, might have joined Collier over the side. He gave a mental shrug; it was pointless to dwell on what might have been – he was alive and Collier was dead and thank Christ it was not the other way around! Hopper returned to the quarterdeck and reported to Rank, and Lamb saw immediately from the midshipman's grave, earnest expression that he had learned of Collier's death and was now filled with delight at the prospect of his own advancement to the glory of a temporary, unconfirmed lieutenancy. Lamb silently wished him joy of it.

Slade had managed to tuck his injured wrist inside his jacket and he stood, large and impassive beneath the weather shrouds, eyeing the activities on the maindeck and in the foretop. Although the frigate was still rolling and plunging heavily and green water was still being shipped on board, it seemed to Lamb that the wind was easing a little, as if that giant wave had been a last, desperate throw by the storm. He made his way down to the maindeck, feeling stiff and sore in the region of his ribs and busied himself in a careful examination of the storm damage and in earnest discussions with the boatswain and the carpenter. When he returned to the quarterdeck and reported his findings to Slade the pumps were sucking and gurgling and throwing black bilge-water over the side, the foretopmast had been secured and the ruined boats had been cleared from the rigging and lashed to the deck, less those pieces which the frantically scavenging cook had managed to steal for firewood, hopping precariously about the deck on his one good leg.

'Very good,' said Slade. He eyed Lamb with a degree of sardonic amusement. 'You appear to be rather in need of a change of clothes, Mr Lamb. One ducking could be put down to mischance – two smacks of sheer carelessness. I was about to ask you earlier to nip down to my cabin and look in on Captain Black. You had better do so now, if you please, before you find yourself a change of clothes. With luck, you should stay dry from now on. The wind is easing and we should be able to come about and resume our proper course very shortly.'

'Yes, sir,' said Lamb. 'May I send for the surgeon to attend your arm, sir?'

'No, you may not. You are presumptuous, Mr Lamb. It is a fault I have noted in you before, on occasion. I am more than capable of deciding when I need the services of the surgeon.'

'Yes, sir. Sorry, sir.'

The captain's cabin was in shadowy darkness, relieved only by a faint gleam of light coming from the low wick of the gimballed lantern suspended above Slade's table. Lamb reached up and turned the little wheel, raising the wick and flooding the cabin with soft, yellow light. He cursed softly and walked over to the open door of Slade's spare sleeping-cabin. Black lay sprawled on his back on the deck, his eyes fixed and staring, his teeth bared in an ugly grin. He had been thrown from his cot, either by the motion of the ship or in his final paroxysm. His feet were entangled in the sheet on his cot and his nightshirt was around his waist, exposing the lower half of his body. Lamb stroked his chin, pondering. Black's wound had scarcely been weeping when he had been brought on board; now his belly and thighs were thickly covered in blood, which had spread in a dark pool over the canvas-covered deck. Had he died by his own hand, Lamb wondered? Had he reached down in black despair and ripped the stitches from his wound, preferring to die rather than face life as half a man? Lamb bent forward to examine the wound more closely but checked himself; let the surgeon make his own discoveries and his own report. He lifted the corpse on to the cot; the man had not been dead for long – his flesh was still warm and his blood tacky beneath Lamb's shoes. He draped the stained sheet over the body and left the cabin, leaving a trail of bloody footprints behind him.

'He is what?' exclaimed Slade angrily.

'Dead, sir,' repeated Lamb.

'Dead?' echoed Slade. 'Jesus Christ! Could he not have lasted a couple more days, the ungrateful bastard?' He gave the rail beside him an angry blow with his good fist. 'Hell!' he said bitterly.

*

'You are talking nonsense, sir, arrant bloody nonsense! I do not believe what you have just told me for one moment and I shall certainly not put such defamatory rubbish in my report.'

Slade had risen from his chair in his anger and stood leaning over his table on his good arm, his chin thrust forward threateningly at the surgeon. Andrews stood his ground stubbornly, incensed that his word should be questioned.

'I can but report what I have found, sir,' he said, his colour high and his chin equally determined. 'The man's sutures had been torn out and the evidence was plain beneath his finger-nails. There is no other interpretation to put on it, sir.'

'Could he not have pulled them out while he was tossing about in a fever, half-conscious, not knowing what he was doing?'

'Aye, it is possible, sir, but very unlikely. I have never known such a thing to happen.'

'Well, if it is possible, so be it. That shall be the cause of his death, loss of blood from grievous wounds, and that is what you shall put in your report. You will put nothing, I repeat, nothing, about dying from his own hand. That is not a suggestion, it is an order – do you understand me, sir?'

'Yes, sir, I understand plainly enough.'

'Good. He will be buried tomorrow morning.'

Andrews raised his eyebrows. 'Buried at sea, sir? Would it not be best to take the body back to Antigua, if only to – ?'

'If only to have more bloody surgeons poking about and finding scandal? No, he shall be buried in the morning. Besides, keeping a corpse on board will only make the hands anxious and nervous, convinced that sharks will be following the ship or that some calamity will befall them. They are a superstitious lot, seamen, and I see little point in worrying them without good cause. That is all, Mr Andrews, thank you.'

The sky rapidly blew itself clear shortly after the ship returned to her original course and just after sunset Lamb and Isherwood took their sextants and observed several sets of lunar distances. Their independent calculations tallied closely, showing the frigate had made considerable leeway from Isherwood's earlier dead reckoning. Slade ordered the necessary course alteration and with the replacement foretopsail bent on, the frigate bowled along merrily under reefed topsails alone over a lumpy, moonlit sea and with a fresh breeze over her starboard quarter. By the morning the sea had decreased to a long swell and at six bells of the forenoon watch the quartermaster seized the clapper of the ship's bell and tolled the funeral call. The body of Captain Black rested on a grating abaft the mainmast, covered with a Union Jack, and in honour of his rank the four lieutenants stood at the corners of the grating, dressed in their best, complete with swords. Opposite them, the stanchions for the man-ropes had been unshipped and an opening made at the after end of the hammock-netting.

'Uncover!' cried Slade, standing at the quarterdeck rail with his prayer-book in his hand. The assembled men removed their hats and the lieutenants lifted the grating and placed its end on the rail, so that Black's feet and the roundshot they rested on projected over the side. Slade immediately began to read the burial service, intoning the words in a loud, clear voice. Out of the corner of his eye Lamb saw the carpenter dart forward and fasten the tethering rope to the end of the grating. The four officers shifted their feet slightly and tensed as their cue drew near. Acting-lieutenant Hopper had been well primed for this ceremony; Lamb had no wish for the nervous youth to act independently and had read the burial service to him, emphasizing the words on which he should act.

'Forasmuch as it hath pleased Almighty God, of his great mercy, to take unto himself the soul of our dear brother here departed, we therefore commit his body to the deep – ' the officers thrust the grating hard over the side, Lamb clinging to the flag, ' – to be turned into corruption, looking for the resurrection of the body, when the sea shall give up her dead – '

The grating hit the water with a sullen splash and the canvas-wrapped body glanced off the end and disappeared. The grating at the end of its rope tapped against the ship's side as it was towed along beneath the main-chains.

Slade finished his reading and closed his prayer-book with a loud slap. 'Dismiss!' he called and turned away from the rail. The hands replaced their caps and drifted forward. The carpenter's mates began to haul in the grating, whistling silently between their teeth. Lamb thrust the balled flag into the hands of the duty midshipman.

'Fold that carefully and stow it away, if you please, Mr Allwyn,' he said and went below to change his clothes.

'Oh, dear me,' said Admiral Upton. 'This is sad news you bring me, Captain Slade, sad news indeed. London will not be pleased with me.' He shook his head sorrowfully, adorned today with an ugly, yellowing wig. 'A pity, a great pity.' He gestured at the chair in front of his desk. 'Bear with me a moment while I glance through your report. I already know the gist of it, of course. England brought his cutter in four hours ago, happy as a two-tailed pup with his news. And now you arrive – ' He sighed and shook his head again.

Slade took a deep breath as he seated himself, determined to hold his tongue no matter what the provocation, vaguely recalling the story of the fate of bearers of bad tidings in ancient Rome – or was it Greece? He eased his throbbing wrist in its sling and studied with some envy the magnificent sideboard fixed to the cabin bulkhead while he resisted with difficulty the temptation to drum his fingers on the arm of his chair as Upton muttered his way through the report.

'You have me baffled here, Slade,' exclaimed the admiral. 'What the devil is the meaning of the phrase "hearing in wind the seed to taste"?'

He slewed the page around, pointing with a bony, yellow finger. Slade leaned forward and craned his neck to read.

'That is "bearing in mind the need for haste", sir,' he said slowly, with great patience.

Upton grunted disdainfully. 'You should really take more care with these reports. Your handwriting is execrable.'

Slade flushed angrily. 'I have but one good hand, sir, as you might have noticed,' he said, his voice rising.

'And it is your right hand, is it not? You are not cack-handed, are you? And do not raise your voice to me, sir.'

The two men glared at each other across the table for a few seconds before Slade looked away, knowing that this was a battle he could not win.

'Your pardon, sir,' he muttered tightly.

'I should damn well think so,' snapped Upton and turned his attention back to Slade's report. Slade sat and simmered, listening with half an ear to the stamp of feet on the deck and the shouted commands of the Marine sergeant as he drilled his men. Upton finished reading and tossed the report in the direction of a pile of other papers at one end of his crowded table.

'Might I ask why you did not bring Captain Black's body here to Antigua? I fail to see the need for the unseemly haste to bury him at sea.'

Slade shifted nervously in his chair. It was a question he had known was certain to be asked and now that the admiral had put it he was still not sure how to answer it.

'It apears, sir, that my surgeon was not altogether happy over the way of Black's passing. He made certain observations to me, which – '

'Observations? Not happy? What are you suggesting, captain?' Upton leaned forward over his table, his eyes narrowed in suspicion. 'Get to the point, man. If you have anything to say, then have the goodness to say it.'

'Very well, sir. You have read of the nature of his wound. It was enough to make any man not want to live and my surgeon deduced from his examination of the corpse that Captain Black had decided – '

Upton held up his hand. 'Enough, enough. I wish to hear no more. You acted very properly, captain, and I would have done exactly the same in the circumstances. No, his death is a great pity but it in no way detracts from your own efforts in the affair. You and your men performed splendidly, sir, and I shall state as much in my report to the interested authorities. I see you write glowingly of your first lieutenant – what is his name, Long?'

'Lamb, sir.'

'Land, yes, of course. Well, kindly convey to Mr Land my very best wishes and warmest appreciation of his efforts. And also to your Marine lieutenant, Mr – ?'

'Vaughan, sir.'

'Yes, Vaughan. Is he quite recovered from his wounds?'

'He is up and about, sir.'

'Good, good.' He drummed his fingers on his desk for a few seconds, looked up and smiled brightly. 'Well, I have delayed your arrival at Port Royal long enough and no doubt Sir John will acquaint me of his displeasure in due course. Now let me see your list of requirements.' He stretched out a thin, liver-spotted hand. 'Good God, man, you are being a trifle greedy here, are you not? It's bloody nigh a complete refit you are asking for, by the look of this. Come, sir, let us try to trim it to a sensible proposition.'

Chapter 8

Captain Mainwaring, Superintendent of the Navy Yard at Port Royal, possessed a fine house and magnificent garden situated on the high ground to the north-east of Kingston. He also possessed a vivacious wife some twenty years his junior, much given to coffee-meetings, poetry readings and vigorous young naval officers. Her present interest in the latter was one Lieutenant Charles Field, a handsome young man of similar stamp to Lamb and due to sail for England and home that very evening. He was an old friend of Lamb – the two had joined their first ship together as midshipmen – and being of a tidy-minded nature and loath to leave the island with loose ends unknitted, he had been delighted to meet Lamb again, seeing in him the means of tying up at least one of those loose ends.

'Mrs Mainwaring,' he called, pulling Lamb forward by the arm. 'Might I present to you one of my oldest and dearest friends, Matthew Lamb? Matthew, Mrs Mainwaring, a poet of no mean talent. Matthew is very interested in poetry, are you not, Matt?'

'Indeed I am, ma'am,' said the well-primed Lamb, bending over the lady's hand. 'Poetry is a great solace to lonely seamen in the long, silent hours at sea.'

'Indeed?' said Mrs Mainwaring, gazing up at the tall officer with keen interest. 'Have you a talent in that direction, sir?'

'Very little in the way of writing it, ma'am, but I have a keen ear for words and metre.'

'How interesting.' She laid a light hand on his arm. 'You must come to my poetry reading tomorrow morning. I shall be reading my latest work, of which I am rather proud. At eleven o'clock, at my house. Charles will tell you how to find it.'

'I shall look forward to hearing your work with much interest, ma'am.'

She smiled and took Field by the arm. 'Now, Charlie, walk

me around Mrs Hill's garden. Do you know how desolate I feel this morning?'

They wandered off through the crowd of coffee-drinkers, leaving Lamb nursing an empty cup and an optimistic tingling of warm anticipation in his breeches.

The *Adroit* had been anchored off Port Royal for several days, snug in the encircling arm of the Palisades, the narrow tongue of land that connected the naval port to the town of Kingston, and well out from the coastline from where, according to the surgeon, the poisonous vapours and swampy miasmas welled up, spreading the killing yellow fever that had put paid to countless brave Jacks and redcoats.

'It is reasonably safe on the island during the daylight hours,' Andrews had assured his colleagues in the gunroom, speaking with all the authority of one who had been entertained at length by the surgeons of Fort Charles. 'It is at night that the miasmas are drawn up as the heat rises from the swamps and as they rise, so they spread, dropping their poisons like invisible raindrops.'

Slade had been impressed by the surgeon's cogent and scientific thesis and once the business of taking on stores and supplies was completed he had allowed the officers and midshipmen a free run ashore each day but with strict instructions to be back on board before nightfall; he had no desire to see fever come aboard his ship.

Slade's meeting with the Commander-in-Chief had left him in the foulest of tempers, which he had proceeded to share out without favour amongst his crew. Sir John Dillforth, who had won much honour at the battle of the Glorious First of June and at the attack on San Domingo two years later, was a man whose bravery and ability were well matched by his hauteur, petty-mindedness and spite. At one time second-in-command to Admiral Nelson, he had gained none of that officer's generous spirit and genuine concern for his subordinates and was detested as deeply as Nelson was adored. Slade had been kept kicking his heels for two days in an ante-chamber at Government House before Sir John had condescended to see him and then but briefly. Slade had emerged with a face like thunder and snorting with pent-up rage. According to the Commander, he had been laggardly in arriving at Port Royal; he had no business to go dashing off on time-wasting errands for Admiral

Upton when his orders specifically required him to report to the Commander-in-Chief with all possible speed; he was, perhaps, unaware that Sir John preferred his ships to cross their yards with something approaching parallelism and would his wrist rest any less comfortably in a sling that was passably clean? Meantime, he would await the Admiral's pleasure, bearing in mind that the wait would not be enlivened by taking black women on board, a custom long established but now causing murmurs at home and one which the Commander-in-Chief was determined to end.

Slade had sulked in his cabin and stamped about the quarterdeck for an hour or two, snarling at anyone who caught his eye, before hitting on a scheme that would cut obliquely but legitimately across Sir John's last order and spread a little salve on Slade's injured pride. He did not himself care for the practice of allowing a King's ship to be overrun with women the moment it touched port and had the Admiral made the prohibition a courteous suggestion rather than an order Slade would have been happy to concur. As it was, having his men rudely denied the opportunity of women coming to them, he was now determined that the process would take place in reverse and by God, each man take advantage of it even if he had to stand over them with a rope's end! The hands were called aft, specific instructions were given (and enthusiastically received) and after lining up for their small advances from the purser the first boat-loads set off, cheered on their way with loud reminders that others were still on board awaiting their turn. The officers, of course, kept aloof from these lustful excursions, albeit not without envy and the midshipmen, to their intense disgust, were barred from enjoining by orders of the captain. A number of the older hands and petty officers declined, many of them decently married and a few deeply pious – one of them, with a keen interest in hagiology, went along lusting solely after the town's churches – but within twenty-four hours Slade's wishes had, by and large, been carried out to the letter, to the satisfaction of those involved and the immediate lightening of the captain's foul mood.

Captain Mainwaring's house lay further from the town than Lamb had realized and it was ten minutes past the hour when he arrived, damp with sweat from his uphill walk. He was shown into the drawing-room by a silent, white-wigged, black footman and eased his way to a chair at the back of the room. Polite but unenthusiastic clapping was taking place as he took his seat and a stout, moustached lady was nodding and beaming from a small dais. She descended with a loud swish of satin and Mrs Mainwaring left her chair and stepped up to the dais in her place.

'I have called this poem "Morning Walk",' she announced in her light, confident voice. She folded her hands over her groin and began her recital, her eyes drifting about her audience. Lamb fancied she dwelt a little longer in his direction.

> 'I scuff the leaves beneath the bower,
> A carpet from the flowers above;
> I tread the rose, the jasmine sweet
> And sadly dwell upon my love.'

Lamb's mind wandered after two or three verses; they were, he gathered, concerned with the moon at dawn, a distant lover and a broken heart, none of which gripped his attention. He found his interest drawn instead to the graceful curve of the speaker's hips, her slim waist and the rise and fall of her bosom, a movement which he found totally absorbing. His imagination was beginning to get a little heated when she clasped her hands, turned her eyes to the ceiling and pitched her voice a trifle higher. Lamb guessed that she was approaching the end of her poem and he dragged his attention back to her words.

> 'But he has grown cold, O moon,
> And he is far from me;
> Buried in a sailor's grave
> Beneath a storm-tossed sea!'

Mrs Mainwaring's audience was composed mainly of the wives of naval officers and a few of their menfolk and her happy blend of pining love and a watery death caught at their imagination. They burst into rapturous applause, with which none joined more enthusiastically than Lamb, bringing a warm flush of pride and pleasure to the cheeks of Mrs Mainwaring and a pinched look to the face of the stout woman who had preceded her. Lamb rose from his chair to ensure that his admiration would not go unnoticed and was gratified to see her smiling gaze linger in his direction. Mrs Mainwaring returned to her chair and her place on the dais was taken by a breastless, hipless woman whose voice seemed to have been crushed by her thin frame. Lamb strained to distinguish the title of her work – he thought it was called 'Thoughts on Breaking a Tea-Cup' but he could not be sure and as her breathless mumble continued he cared even less – and sat back in his chair with every evidence of rapt concentration on his face while a colourful succession of lustful images passed through his mind.

Coffee and little cakes were served at the end of the readings and Lamb hovered at the edge of the group surrounding Mrs Mainwaring wondering how he might effect an entry. He need not have worried; she caught sight of his tall figure and broke through her cordon of admirers to lay her hand upon his arm and smile up at him.

'Mr Lamb! How good of you to come to our little meeting. Did you find it interesting? We are rather proud of our little group – we have some very talented poets, you know, and I am sorry you did not hear the best of them today.'

'Oh, I am quite certain I heard one of them, at least,' said Lamb, gallantly.

Mrs Mainwaring looked a little arch. 'And to whom would you be referring, sir?' she enquired coyly.

'Why, to the author of "Morning Walk" ma'am, who else?'

She smiled and bowed her head in graceful acknowledgement. 'Your coffee-cup is empty, Mr Lamb. Allow me to refill it for you. Come.'

They walked to the white-clothed table set against the window and Mrs Mainwaring filled his cup from the silver jug keeping warm over its little heater. Lamb gestured to the magnificent blaze of colour and the winding, shaded walks of the garden.

'Your garden is truly a picture, Mrs Mainwaring, a feast to the eye.'

She studied him over the rim of her coffee-cup. 'You are very kind, Mr Lamb. You cannot see all of it from here, of course. Perhaps one day you would allow me to show you the rest of it.'

Lamb smiled and they held each other's gaze for a long second. 'That would be a great pleasure, Mrs Mainwaring,' he said softly.

'Would tomorrow morning be inconvenient? About eleven o'clock?'

'It would not be at all inconvenient, ma'am. I look forward to it with much pleasure.'

Slade dined ashore that night, evidently concluding that his exalted rank rendered him immune from the deadly night-time miasmas of the island. Taking advantage of the quiet anchor-watch the officers decided to dine on the quarterdeck, considering an hour of sweated labour by the carpenter's mates a small price to pay for the pleasure of sitting at table in the cool evening air beneath a canopy of bright stars. The arrangement did not suit Sykes in the slightest, involving, as it did, the climbing of the aft companionway a dozen times during the meal and he made his displeasure plain, puffing and panting exaggeratedly each time he came to the table, banging the dishes on to it, clattering the dirty ones loudly on his tray and allowing muttered swearing to drift up from the companionway as he descended. The officers, well used to his domestic ways, ignored him and chatted comfortably amongst themselves through his noisy clatter.

'Well, Mr Hopper,' said Lamb, leaning back easily in his chair and stretching his long legs, 'and how do you like life as a lieutenant?'

'Oh, I like it fine, sir,' said Hopper eagerly. 'It will be a wrench for me to go back to the cockpit.'

'Yes, enjoy our august company while you may,' said Rank. 'It will not be long, I expect, before the Commander-in-Chief sends one of his favourites to replace you.'

'Yes,' said Hopper gloomily. 'One thing, though,' he exclaimed, brightening, 'it has made me determined to stick to my studies and go for lieutenant at the earliest opportunity. My six years are almost up now.'

'You can always try for it here at Port Royal,' said Lamb. 'There is sure to be a board sitting sooner or later. I dare say you would find it easier here than at Somerset House.'

'Aye, or Malta!' cried Bell, wincing at the memory.

'Yes, I took mine there,' said Rank. 'Walking through fire would have been less painful, I'm certain; and it's a curious fact that all the middies there without a master's ticket failed. You haven't one, have you, Hopper?'

Hopper shook his head. 'No, I never saw the need to work for it.'

'What he means is he was too damned idle and too fond of the bottle,' snorted Ball, causing amused eyebrows to be raised around the table and a murmur from the surgeon about the relative blackness of the pot to the kettle.

'You took your examination at the Navy Office, did you not, sir?' asked Hopper of Lamb, anxious to keep the conversation on a topic close to his heart.

'I did.'

'Was it very difficult? Did your parents go with you?'

'Difficult? Well, some found it so. As for my parents, no, I went on my own. My mother was dead and my father was with his regiment in Ireland. I had taken lodgings in Stepney. It had rained in the night and I had to walk some way to the nearest cab-stand and I remember how worried I was about the mud on my boots. I stopped the cab-man at Charing Cross and walked the rest of the way so that I could wash my boots in the puddles. When I reached Somerset House I realized that I had left my precious copy of *The Complete Navigator* in the carriage. I could have wept! It was like losing an old friend. I was convinced it was a bad omen and I went into the Navy Office quite certain that I was going to fail.'

'Oh, I am sure everyone feels like that,' cried Ball. 'I know I did and I can remember gaping like an idiot when I was told I had passed.'

'Yes, you probably deserved to gape,' said Rank unkindly. 'I was asked by one of the board how often I said my prayers. "Oh, every night, sir, without fail," I said, looking him straight in the eye. "Every night?" he said, looking at me a bit narrow. "Yes, sir, I was brought up pious, sir," I said, looking as holy as I could, "and I never let the good book leave my person, sir," and I whipped a pocket Bible out and held it up for him to see. The old boy was so moved he had to wipe his eye. "Oh, would that there were more youngsters like you, Mr Rank," he said and I knew then that I had passed.'

There was a long silence. 'You?' said Ball at last. 'Pious? Prayers every night? Pocket Bible? My God, you have changed!'

'No, not at all,' said Rank. 'I got wind that Billy Burton was to be one of the examining captains – Bible Billy, he was known as, because he always carried one – and I prepared myself accordingly. I deserved to pass for sheer forethought and anticipation, if nothing else.'

'La, Mr Lamb!' cried Mrs Mainwaring, giving him a playful little poke in the arm. 'I do not believe you are at all interested in my poincianas – you have scarcely given them a glance since we came outside. Do you not care for them?' She looked up at him, wide-eyed. 'Do you not find them beautiful?'

Lamb looked down into her blue, smiling eyes and decided it was time to come alongside, grapple and probe his chances of boarding.

'My dearest Mrs Mainwaring, dearest Fanny,' he said, dropping his voice an octave or so to a seductive purr, 'with eyes like yours to gaze into, what chance has a mere flower of holding my attention? With you beside me, why should I turn to look at these dull things?'

He gestured at the magnificent flowering trees which ranged along the high wall of Captain Mainwaring's garden, thinking that perhaps he had come over a little too strong. Mrs Mainwaring did not seem to feel so, however; she closed her eyes and shivered with delight, pressing her small bosom against Lamb's elbow and digging her fingers hungrily into his arm.

'Fie, Mr Lamb, you are outrageous,' she protested weakly. 'You make me feel quite faint. Come, take me out of this hot sun into the gazebo.'

Mrs Mainwaring was a slight, slim woman and if one ignored the low forehead and the eruptions which peeped shyly through the thick layer of powder, almost pretty. Keenly aware of certain stirrings and upliftings, Lamb followed the lady into the cool darkness of the gazebo, set in a discreet corner of the garden surrounded by a blaze of poincianas, angel's trumpets and ginger-lilies.

She turned to face him, her eyes fixed on his, her bosom heaving. Lamb stepped close; she reacted like a pin to a magnet. They kissed. She gave out little mewing noises, her fingers digging hard into his back. Lamb slipped his hand down to the firm rise of her buttocks and pressed her close to his groin. Her mewing changed to a squeal of wonder and delight.

'Oh, Mr Lamb!'

Lamb brought his free hand up between them and pressed home the attack with an exploratory squeeze of a small, unfettered breast.

'No, no, you must not!' gasped Mrs Mainwaring, gripping his biceps tenaciously. Lamb sensibly ignored this token protest and kissed her again, pressing her down on to the long seat that ran round three of the gazebo's walls. He lowered himself beside her, squatting awkwardly with one haunch on the edge of the seat. Her hand strayed down towards his jutting breeches and probed and pressed and gripped. Lamb's free hand inched at her skirt and petticoats, endeavouring to hoist them over her knees without appearing so to do.

'Wait, wait,' she murmured urgently, and lifting her buttocks off the seat a trifle she gathered up her skirts beneath her. Lamb's hand fell on a smooth, warm thigh. Her legs parted, her breathing quickened. Boarders away! thought Lamb, sliding his hand along, hoping he would find no boarding nets rigged. There were none. Mrs Mainwaring clung to his lips, shifting slightly to assist his exploration, her fingers fumbling urgently at his buttons.

Lamb crouched over her, his toes braced firmly against a conveniently proud stone flag. 'Darling Fanny!' he breathed as her hand pulled and guided.

'No, no, call me Mrs Mainwaring, always – it is safer,' she panted.

Lamb thrust home.

'Ah! Ah!' she squealed. 'Yes, yes, yes!'

'Darling Mrs Mainwaring!' grunted Lamb.

The noonday Jamaican sun sparkled glitteringly off the blue water of the harbour and struck with baking heat on to King Street facing it but the select room of the Blue Boar, with doors and windows flung wide, was an oasis of shady coolness, gurgling spigots and clinking glasses. Lamb stepped gratefully inside, hot and perspiring from his long walk in the sun and his exertions in Captain Mainwaring's gazebo. The room was hazy with blue tobacco smoke and for a second Lamb was almost sightless after the glaring brightness of the open air. He heard his name called and saw Rank waving an arm from a corner. Lamb made his way through the press of blue and bright scarlet uniforms and the drab black and grey of the few civilians to where Rank kept company with two other lieutenants.

'Hello, Lamb. A damned peculiar twelve o'clock this is,' cried Simms, first lieutenant of the sloop *Diadem* which was anchored close to the *Adroit*. 'What tricks have you been up to, all on your own, you hound?'

'On his own?' murmured Rank questioningly, raising a guffaw from Simms and a smile from the other officer.

'I am sorry to be late,' said Lamb. 'I was browsing amongst some truly magnificent poincianas and I clean forgot the time. You know of my deep interest in flora, do you not, Rank?'

'No,' said Rank in a firm tone.

Simms introduced the third lieutenant sitting at the table as Edwin Wheelwright, who struggled awkwardly to his feet to take Lamb's outstretched hand. Lamb noticed the heavy stick propped in the corner and Wheelwright caught his glance.

'A broken tibia,' he explained, with a wry grin.

'Shin bone to you, Lamb,' put in Simms, rudely. 'The bloody fool fell down a companionway and now he is without a ship. He will not get one either, until he can throw that bloody stick away. How long has it been now, Wheelwright?'

'Four months – but it improves each day, I am sure of it.'

Lamb poured himself some wine and surveyed Wheelwright over the rim of his glass. Four months and he still needs a stick to get about? He will never get a ship now, only as a supernumary, to be paid off for good when he reaches England, the poor sod. For some reason the instance of Collier's death came into his mind and looking at Wheelwright he reflected on the narrow path that man trod and how easily he was nudged from it. Here was a young officer, until a few months ago an undoubtedly energetic and ambitious man with a long and active career stretching before him; and now, a momentary stumble, a second's carelessness, has put paid to all his hopes and probably crippled him for good into the bargain. Lamb gave a mental shake of the head and drained his glass.

'I have ordered a leg of pork,' said Simms. 'Roasted crisp,

162

with every vegetable they can lay their hands on and plenty of fresh bread to fill up the holes. With luck we should get through that and still make the first race. Wheelwright has promised to mark our cards for us – he spends a great deal of his time at the race-course, he tells me.'

'There is precious little else to do,' smiled Wheelwright apologetically.

'That all sounds splendid,' said Lamb. 'And in the meantime we'll have a couple of fresh bottles here.'

The wine arrived, the food arrived and in due course, after a short and merry journey during which they managed to make their driver nearly insensible with drink, the first race arrived, leaving Lamb less merry and a good deal poorer. On the next race his stake was more modest; he decided this time to ignore Wheelwright's advice and put his money on a pretty brown filly with a fetching white blaze to her forehead. He cheered her on to a narrow win, a short neck in front of Wheelwright's choice and went off flushed with cheering and excitement to collect his winnings. With his pockets jingling he threaded his way back through the crowd but stopped short and turned as a feminine voice called his name.

'Mr Lamb! It is Mr Lamb, is it not?'

It was Mrs Mainwaring, bright and elegant in white beneath a pretty parasol, her hand on the arm of a stout, jovial captain considerably older than herself.

Lamb bowed. 'It is indeed, ma'am. I am gratified that you remember me.'

Mrs Mainwaring's face was a picture of innocence. 'I rarely forget a name or a face, sir. My dear, this is Mr Lamb – he came to my poetry reading yesterday. Mr Lamb, this is my husband, Captain Mainwaring.'

Mainwaring's handshake was hearty. 'Delighted to make your acquaintance, Lamb. You don't look like a bloody poet, I must say,' he added, in a tone that suggested he had little time for the species. 'What ship?'

'*Adroit*, sir.'

'Ah, Captain Slade,' said Mainwaring, his smile vanishing. 'You have my sympathy, young man.'

'Mr Lamb expressed a keen interest in Jamaica's flowers – he is something of an expert in that field, I gather. We shall have to show him our garden – it is quite famous in its way, is it not, Charles?'

Lamb regarded Mrs Mainwaring with silent amusement as she spoke, her voice light, looking cool and contained beneath her pink parasol, a vastly different creature altogether from the one he had known beneath him in the gazebo a few hours earlier.

'Yes, come any time you are free, Lamb,' said Mainwaring absently, studying his card, clearly anxious to be rid of him. Lamb could almost hear the thoughts in his mind; flowers *and* poetry, by God! – what sort of men are we getting in the Navy nowadays?

'Perhaps tomorrow morning, sir, if that is convenient to you?' suggested Lamb, carefully avoiding Mrs Mainwaring's eye.

'Yes, by all means. I shall not be there, of course; I shall be at the Navy Yard, no doubt fending off the inordinate demands of your captain, if the past few days are anything to go by. But I am sure Mrs Mainwaring will be only too pleased to show you her pretty flowers. Huh!'

'It will be a pleasure to do so, Mr Lamb. Shall we say ten o'clock, before it grows too warm?'

Lamb bowed. 'You are very kind, ma'am. Your servant, sir.'

Mrs Mainwaring gave a demure smile in return and for a brief instant showed the red, lascivious tip of her tongue. Her husband gave an abstracted nod and a grunt, and Lamb walked away towards his companions, striving to control the involuntary stirrings in his breeches.

'No, wait, do not move yet,' panted Mrs Mainwaring, pulling Lamb close again and locking him there with clamped legs and clinging arms. 'Wait just another moment or two.'

Lamb lowered his head and brushed the perspiration from his forehead with his outstretched arm, listening to his heart beating so hard he thought it might jump from its moorings and keenly aware of his naked buttocks presented to the opening of the gazebo. Mrs Mainwaring gave a grunt of animal content-ment and tightened her arms around his back; for an uneasy moment he thought she might be making renewed, impossible demands on him. There has been nothing in the way of coy protests from the lady this morning; the angel's trumpets and the ginger-lilies might have been ragwort and bindweed for all the attention they received during her rapid progress from the house to the gazebo with a delighted but slightly alarmed Lamb stepping out briskly beside her. He wondered now, as his heart slowed its frantic pumping and his buttocks cooled in the shade of the dark arbour, if he had not bitten off more than he could comfortably chew; the urgent, wanton demands that she had made on him in the past hour had not only astonished him – and, if he had dared to admit it, shocked him more than a trifle – but had also sown unfamiliar seeds of doubt in his mind concerning his own stamina. His performance, he was quite sure, had been more than adequate but he was not so certain of his ability to keep pace with her future needs.

Mrs Mainwaring stirred beneath him and traced a finger along his spine. 'Mr Lamb,' she murmured, in a playful tone, 'do you think it might be possible for you to – ?'

She stopped abruptly, her body stiffening.

'Hush!' she hissed, cocking her head to one side. 'Do you hear wheels?'

Lamb raised his head and listened. The sound of iron-shod wheels crunching over the gravel drive at the front of the house was faint but distinct.

'Yes.'

'My God, it is Charles!'

Lamb sprang as if stung from his fleshy prison and shuffled in ungainly fashion to one side, his breeches coiled around his ankles. As he hurriedly stooped and pulled and struggled Mrs Mainwaring rose from the seat, allowed her skirts to fall modestly back to her shoes and patted her hair into place.

'Let me have the use of your handkerchief,' she demanded. Lamb held the waistband of his breeches somewhere between his knees and damp thighs while he delved awkwardly into his pockets.

'Thank you, sir,' she said prettily and dabbed at her shining face. 'There!' she smiled, twirling around for his inspection. 'All quite decent again and quite unruffled. I shall go and meet Charles while you finish dressing yourself.' She gave a girlish giggle and kissed him on the tip of his nose. 'Do not look so alarmed, Mr Lamb. Charles did invite you here this morning, did he not?'

Her light footsteps disappeared along the paved walk to the house as Lamb continued to force his perspiring lower half into his tight breeches. He swore savagely as a button came free from the flap. Buttoned up tight at last, he tugged and straightened, sweat bursting from every pore. He smoothed back his hair, pulled at his queue, fingered his sodden stock and ran his handkerchief around his face and neck, the scent of Mrs Mainwaring's face-powder coming to his nostrils again. He stepped from the gazebo and made his way along the curving path to a little wooden seat placed beneath the overhanging trees. He sat, crossed his legs and endeavoured to look the picture of a man cool and composed, fixing his gaze with apparent deep interest on the flowering shrubs across the far side of the little lawn. Captain Mainwaring, he was convinced, would instantly detect from his hot, flushed face and rumpled clothing the game he had been at and would no doubt call him out on the spot. He heard the murmur of voices and footsteps on the garden path and quickly rehearsed a casual, disarming smile.

Mrs Mainwaring appeared around the curve of the path but it was not her husband that accompanied her, unless that aging officer had shrunk by half, lost three-quarters of his bulk and gained a great deal in the way of hair.

'Mr Allwyn!' exclaimed Lamb in surprise. 'What the devil brings you here?'

'I beg your pardon, sir,' said the midshipman. 'The captain sends his compliments and would be obliged if you returned to the ship forthwith. We have our sailing orders, sir.'

As the phaeton rattled its way down the hill to the harbour and the waiting boat Lamb gave the boy a sidelong glance.

'How did you, um, know where I was, Mr Allwyn?' he asked casually, curious as to how the midshipman, in spite of Lamb's utmost discretion concerning his acquaintance with Mrs Mainwaring, had known where to look for him.

'Oh, the captain said he thought you might be here, sir, and Mr Rank said he was certain of it and so did Mr Ball; but I knew already, sir, anyway, because Sykes told me earlier.'

*

'Steady as she goes, Latimer,' called Slade over his shoulder.

'Steady as she goes, sir,' murmured the quartermaster.

The Blue Mountains of Jamaica lay astern as the *Adroit* headed north-east under clear skies and a quartering wind. Ahead lay the Windward Passage, separating Cuba from Hispaniola and a main gateway from the Caribbean to the Atlantic for homeward-bound British merchantmen. Another gateway was the Mona Passage, east of Hispaniola and it was here the frigate was to take up her patrolling duties, roaming the waters between Hispaniola and Puerto Rico and attempting to keep the passage clear of privateers. Slade had received his orders early in the forenoon watch just as he was about to leave the ship to join a party of senior officers for a pig-hunt in the mountains. His orders had been brought to him by a supercilious young flag lieutenant who was clearly more accustomed to treading the grander boards of the flagship and the marble floors of Admiralty House than the narrow, cramped deck of a lowly frigate. He came and went with his lip firmly curled and Rank had barely seen him frostily over the side before the captain was bellowing from the quarterdeck for a boat to be sent to find his first lieutenant and another to Fort Charles to pick up the surgeon.

It was with mixed feelings that Lamb had watched Port Royal recede astern. Mrs Mainwaring, her gazebo and her poincianas had been a warm and satisfying interlude and her warm thigh beneath his hand a good deal softer and more interesting than the unyielding oak of the quarterdeck rail. However, he thought philosophically, there is little in the way of promotion or prize-money to be won in climbing aboard another officer's wife – better by far to climb aboard a Spanish treasure-ship!

The wind was comfortably on the starboard quarter and having seen the topgallant royals and the studdingsails set alow and aloft Slade withdrew to his cabin for a private jug of coffee and a more leisurely perusal of his orders. The admiral's clerk had evidently dashed off the orders in some haste; the paper was decorated with a spattering of tiny ink spots from his racing pen and his inadequate blotting had left some letters badly smudged. But they were clear enough for all that. The *Adroit* was to relieve the brig-sloop *Rosemary* and patrol the Mona

Passage; she was to close and destroy enemy privateers and to engage enemy men-of-war at the captain's discretion; she was to render such aid and assistance to British ships as might be found necessary. Enemy merchant ships could be taken, again at the captain's discretion, provided this did not interfere with or prejudice his main duties, bearing in mind the danger of weakening his command by the provision of prize-crews. Slade grunted sardonically at this last paragraph. The Commander-in-Chief collected one eighth of all prize-monies won under his command and any independent-cruising captain who placed too much importance to this cautionary formality would swiftly find his ship placed on mundane duties that gave very little scope for independence or prize-money. He locked his orders in his table drawer and made his way up to the quarterdeck deep in thought, turning over in his mind again the least number of men needed to sail and fight the ship and the names of those undesirables amongst his crew whom he would place at the top of his prize-crew list.

Slade was by no means a poor man; service on the American station had brought him little in the way of financial gain but since then he had more than made up for that in the Mediterranean and the Channel. He was cursed, however, with three daughters, two of them of marriageable age and the third not far short, and the thought of funding their matrimonies hovered constantly and darkly at the edge of his mind. As he took up his slow pacing on the weather side of the quarterdeck he closed his eyes and sent up a silent prayer: Send me a fat treasure-ship, O Lord, heavy with gold and silver. He quickly added an afterthought. And a clear sea – I would rather not share it, if it is all the same to you.

Twenty-four hours later the *Adroit* snapped up a Spanish felucca making a dash across the Windward Passage. Armed with only a rusty six-pounder the sight of the *Adroit*'s gun-ports opening was sufficient threat to make her heave-to and the frigate swept down on her like a shark to a sprat. She was carrying tobacco and copper ingots and after prudently removing her wine and distributing it between his own cabin and the gunroom Slade promptly despatched her southwards under the command of a master's mate with four of the *Adroit*'s incorrigibles as crew. Slade performed certain rough and ready calculations in his head and smiled as the frigate continued north, leaving the original crew of the felucca pulling glumly for the coast of Hispaniola, some fifteen miles to the east.

Flying French colours the *Adroit* rounded Tortuga, the one-time haven for French and British privateers, and sighted an armed brig ahead drawing away from the land, on a similar but converging course to that of the frigate. Slade studied her briefly through his glass and ordered the ship's head edged away a trifle, hoping that this display of non-interest coupled with the tricolour flying from the mast would be enough to lull the brig into believing that she was in no danger. For a time the ruse succeeded and when the brig suddenly woke up to the fact that the frigate overhauling her was certainly not French the *Adroit* had closed to within a couple of miles. The brig dithered, started to make a run for it and then decided it would be safer to make a dash back to the island. She tacked and put her stern to the wind. Slade brought the frigate's head round to intercept her.

'Run up the colours, Mr Hopper,' called Slade, overflowing with good humour, a beaming smile fixed on his broad, red face, and in a roar along the maindeck, 'Open gun-ports! Stand by the starboard guns! Stand by the fo'c'sle guns!'

For her size the brig was a fast sailer but on this tack Lamb considered her to be somewhat overpressed with sail; in any event the frigate was a knot or two faster and within half an hour Slade ordered the long six-pounders on the forecastle to open fire.

'Take your time and aim well, my good lads!' he bellowed. 'I want every shot to drop on to her poop.'

He chuckled and grinned widely around the quarterdeck, anxious that no one should have missed this piece of sparkling wit; the brig had no poop-deck, of course, not even a quarterdeck to speak of but his humour raised a dutiful laugh from the officers crowded on to the lee side. All the officers not committed to duty at the guns and who had a right to walk the quarterdeck had decided to exercise their privilege this morning and the surgeon, purser and lieutenant of Marines were there, getting in the way of the officer of the watch and the duty midshipman and squabbling over the use of a ship's telescope. Lamb shot them a dark look, surprised that Slade had not blasted them into silence but today he was full of smiles and bonhomie and even went so far as to join in the cheers which went up when a well-aimed shot cut away the brig's spanker gaff and collapsed her driver into useless folds over her boom.

'Ha! ha!' laughed the purser knowingly. 'That has fixed her capers.'

The forward guns were hitting regularly on the brig's aft section and stern and within a few minutes of her spanker falling the little ship slewed to starboard with a shattered rudder, exposing the line of carronades run out through her open ports.

'Starboard the helm!' shouted Slade.

'Starboard the helm it is, sir,' murmured the grave-faced quartermaster.

The frigate's bow swung obediently to starboard, bringing her starboard guns to bear.

'Steady – keep her so.'

'Steady it is, sir.'

The two vessels fired their guns at the same instant but the range was too great for the brig's short guns and her twenty-four-pound roundshot tore up the water two hundred yards short of the frigate. The *Adroit*'s long twelve-pounders, however, were comfortably within range and smashed home on the privateer's side and low bulwarks, extending her gun-ports and sending wicked shards of timber flying. The brig wallowed helplessly in the water, unable to steer, unable to hit back as the frigate's guns struck heavily again.

'We will have a crack at her stern, Mr Goode,' called Slade. 'And let the larboard guns show us their mettle this time. Keep her at this distance, if you please.'

The sailing master issued the necessary orders and the frigate swept in a long curve to starboard around the shattered stern of the brig.

'Fire as you bear!'

The bright flash of darting flame and the rolling thunder of exploding gunpowder travelled swiftly along the larboard side, the noise merging into one long roar, the rising clouds of smoke caught and shredded by the wind. The gun-captains, who much preferred to exercise their skills individually in this manner rather than in the collective broadside, raised their grinning, smoke-stained faces to the quarterdeck, delighted with their work. The stern of the brig was a shambles; the low taffrail had been blasted away, the wheel was gone and the narrow deck was littered with overturned guns, splintered timber and the bodies of men cut down by the lethal passage of iron and timber missiles. Lamb cocked an eye at Slade as he examined the vessel through his glass, wondering whether the captain would order the guns to fire again. In his opinion it would be a waste of powder and shot; the brig was so badly cut about that he doubted her ability to stay afloat for very long, let alone make it back to Tortuga. In either case, her days as a privateer were finished.

Slade lowered his glass. 'Secure the guns, Mr Lamb. Helm a-lee, quartermaster. Set the courses again, Mr Goode, if you please and resume our course.'

Slade left the quarterdeck without another glance at the devastated privateer. Lamb descended to the maindeck and advanced along it as the men secured their guns, sponging and swabbing and hauling at their ropes in high good humour, delighted with their quick success, happy to have remained unbloodied and glancing at Lamb with wide grins as he passed, clearly hoping for a complimentary word. Lamb did not disappoint them.

'Well done, my lads. Every shot told. You will be busy again before long, I feel. Well done, boys.'

He repeated the litany with minor variations as he went along. It was little enough but it delighted the men and brought on much hitching-up of trousers and spitting-on of hands, as if the next round of action could not come soon enough. Lamb pushed aside the damp canvas covering the forward hatchway and descended to the orlop-deck, where he held a shouted exchange with the unseen gunner in the screened-off magazine about the availability of cartridges. Winter's replies were short and Lamb grinned, knowing of the stupefying heat within that airless compartment. He returned to the bright breeziness of the open deck in time to hear a hail from the masthead.

'Deck there! A sail fine on the larboard bow.'

Lamb beckoned to little Bird and sent him to inform the captain and whilst he waited for Slade's arrival he took his glass aft to the taffrail and levelled it at the distant brig. She was now several miles astern but he fancied he could see movement on her deck and masts and envisaged the frantic efforts of those left more or less whole in rigging a jury rudder and to keeping the vessel afloat. Lamb had no love for privateersmen but they had defended themselves bravely and he silently wished them luck.

The captain arrived on the quarterdeck hard on the heels of young Bird, slopping coffee from the cup in his hand.

The lookout hailed again. 'Deck there! Make that two sail, both fine on the larboard bow!'

Slade caught Lamb's eye and raised his cup to him in a cheerful salute. He was smiling broadly. 'A busy morning, I think, Mr Lamb.'

'I am happy to have it so, sir,' said Lamb, smiling in return.

'We will have a good man with a glass aloft, Mr Lamb,' he said, advancing to the quarterdeck rail. 'Mr Isherwood!' he called out to the master's mate, bent over a cask of beef in the waist in earnest consultation with the purser and the cook. Isherwood straightened and touched his hat.

'Sir?'

'Do me the kindness of taking a glass and your best pair of eyes aloft and report down what you see of those two sail.'

'Aye aye, sir,' responded Isherwood, smiling at Slade's cheerful and uncommon courtesy and two minutes later he was standing on the jacks at the top of the maintopgallantmast with his arm curled round the spar and his telescope fixed to his eye.

'And as for you, my brave lads,' roared Slade at the men standing at their guns on the maindeck, 'do not think that you have yet earned your pay and grog with those few minutes' work this morning. With a little luck I shall be sweating that rum and wickedness out of you before the day is over and who knows, by nightfall you might have earned yourselves a handful of guineas or more!'

A ragged cheer went up from the gun-crews at these words and Slade turned his back on them, chuckling. The captain was far from being a morose man but by no stretch of the imagination could he be described as affable and even-tempered. His mood, in general, hovered about that of prickly irritability, sometimes erupting into a volcanic outburst of foul temper and filthy language, times when the prohibitions placed on such language by the Articles of War and so often earnestly delivered by him to the crew on Sunday mornings were wholeheartedly ignored. His bubbling good humour of today spread its happy influence throughout the ship, so that the men at the guns hummed and whistled between their teeth as they worked at reloading their charges and replenishing the racks of roundshot and the officers on the quarterdeck smiled and laughed and chatted together in an uncommonly liberal fashion under the benign eye of their beaming captain; even the master, that most determinedly dark-tempered man, was sufficiently infected to allow the set of his mouth to edge into something approaching a smile.

Isherwood's clear voice sang down from the masthead. 'Two French barques, sir, stern-on. One has just sent up her royals – t'other one too, now, sir.'

They had sighted the *Adroit*. Lamb glanced aloft. Their colours had again been replaced by the vertical stripes of the French tricolour which was streaming bravely in the wind but it was clear that the distant masters were not going to take that at its face value. 'Better flight than fight' were words engraved on every merchant captain's heart.

The wind was blowing warmly from the dim blue haze of Hispaniola to the south across the frigate's starboard quarter, her best point of sailing, and she bowled merrily along at a slight heel, her bow cutting through the blue water and sending the white furrow hissing and singing along her sides. Six bells sounded and Allwyn moved aft followed by a quartermaster bearing a sand-glass. The captain of the mizzen-top crooked a finger at one of his gang and silently pointed at the lee quarter. Lamb walked to the side and glanced down at the rush of water along the timbers.

'Eleven knots,' he said confidently to Rank.

Rank joined him and took a calculating look over the side. He shook his head. 'No. Ten and a quarter at the most.'

'A guinea?'

'Done!'

They walked aft to where the midshipman clutched the log-ship in his hand along with about twenty feet of the line pulled from the reel held high above the seaman's head. Allwyn glanced behind him at the approach of the two officers and instinctively straightened, donning his diminutive mantle of authority and clearing his throat in an endeavour to lower his piping treble to what he optimistically imagined would be a deep, stern, authoritative note.

'Is the glass clear?' he enquired, in a curious, strangled tone.

'All clear, sir,' replied the ancient quartermaster, solemnly eyeing the top half of the half-minute glass.

The midshipman drew back his arm and cast the lead-weighted log-ship well out to the lee of the ship; the stray line attached to it immediately began to run rapidly through his cupped hand.

'Turn! he cried, feeling the piece of red bunting marking the end of the stray line pass through his fingers. The quartermaster, whose keen old eyes had seen the bunting fly from the reel, instantly turned the glass, holding it up to the sky close to his face. Exactly twenty-eight seconds later, as the last of the grains of sand tumbled into the neck, he called, 'Stop!' and Allwyn closed his hand upon the line. The seaman lowered the reel and as the midshipman gave the line a jerk to release the peg from the log-ship he began to haul it in hand over hand. Allwyn examined the mark on the line below his hand, turned his eyes to the sky and muttered to himself as he ran through his catechism of markings, and gave a questioning glance at the quartermaster. The old man gave a slight nod and Allwyn trotted up to Rank.

'Eleven knots and a fathom, if you please, sir.'

Lamb smiled. Rank scowled and moved his lips in a silent curse. The midshipman waited, puzzled at this strange reaction.

'Very well, Mr Allwyn,' said Rank with a disgusted nod. 'Make it so.'

The boy ran off to mark up the log-board and Rank delved reluctantly into his pocket.

'Mr Rank,' called Slade from his side of the quarterdeck. 'Warn the cook – the men will eat early today, whether it be ready or not. I shall do the same; let my steward know, if you please, that I shall be eating up here.'

'Aye aye, sir. Mr Allwyn!'

'Perhaps you will be kind enough to join me, Mr Lamb?' enquired Slade.

A captain's suggestion was as firm as an order and without

waiting for a reply Slade leaned over the quarterdeck rail. 'Tell Donovan to make enough for two, Mr Allwyn!' he bellowed at the running midshipman's back.

Donovan arrived as the hands tumbled below, happy to have their beef and grog early. Slade lifted the cloth on the tray and inspected the offerings beneath. The smell of freshly brewed coffee wafted deliciously across the deck.

'Shall we sit here?' suggested Slade and the two men squatted on a carronade slide apiece with the tray between them and munched with keen appetites on cold ham, cheese and bread from Port Royal not yet grown hard while Allwyn stared fixedly with deep longing from the lee shrouds. Slade was a hearty eater and devoted all of his attention to the task in hand and none to conversation. The silence, however, was not uncomfortable; the captain exuded good humour as he chewed, his eyes narrowed against the sun, his forefinger pointing to the tray as he silently urged Lamb to help himself to more.

Rank clambered up on to the lee bulwark and levelled his glass at the distant ships.

'Well, Mr Rank?' demanded Slade.

'No change in their course, sir. We are clearly gaining on them but it will be an hour or two yet before we get within range, sir.'

Slade grunted and glanced aloft, wiping his mouth with his napkin. Short of fixing that square foot of linen to the yards, there was little else he could add in the way of sail.

'Enough, Mr Lamb? More cheese? Coffee?'

Lamb patted his stomach. 'Thank you, sir, but no. Enough is as good as a feast, they say, sir.'

Slade raised a finger to the midshipman. 'Mr Allwyn, be so good as to dispose of these leavings over the stern.'

Allwyn's eyes gleamed as he surveyed the tray's contents.

'Aye aye, sir,' he said eagerly, snatching it up with all the avidity of a beggar coming across a golden guinea.

Eight bells sounded. The hands came up from below and went to their guns and action stations, the helmsmen were relieved, a fresh lookout climbed aloft and Ball took over the quarterdeck watch. Midshipman Allwyn exchanged a few words with Midshipman Bird and left the quarterdeck with the captain's tray tucked beneath his arm and a scattering of crumbs down his jacket whilst Lamb moved over to the lee side, leaving Slade to enjoy the solitude of his part of the deck. The afternoon wore on. Rank's estimate of an hour or two proved to be sadly astray. The frigate's greater sail area and length at the waterline gave her a distinct advantage but the smaller, three-masted vessels were no laggards and it was not until near the end of the afternoon watch that the barques were within the extreme range of the *Adroit*'s guns. The coast of Hispaniola had been a dim, blue thickening of the starboard horizon for most of the way but in the past hour or so the mountainous shoreline had begun to bulge and the peaks and heights were now clearly visible from the quarterdeck. Lamb studied the Frenchmen through his glass. They were as like as two peas in a pod but one had managed to creep ahead to lead the other by half a mile or so. There was a good deal of activity on the deck of the nearest barque. She carried three small guns to each side and a larger one at her stern, three- and six-pounders, Lamb judged, and her crew was spread in busy knots about them. He smiled; she evidently did not intend to be taken without at least a show of resistance. He lowered his glass to her stern. Her name was the *Jeanne-Marie*.

'Run up the colours, Mr Bird,' ordered Slade and leaning out over the quarterdeck rail bellowed 'Open ports! Stand by to run out! Stand by the bow guns!'

The barques gave instant and simultaneous reaction to the sight of the British colours, as if they had been waiting for just such a signal. The nearest ship immediately tacked to starboard, pointing her bow at the jutting coastline some eight or ten miles distant, while the other swung north-east, putting the wind almost directly astern. Slade did not hesitate in his selection.

'Larboard the helm! Man the weather braces! Harden-in those sheets there!'

Lamb gave a mental nod of agreement; far better to keep the advantage of the wind and open sea and chase the more distant vessel than beat to windward towards an unknown coastline.

'Keep your eye on that other one, Mr Lamb,' shouted Slade. 'We may yet manage to take both.'

Lamb glanced astern. The barque was tacking, close-hauled, making for the coast. She could hide in any of a dozen bays and coves there, he thought, in water too shallow for the frigate's deeper draught. He turned his attention forward.

'At your pleasure, Mr Ball!' roared the captain.

The third lieutenant, standing on the forecastle, touched his hat in acknowledgement and turned to his guns. The six-pounders barked as one and Lamb raised his telescope to his eye. A series of white splashes showed where one ball skipped along the surface close to the barque's larboard side; he saw no sign of the other. He levelled his glass at the group of men at the stern of the vessel, bending over her long gun. The half-naked figures on each side stepped back and the man crouching over the breech jerked at the lanyard. To Lamb's astonishment the gun leaped a foot or so into the air and crashed down on to its side, bringing men down with it and scattering the others in panic. The muffled sound of an explosion reached his ears.

'Ha! Did you see that?' shouted Slade in considerable excitement, turning his large, red face to Lamb. 'The bloody thing has burst!'

The *Adroit*'s forward guns fired again. The exploded gun at the barque's stern slewed as it was hit by a six-pound ball and splinters flew as a section of her taffrail vanished. These two shots, following on the terror of the bursting gun, were enough. The wind spilled from her topsails and she lost way, rolling sullenly on the shallow swell as she lay-to, waiting for the frigate to come alongside.

'Isherwood can take her in,' said Slade. 'He can have young Bird, one bo'sun's mate – Blakely will serve – six Marines and twenty men. I can spare no more.' He produced a folded sheet of paper from his pocket and handed it to Lamb. 'Take the first twenty names from that list.'

Lamb quickly ran his eye down the list of names and managed with difficulty not to grin. Slade had clearly given careful thought to it – the list contained the names of all the trouble-makers, habitual drunkards and useless landmen in the ship.

'Go across with Isherwood,' Slade went on. 'See him settled and get back as quick as you can. Bring her master and the ship's books with you. Do not waste a minute, Mr Lamb – there is still the other barque to deal with.'

The ship's master did not present himself when Lamb clambered on board the *Belle du Sud*. He issued terse orders to the Marines and strode towards the little group of sullen officers standing abaft of the mainmast. Blakely stepped beside him, his cutlass in his hand.

Lamb scanned the dark, bitter faces. '*Où est le capitaine?*' he demanded. They gave no answer. He looked at one man whose shirt seemed less grimy than those of his fellows. '*C'est vous?*'

The man shook his head, jerked his thumb aft and muttered something. Lamb waved his arm forward to where the Marines had gathered the seamen round the hatchway.

'*Allez*,' he said firmly to the ship's officers.

The captain was seated at his table when Lamb ducked into his cabin. Beside him was a bottle of brandy, two-thirds empty, and at the sight of Lamb's uniform he leaped to his feet with a screech of rapid French, hurled the bottle at Lamb's head and burst into tears. Lamb's lip curled in disgust.

'Take the drunken fool on deck,' he said to Blakely.

Isherwood came aft to meet him when Lamb emerged on deck with the ship's books tucked beneath his arm and a heavy, canvas bag that jingled pleasantly as it swung against his leg.

'She is crammed full of gunpowder, sir, from top to bottom, keg upon keg. It only needs one spark, sir, and we are all dust.'

Christ! No wonder she was so quick to heave-to, thought Lamb. So would he have been, by God! His feet itched to get off the ship but the face he showed to Isherwood was one of unconcern and only mild interest.

'Gunpowder, eh? Well, take the usual precautions, Mr Isherwood. No lanterns, candles, pipes or nailed shoes below. It will be no great hardship for you for a few days. When you arrive at Port Royal it would be best for you to anchor well outside and send in a boat first; if you sail in with this lot unannounced you will give the Port Admiral a heart seizure!'

The French master sat slumped in the bottom of the boat,

178

weeping and muttering as Lamb was pulled back to the *Adroit*. He was quite incapable of climbing up the side and was hauled unceremoniously to the frigate's deck with a rope beneath his armpits.

'Captain Didot, sir,' announced Lamb.

Slade ignored the Frenchman slumped at his feet. 'What was she carrying?' he asked, his priorities firmly fixed.

'Gunpowder, sir.'

Slade raised his eyebrows. 'Ah, yes? Well, at least there should be no problem about getting that purchased, although personally, I would rather not be issued with the stuff – the French use too much charcoal and not enough sulphur in their powder, in my opinion. As soon as the boat is inboard we will get under way, if you please. We still have the matter of the other barque outstanding.'

'Aye aye, sir. Her name is the *Jeanne-Marie*, sir.'

'Really?' Slade bent down and plucked the frail little Frenchman to his feet, supporting the swaying figure with a hand the size of a moderate ham.

'Come, m'sewer, let me assist you to my cabin.' He led the Frenchman aft, smiling solicitously. 'Perhaps we can find you another bottle, *mon capitaine – encore du bateau!* Send Jackson aft,' he called over his shoulder.

The quartermaster was a Channel Islander and was as fluent in French as he was in English. Lamb smiled as he sent Allwyn off to find him – the captain would have need of Jackson by the sound of it, he thought.

Lamb had not forgotten to keep a watchful eye on the *Jeanne-Marie* as she fled towards the coast, and before she had disappeared from his view, blending into the blur of the land, he had noted her bearing and the shape of the high peak beyond. It would be a rough guide at best; she could have turned east or west and now be sitting securely in one of the fortified harbours strung along this coastline. He gave directions to the master and as the frigate beat her way southwards he glanced over the starboard quarter. Isherwood's command was under way, heading westward, close-hauled. Lamb felt a twinge of guilt as he recalled his last brusque words to the young master's mate. His first command would be no pleasure cruise, sailing an undermanned, floating powder keg back to port. There would be precious little sleep for Isherwood for the next few days!

An hour or more of slow work beating towards the coast of Hispaniola by a long series of opposite tacks brought the frigate to within a couple of miles of the shoreline and approximately at the position where Lamb had last noted the barque. The sun was below the maintopmast yard as Lamb raised his telescope to his eye and scanned along the coast. To left and right the dark green vegetation started close at the water's edge and swept back over a rising series of hills to the distant, blue-grey mountain peaks. There was no sign of an anchorage or a bay or the work of human hands.

Lamb beckoned to the midshipman. 'My compliments to the captain, Mr Allwyn. We are two miles from the coast. Does he wish us to sail east or west?'

Allwyn was back within the minute.

'The captain's compliments and sail east, sir, if you please, and could you spare him a moment of your time, sir?'

'Well, just the one, perhaps,' Lamb conceded graciously. 'Starboard the helm, quartermaster. Steer due east.'

Slade was standing with splayed arms over a chart spread on his table; behind him Captain Didot was stretched out on the windowseat, snoring loudly. The cabin reeked of brandy. Slade looked up as Lamb knocked and entered. He smiled.

'It is amazing what a few glasses of brandy and a little sympathetic probing can reveal. The barque we are after is the *Jeanne-Marie*.'

'Really, sir?' said Lamb.

'Yes, but that is not important. Do you know what she carries? Allow me to inform you. Silver, Mr Lamb! Silver bars and specie! How much she carries I could not ascertain but she could well be crammed full of the stuff. Come round this side of the table.' His finger stabbed at the chart. 'The two barques sailed together from Havana under the protection of an armed brig, the *La Citoyenne*, fourteen guns.'

'The *La Citoyenne*? Was she not –?'

Slade chuckled. 'She was indeed. Our brig of this morning. According to our gallant Didot the brig was not averse to adding a little privateering to her main duty and yesterday she picked up a Danish schooner. She took her into Tortuga and

180

that is how we came across her this morning. Didot's comments about his escort were almost too strong for Jackson to repeat!

'Now, according to the barque's papers, Didot was to deliver his powder to San Juan in Puerto Rico and the natural assumption is that San Juan is also the destination of the *Jeanne-Marie*. From what Jackson and I gathered from Didot's papers, both ships and escort were jointly chartered by French and Spanish government officials but that is by the by. The important thing is that I know where to find that silver-laden barque.'

Lamb glanced over his shoulder at the snoring Frenchman and grinned. 'Potent stuff, your brandy, sir.'

'No, no, give the man his due, he told me precious little, after that one slip about the silver and specie. From then on he shut up like an oyster, in spite of my precious brandy going down his throat as if from a pump. No, Jackson found – wait, I'll show you.' He lifted the chart and scrabbled among the papers beneath, muttering. 'No, that's not it. Nor that. Now where the devil did Jackson –? Ah, here it is.' He produced a document and slapped it down in front of Lamb. 'There! – an appendix to Didot's orders. What is your French like?'

'Not all that good, sir, especially their handwriting. They all seem to write in such a spidery hand. In any case – '

Slade cut him short with an impatient gesture. 'No matter. I made out the gist of it, with a little help from Jackson. It instructs Didot to stop off at Luperon and deliver a quantity of his powder to the garrison there.' He tapped at his chart. 'Luperon is here, on Cape Isabelo, just a few miles east of where we are now. And that is where we shall find the *Jeanne-Marie*.' He gave Lamb a knowing, triumphant beam.

'Excellent work, sir.' Lamb frowned thoughtfully at the chart, rubbing his chin. 'Of course, sir, it is possible that the order to call at Luperon applied only to Captain Didot, in which case the *Jeanne-Marie* – '

'Nonsense!' snapped Slade, replacing his beam with a scowl. 'Use your bloody head, man. The two barques sailed together under escort, did they not? They were both bound for San Juan, were they not? No, where one went, so would the other, and the *Jeanne-Marie* will be at Luperon now, waiting for the *Belle du Sud* or the brig to turn up, you can take my oath on it. Now kindly pass me those sailing instructions and try and show a little more damned enthusiasm.'

Chapter 9

Lamb hooked his leg round the shroud and settled his back against the Baltic pine of the maintopgallantmast. The sun was descending in a glorious red blaze towards the hazy western horizon but there was still sufficient light to pick out the masts and yards of the ship anchored in the enclosed waters of the natural harbour. He felt a prickle of excitement as he recognized the distinctive narrow yards; yes, it was the *Jeanne-Marie* right enough, snug and safe under the protective guns of the Spanish garrison. The *Adroit* was some two miles out, spilling the wind from her sails as she passed very slowly across the mouth of the almost circular harbour. The sandy beaches at the sides of the anchorage and the barque's position in the centre of the available water suggested shallow depths, confirming one of the few, meagre pieces of information about the place that Slade and Lamb had managed to glean. The town of Luperon was spread thinly round the sides of the harbour and more thickly at its southern shore; beyond, on a low hill, was a squat fort and cultivated fields covered the rising ground at the rear of the town. Lamb shifted his glass to the harbour entrance and the land on either side, seeking out the inevitable guns. The coastal strip here was low, with no high ground near enough to give the guns extra range over the sea, so the Spaniards had built a series of round towers connected by a wall on each side of the curving entrance to the harbour. Earthworks, Lamb guessed, clad with stone, but no less effective for all that and a considerable feat of labour and determination for such an isolated outpost. Atop each tower he could see the muzzle of a gun pointing seaward through a low embrasure; there were twelve in all, thirty-six-pounders, Lamb judged, covering the harbour mouth from each side and a considerable area of sea. He swept the harbour again with his glass. There was little in the way of other vessels apart from a small xebec moored a cable or so from the barque and a collection of boats and barges tied up to a small stone jetty projecting into the harbour from the southern shore.

Lamb had seen enough. He gave a last quick scan of the round towers prior to descending to the deck when a movement on the easternmost one caught his eye. A dozen or so men were clustered round the gun, one of whom stood behind the embrasure with a telescope pointed, it seemed to Lamb, directly at him. The frigate had been seen and from all appearances was about to be warned off. The French colours had not deceived the Spanish for an instant, but, in any case, the master of the *Jeanne-Marie* had undoubtedly described the *Adroit* down to her last spar.

'Deck there!' yelled Lamb, peering down at the tiny figures on the shrunken quarterdeck. 'Stand by to receive gunfire!'

He swung himself into the shrouds and began to lower himself to the deck, gripping tightly on the leaning mast as Slade brought the ship's head round, putting the wind on to her starboard quarter. A brief, white plume of water showed on the darkening sea a quarter of a mile from the frigate's stern as Lamb reached the maintop and a few moments later the dull boom of the report reached his ears.

Slade was smiling broadly when Lamb mounted the quarterdeck. He jerked his head at the distant guns. 'They'd have trouble hitting a cow's arse with a stick!'

Lamb gave his report. Slade listened attentively, his head thrown back, his hands clasped behind him.

'No sign of a boom?' he asked when Lamb had finished.

'None that I could see, sir.'

'Hmm.' He pondered for a moment or two. 'Well, it is doubtful if they can lay a boom in the next few hours. There are bound to be patrolling boats, of course, and no doubt some very wide-awake men on the barque and on those gun-towers. So, silence and stealth must be our watchwords.'

'Tonight, sir? You intend to cut her out?'

'Yes, indeed, Mr Lamb. And I shall take command of the boats.'

'Call the hands aft, Mr Lamb,' ordered the captain as he stepped from the ladder on to the dark quarterdeck. He paced to and fro beside the gap in the rail as the hands pattered their way aft, his head sunk on his chest and his hands clasped in habitual fashion behind his back as he prepared his words in his mind. Slade was not one of those men who believed that the crew should be fully informed at all times as to the whys and wherefores of their orders, a practice unheard of in his younger days but gaining some popularity amongst certain youthful captains; indeed, he was totally opposed to the notion, considering it to be bad for discipline, unnecessary and French-inspired, the last reason more than enough to ensure his complete resistance to it. Tonight, however, he had decided to make one of his rare addresses to the crew; a boat action at night was always one of the most hazardous of operations and a few hard words of warning beforehand could do much in lowering the numbers of casualties that were bound to occur. In addition, he aimed to enlist their enthusiasm, a factor which could mean all the difference between success and failure.

It was a warm night and very dark; southerly winds had brought clouds that blanketed the high mountains of the island and made a low, thick cover over the sea. The hands settled themselves abaft the mainmast and below the break of the quarterdeck, whispering expectantly amongst themselves. They knew something was in the wind and they had more than a suspicion that it was connected with the barque and the harbour in which it was anchored. Lamb stood by the quarterdeck rail, listening with some amusement to the muttering of the hands as they squatted waiting for the last of the men to arrive from the bowels of the ship. 'Stand by, Jem,' he heard one anonymous voice murmur. 'Old Far-be-it has got something nasty in mind for us. I can feel it in my water.'

He heard the boatswain's deep growl and Allwyn's quick feet on the ladder. 'Please, sir,' he reported to Lamb, 'all present and correct, sir.'

'Very good,' said Lamb. He turned to the captain, all of six feet from him. 'Hands all present and correct, sir,' he said formally, with a touch of his hat.

'Very good,' said Slade and moved forward to lean his belly against the quarterdeck rail.

His voice was warmly avuncular. 'My lads, a little barque escaped us this afternoon and is now holed up in a snug harbour yonder. That is no great loss, what is one little barque, I hear some of you say?' Lamb grinned to himself at this wild claim – who would dare utter a peep when Slade was talking? 'Well, I shall tell you what she is. She is stuffed with silver bars and gold coins, that is what she is! It could be worth fifty, a hundred guineas – two hundred, perhaps – to each and every man jack of you if we can cut her out. Think of it, my brave lads, all that gold weighing down your pockets! It will not be an easy task, that I can promise you, and it might well be a bloody one but if we succeed it will be happy times for us all when we get home. Now far be it from me to expect you men to go where I would not, and as proof of that I shall be leading the boat party myself. Is there any man here who has no wish to follow me?' One lone fool began to cheer but was quickly punched silent. 'And who will follow me?' A thunderous cheer rose into the night air. 'That is what I expected to hear, my brave lads. Now listen carefully. Those dagoes will be half-expecting a visit from us tonight so, if you wish to live to spend your money, absolute silence is a must until we board her – after that you can cheer your hearts out. You will assemble in a moment or two to be assigned to your boats. Listen to what your boat officer tells you – every man must know his task. Make sure you know your officer. You must all wear dark clothing – I want no white cuffs showing! That is all, men. Assemble now in your divisions.'

As the hands moved forward and the officers followed, clutching their lists of names, the surgeon bounded up the quarterdeck ladder and approached the captain.

'Sir! Sir! With your permission, sir?'

'Yes, Mr Andrews, what is it?'

'With the greatest respect, sir, I must protest. I find I have not been given a boat, sir.'

Slade gave an amused laugh. 'You, Mr Andrews? A boat? It is hardly the thing for a surgeon, is it?'

'I see no reason why not, sir. I have a strong right arm and I can climb a rope as well as the next man.'

Slade clapped him on the shoulder. 'Very well, Mr Andrews, you shall have your boat. We are short of a midshipman as you know. You can take the jolly-boat with the bo'sun. Tell Mr Allwyn he is now assigned to the launch with Mr Lamb.'

'You are very kind, sir,' said the surgeon and turned to leave but was stopped half-way down the ladder by a call from the captain.

'One thing, Mr Andrews – I want no heroics from you. I am not too sure about the morality of taking a surgeon on a cutting-out expedition and if you are killed I shall have some awkward questions to answer later. And in any case, some of us may have need of your services when it is over.'

The boats took the water a mile from the harbour mouth and Goode turned the frigate to the north, to lay-to out of range of the Spanish guns. From the stern of the launch Lamb kept an eye on the oar splashes of Slade's pinnace a few yards to starboard. He was still feeling a little piqued that Slade had decided to lead the expedition himself – this sort of boat action was normally commanded by the first lieutenant and was one of the ways he could expect to earn a little glory and get his name known. However, he had consoled himself somewhat with the thought that the captain could, with some justification, have ordered him to command the frigate in his absence.

He eased the tiller a trifle. It was important that the two divisions of boats entered the harbour together and attacked the barque simultaneously. From the stern of the launch trailed a rope attached to one of the cutters, commanded by Ball. It continued on to the gig, under Rank's command. Astern of the captain's pinnace was the other cutter, under the theoretical command of Acting-Lieutenant Hopper but rather more under the actual command of the carpenter, Mr Armstrong, and trailing that was the surgeon's jolly-boat. Lamb had reported the barque as being moored fore and aft with her bow pointing at the harbour mouth and with this in mind Slade had arranged the boats in the order in which their crews would board the ship, at her stern, waist and bow. Lamb's task was to board at the stern, cut her cable and set the mizzen course. The bower cable was to be cut by the crew of the jolly-boat, who had strict instructions to ignore the fighting and to attend directly to the setting of the foretopsail. Further, private instructions had been given to Mr Clegg to keep the fiery little surgeon on a very tight rein.

The wind was fresh and the sea threw up short little waves that had very soon soaked every man in the launch. At least the wind and the clouds were in their favour, thought Lamb; conditions could not be better for them. A bright moon and an onshore wind might have given even the impetuous Slade second thoughts. As it was, he considered the captain to be taking a severe risk with this little outing, from the point of his career; the indulgence of the Commander-in-Chief at this liberal interpretation of his orders would be strained even with success – failure would bring swift and angry retribution. Not that Lamb disapproved in the smallest degree of Slade's enterprise; on the contrary, he was filled with admiration and enthusiasm for his audacity and grimly determined that his boat, at least, would not be found wanting.

The lights of the town and the night-lanterns of the *Jeanne-Marie* provided a clear beacon for the boats and the oars of Slade's pinnace slowed as the black shapes of the round towers loomed dimly on either side. Lamb hissed a quiet order and his oarsmen slowed their rate to match that of the pinnace. The opening of the harbour was some five hundred yards wide and by the relative distances of the towers at each side it seemed that Slade had taken his flotilla directly through the centre of it. There was little fear of being seen by the sentries on the towers – the pinnace and her crew, not ten yards away, were barely discernible from where Lamb sat and the oarsmen, conscious of the need for stealth, were plying their blades so carefully that the boats appeared to be tip-toeing through the black water. Lamb's hands were damp as they gripped the tiller ropes and he was aware of the increasing tempo of his heart-beat. He pressed his elbow against the reassuring solidity of the cutlass hilt at his belt; he had forsaken his own sword for the seaman's weapon – its greater weight and shorter length made it a more convenient weapon for close-quarter work.

The boats pulled slowly and steadily in the direction of the barque; the creaking of the stealthily pulled oars in their rowlocks and the harsh, grunting breaths of the men, tiring now after their long pull, seemed extraordinarily loud to Lamb and it was with a sense of foolishness that he found himself holding his breath in an unconscious attempt to lessen the noise. A loud and rapid burst of Spanish suddenly sounded from the darkness beyond the captain's pinnace, the voice urgent and excited. Fuck! The bloody guard-boat has seen us, thought

Lamb, twisting in his seat to peer across the black water. The voice sounded again, and then others, shouting in alarm. Answering shouts came from the barque and the darkness immediately to starboard of the pinnace was split with the bright yellow flashes of musket-fire. The pinnace rocked and slewed as the bow of the guard-boat ploughed into its oars and Slade's voice roared out in furious, cursing rage.

'Fend the bastards off! Kill the bloody swine! Mr Armstrong, lend a hand here!'

There was little that Lamb could do without working his line of boats around Slade's flotilla and with the element of surprise and the need for caution gone he urged his men to bend their backs with a will as he steered for the larboard side of the ship. Muskets were being fired from her deck now, indiscriminately and blindly into the darkness from both sides.

'Pull, lads, pull!' yelled Lamb, wildly excited, half-standing in the stern of the launch. The bow of the barque loomed up ahead. He hauled on his left-hand tiller rope to narrowly shave past the mooring cable and the launch shot down the side of the barque just as a second guard-boat rounded her stern.

'In oars!' screamed Lamb and with a crunch of splintering timber and a chorus of Spanish yells the bow of the launch crashed into the side of the guard-boat. The shock of the collision knocked Lamb backwards from his crouching position on to the stern transom and for a second he teetered on the edge, scrabbling wildly for a handhold. An unseen hand grabbed his sleeve and jerked him undeferentially forward. Bright flashes came blindingly from overhead as the muskets on board fired downwards into the locked boats, unknowing or uncaring whether they were directed at friend or foe.

'Secure the boat!' shouted Lamb, remembering even in this mad moment one of Slade's sternly repeated instructions, and flung himself at the mainmast chains. Other dark figures were already there, scrambling up the outer shrouds and hacking at the faces lining the rail. Lamb snatched a hold on the ropes and pulled himself up, cursing as a bare foot kicked backwards at his face when the seaman above him swung himself over the rail. A musket flashed from his left, the report drowned in the continuous rattle of others and he felt a blow on his thigh as if he had been kicked by a horse. Gritting his teeth he scrambled

189

upwards until his feet were on a level with the rail and hooking an elbow through the ropes he snatched the pistols from his belt. Levelling at the pale faces below, he fired first one and then the other, hurling his pistol on board after each shot – with luck he would retrieve them later. Drawing his cutlass he lowered his feet on to the rail and immediately jumped on to the deck of the barque, pain flaring from his thigh as he landed. Six or eight of his men had arrived before him and were swinging and hacking at the press of men around them, swearing viciously and grunting with each stroke. Out of the corner of his eye he saw a struggling mess of men in the waist as Vaughan and his Marines fought their way on board with bayonets. More of the launch's men were now pouring over the rail and springing forward he began to cut and slash at the close-packed Spanish soldiers and their jabbing pikes and bayonets, striving to force his way aft. Young Allwyn appeared beside him, his dirk in one hand and a cutlass in the other, his face white, his eyes huge at the horrors around him but swinging his arm bravely for all that. Lamb stretched out an arm and pulled the boy behind him, out of reach of the murderous Spanish steel.

'Guard my back for me, Mr Allwyn!' he roared, anxious not to dent the midshipman's pride.

A lunging musket-butt came from nowhere and he found himself on his knees, shaking free-running blood from a head that sang like a cracked bell. The noise of clashing steel, shouts and musket-fire seemed to come from a vast distance away and the deck seams before his eyes swam in and out of focus. Someone was shouting, calling his name and tugging at his shoulder. He shook his head again in an attempt to clear it, scattering blood like rain and with an effort, levered himself to his feet.

'Are you all right, sir? Mr Lamb, sir!'

It was Allwyn, his anxious face peering up at him.

'Never better!' said Lamb thickly and swayed, the world spinning. 'Lend me your shoulder for a moment.'

His vision cleared and he saw that his men had surged aft, leaving him surrounded by the sprawled bodies of Spanish soldiers. Across the deck he caught sight of Slade, roaring like a bull and swinging his sword at a tall Spanish officer whose rapier was flashing like quicksilver. Slade's coxswain, Leyton, stepped forward from beside his captain and cut the officer down as casually as he would a thistle. Amidships, the Marines knelt in the space they had won with their bayonets and fired a single, devastating volley into the mass of soldiers struggling to retreat from them.

This will not do, thought Lamb, standing here like a spectator at a twopenny theatre. He clenched his teeth and shook his head, striving to clear his mind. Something was missing from his grip and he stared at his hand in bewilderment for a second. Of course, his cutlass! Suddenly the fog was gone from his mind like a sleeve being wiped over a misted windowpane and he could think clearly again.

'Do me the goodness of retrieving my cutlass, Mr Allwyn,' he said, pointing, and with the hilt warmly in his hand again, made his unsteady way aft to join his men. There was little in the way of fighting left to do; caught between Lamb's men from the larboard side and the arrival of Slade's men from the starboard side, albeit belatedly, the Spaniards had melted away forward to join the struggling mass of soldiers and Marines in the waist. One of Lamb's men was already hacking at the anchor cable with his axe and two others, with bloody cutlasses raised threateningly, stood guard over the wheel. Lamb's task was almost complete; as his men busied themselves about the mizzen gaff and boom he clapped Allwyn on the shoulder.

'See to the spanker, Mr Allwyn,' he said, and dashing his sleeve across his forehead to remove the blood that threatened to drip into his eyes he limped painfully forward, suddenly aware of the hot agony in his thigh.

The fighting was over; the ship was theirs. The Marines were already driving the surviving soldiers below at the points of their bayonets and Slade's men were swarming along the yards setting the maintopsail. The captain was standing between the foremast and mainmast, leaning on his sword, his head craned upwards, looking at his men. Blood coated his fingers from a wounded arm. He turned his head and raised his eyebrows as Lamb approached.

'Good God!' he exclaimed, surprise in his voice. 'Someone told me you were dead.' He peered at the blood on Lamb's face and glanced down at his holed and gory breeches. 'And I am not altogether convinced they were wrong.'

'For a moment back there I shared the same opinion, sir,' said Lamb, then went on formally, 'I beg leave to report the stern cable is cut, the mizzen course set and the wheel secured, sir.'

'Very good, Mr Lamb. Well done, in fact.'

The topsails slapped and billowed; the ship trembled and gave a little sideways dance.

'Stay for'rd and assist Mr Vaughan, if you will, while I go aft. Douse all lights immediately he has cleared the deck.'

Lamb saluted. 'Aye aye, sir.'

The Marine lieutenant needed no assistance from Lamb. The last of the prisoners were being herded down the forward hatchway as Lamb picked his way amongst the corpses and whimpering wounded to meet him. He greeted Lamb with an enormous grin on his face.

'Well, the Marines have come up trumps, as always, Matthew. We have taken the ship for you and got the Navy out of trouble yet again, with nary a single man lost.'

'Yes, I really do not know why we bothered to come along at all,' said Lamb.

Vaughan laughed. 'Someone has to pull the ropes and do the donkey work!'

Ball approached, quite clearly bubbling with excited triumph. Lamb's head was throbbing and he was in no mood for Ball's ebullience; he turned him smartly round to see to the dousing of the ship's lights. Satisfied that Vaughan's men had the deck under firm control he made his way back to the stern as the ship began to pick up speed. Muskets were firing from both sides of the harbour as the darkened ship drove towards the entrance and the dim outlines of the towers came into view.

'Steady as she goes,' muttered Slade to the helmsmen and in a loud voice along the deck, 'Lay flat now, men. There may be a few splinters flying soon.'

He turned to Lamb. 'I shall turn to starboard and hug the coast for a mile or two as soon as we are clear of the harbour,' he said, unusually informative.

A sensible notion, thought Lamb; that would take them out of the vector of all but the easternmost guns. First, though, they would have to run the gauntlet of all of them.

The first gun sounded as soon as the barque had cleared the harbour entrance, the shot passing low between the helm and the mizzenmast and causing Slade to stagger in the wind of its passing as it vanished without touching so much as a rope strand.

'Jesus!' exclaimed Slade.

A second gun fired as he spoke, from starboard this time, the ball whistling between Lamb and the captain close enough to make them both rock on their feet and tearing away a section of the larboard rail, the splinters whirring harmlessly out to sea.

'Christ Almighty!' shouted Slade angrily. 'The bastards are aiming straight at me! Larboard the helm!'

'Larboard the helm it is, sir,' repeated the quartermaster quietly.

Several guns fired at once. The loud crash of an immense ball of iron smashing into timber came from the starboard bow, the shock trembling along the deck and through Lamb's shoes. A fountain of water rose high into the air as a roundshot ploughed up the sea close to the larboard quarter.

'Midships the helm.'

'Helm amidships, sir.'

A shot glanced along the timbers of the larboard side, tearing away part of the mainmast chains. A spout of water appeared directly astern, the shot missing the rudder by a hand's breadth, spray flying over the taffrail. Although the guns were firing from both sides of the harbour entrance, most of the shots were going nowhere near the barque. The Spaniards were still energetically aiming for a dark ship slipping away on a black sea ten minutes later, as the *Jeanne-Marie* pointed her head northwards and headed out to meet the *Adroit*, the bright, scarlet flashes and the rolling thunder of the huge guns continuing in an impressive and completely wasteful display of Spanish gunnery.

Two hours after dawn the last of the prisoners were ferried to a narrow, sandy strip of tree-lined beach some ten miles east of Luperon. The dead had long been put over the side, entirely without benefit of prayer book or service or the smallest degree of reverence and the deck of the barque now showed shrinking patches of damp from an energetic hosing and scrubbing. It is probably cleaner now, thought Lamb as he glanced about the deck, than it has been for many a long day. Astonishingly, not one of the *Adroit*'s men had been killed, a point of much satisfaction for Slade and very little for many of his men, who considered a fight to be no fight at all unless there was a row of dead to be buried at the end of it, always providing it did not include any of them. Andrews, who professed not to have enjoyed himself so much for years, donned his surgeon's hat again to stitch and bind and probe the flesh of the two dozen or so wounded men. Both the captain and his first lieutenant were amongst that number and Lamb now stood beside the barque's main hatchway with his head bandaged and his thigh smarting cruelly from the surgeon's hasty sutures.

'Remove the covers,' ordered Slade, the bulge of his bandaged arm showing through the torn sleeve of his coat. A dozen armed Marines stood guard around the hatchway; in the rigging above some fifty faces gazed excitedly downwards and at the rail of the *Adroit* half a cable to starboard a jostle of men craned for a better view. The canvas cover and the grating were hauled to one side.

'Down you go, Mr Clegg.'

The boatswain, clutching a lantern in his hairy fist, lowered himself into the darkness of the hold, closely followed by the captain and then Lamb. Lamb was as curious and excited as the men in the rigging. None of the ship's officers, dead or alive, had been found on board and a careful search of the captain's cabin had failed to reveal the ship's papers; presumably, both these and the captain were safely ashore at Luperon. A strong smell, familiar but indefinable, caught at Lamb's nostrils as he descended and looking around the hold as the boatswain held the lantern high he saw hundreds of small kegs securely stacked and roped on both sides of the narrow walkway. Slade was sniffing loudly, his broad nostrils flaring.

'Brandy, by God!' he pronounced.

Lamb peered at the lettering burnt into one of the casks. 'Angoulême – Charente,' he mouthed. He was none the wiser but the captain's nose was clearly not to be faulted – the smell was most certainly that of brandy. He followed Slade and the dancing light of the boatswain's lantern past tier upon tier of brandy kegs until they came to a massive, timber, box-like structure erected against the aftermost bulkhead. It was the size of a small room but without the convenience of a door. Slade shook at its thick timbers.

'We'll have two good men down here with axes and crowbars, Mr Clegg, if you please.'

Slade leaned his back against the structure as Clegg trotted off towards the light of the hatchway.

'Well, the ship is obviously not stuffed with silver and specie but this behind me could prove interesting. How do you view the prospect of sudden wealth, Mr Lamb?'

'With equanimity, sir,' lied Lamb firmly.

Slade chuckled. 'Well said but hardly honest, I'm sure.' He turned and kicked at the base of the structure. 'I shall tell you one thing, though. Whatever is in here is not such a concern as the stuff outside of it. If any of the hands ever got down here they would drink themselves insensible. We must take suitable precautions, Mr Lamb. Some of our men would walk through fire for an extra pint of liquor.'

Clegg arrived with two of the carpenter's mates, followed by the carpenter himself.

Slade frowned. 'I asked for two men. I do not recall inviting you down here, Mr Armstrong.'

The carpenter was unabashed. 'They may have the stronger arms, sir, but I have the knowledge and experience.' He tapped his head. 'A little of this can often win where brute muscle fails, sir.'

'Poppycock! It was your long nose that brought you down here. Now stand back and give them room to swing.'

The structure was stoutly built. It took ten minutes of grunting effort with axe and bar before a hole had been made sufficiently large for a man to squeeze through.

'That will do,' said Slade. 'Stand aside.'

He picked up the lantern and crouching low, insinuated his large frame with some effort through the small gap. Lamb, agog with anticipation, ducked through with considerably more ease after him. His eyes widened. Timber racks reached from the deck to above his head and nestling on them, securely wedged, were hundreds of ingots of bright, white silver, gleaming in the yellow light of the lantern. Slade slowly revolved, holding the light high.

'Jesus, Mary and Joseph,' he breathed reverently, awe-struck.

Faces peered in through the aperture, eyes round and mouths open.

'Fuck me gently!' muttered Clegg, his bald head turning from side to side.

For a long moment there was silence as the men gazed at the magnificent spectacle of so much wealth in so small a space. Slade reached out and lifted a bar, hefting its weight. He handed it to Lamb.

'Ten or twelve pounds, would you say?'

Lamb raised and lowered it in his hand, considering. 'At least that, sir, probably more.' He ran his thumb over the smooth, cold surface of the metal.

'I've had a lot of practice at judging weights, sir,' said Armstrong hopefully, pushing his way inside.

Slade glared. 'You have? Then practise waiting outside! This is not a bloody free-for-all.'

He carefully placed the ingot back on its rack.

'I want all these bars counted, Mr Lamb, and a permanent guard put on the hatch. In addition – hello, what is this? Lend a hand here.'

It was a small, padlocked chest tucked away beneath the bottom rack. Together, Slade and Lamb dragged it out.

'Give me the loan of your axe, Keo,' said Slade, stretching out his hand.

Several heavy blows broke the lock free from its hasp. Slade lifted the lid and grunted with satisfaction. Packed neatly inside, almost up to the level of the lid, were short, paper-wrapped cylinders. Slade picked one up and with a sharp twist broke open the paper wrapping. Several gold coins fell on to the cylinders beneath and others gleamed brightly from each end of the broken package.

'This must be the specie Didot spoke of. *Louis d'or*, Mr Lamb – twenty-franc pieces. There is a tidy little sum in there.'

He replaced the opened cylinder in the chest and closed the lid.

'Yes, a tidy little sum,' he said again slowly. He stood in thought for a few moments, stroking his chin and studying the shining ingots of silver.

'Yes, that is best,' he said at last, apparently coming to some agreement with himself. He lowered himself to squat on the chest, his legs stretched out before him. 'That's better – it has been a damned long night,' he grunted. He flexed his arm, wincing. 'Blast this bloody arm! The silver will remain here, Mr Lamb. The chest will be taken aboard the *Adroit* and placed in my cabin. Once it has been counted we can have a little share-out – from the look of it, there will be a couple of guineas for each man. I do not see the need to bother the Commander-in-Chief with such trifling sums, do you, Mr Lamb?'

'Oh, indeed not, sir,' agreed Lamb wholeheartedly, not at all unhappy to have his share increased by a proportion of the Commander's eighth part.

'Now so far as the barque is concerned, I want you to take command of her – I dare not entrust her to a less senior man. You will keep company with the *Adroit* until we meet with the *Rosemary* in the Mona Passage. She can then escort you to Port Royal. This strong-room will be repaired by Mr Armstrong as best he can and a Marine sentry stood outside it night and day. You will also place a Marine on guard over the hatchway. Take no risks, Mr Lamb, and bear constantly in mind the men's predilection for drink. Allow no one but yourself and the sentries down here and trust no one. Is that all quite clear?'

'Yes, sir.'

'Good. I shall see that this chest reaches my cabin safely. Count the bars and then set Mr Armstrong to work.'

There were one thousand, nine hundred and sixty ingots of silver on the racks. Lamb counted them twice, certain he had jumped a hundred during his first tally. He stood in the strong-room, still scarcely able to take in what was around him, attempting to calculate the value of it all. It was a process rendered difficult because he had not the slightest notion of the price of silver. Five shillings an ounce? Ten, twenty? Call it ten shillings an ounce. At sixteen ounces to the pound, that makes each ingot worth, um, say ninety-six pounds sterling – well, call it a hundred. And a hundred multiplied by one thousand, nine hundred and sixty is, let me see, add two noughts, that comes to one hundred and ninety-six thousand pounds! And if silver is worth twenty shillings an ounce, then close on four hundred thousand pounds! He reluctantly abandoned this fascinating little exercise, gave the nearest ingot a friendly pat and ducked out into the hold, where stood a wide-eyed Marine and a grinning Armstrong with his tools.

Chapter 10

Slade kept the *Jeanne-Marie* closely under his wing as the *Adroit* continued along the northern coast of Hispaniola to her rendezvous with the *Rosemary* in the Mona Passage. The winds were slack and what there were came at the frigate's starboard bow; during the three days it took to reach the Passage a number of sails were sighted, none very close except for one fat Spanish merchantman which sleepily allowed the two ships to approach within two miles before suddenly waking up and sheering off to the north. Slade resolutely ignored them all, although the merchantman caused considerable anguish on board the *Adroit* as the crew watched her waddle slowly out of sight. The hands had already tasted the flavour of prize-money – three golden *louis* had been paid to each man as they lined up at the capstan-head – and it was very much to their liking; they gazed after the vanishing merchantman like hungry wolves watching a well-fed sheep beyond their reach, muttering amongst themselves. Why, she could be stuffed from stem to stern with gold, jewels, chests of coins, the entire treasures of Spain – it would not take but a moment to snap her up! Slade gave orders for the frigate to maintain her course and retreated to his cabin; he had made his own calculations of the value of the silver aboard the barque, with considerably more accuracy than had Lamb, and while his own thoughts, unlike those of the hands, did not revolve about the purchase of taverns, carriages, untold amounts of rum and women, he was a reasonably happy man. Until he had handed over the barque to the safe-keeping of the *Rosemary*, however, he did not intend to let her out of his sight.

Lamb was also a happy man. True, he would have found life on board the barque a little easier with more in the way of watch-keeping officers – these consisted of Midshipman Allwyn and himself – but he could call on the experience of a

199

quartermaster, a boatswain's mate and a sergeant of Marines, and with twenty seamen and a dozen Marines to work the ship he was quite content. For the first time in his career he had a large stern cabin to himself, with wide windows and a separate night-cabin for his cot. Ahead lay a pleasantly short voyage back to port in company with a powerful escort, a warm reception from an undoubtedly grateful Commander-in-Chief – grateful enough, perhaps, to find a little sloop for Lamb to command – and the even warmer pleasures of Mrs Mainwaring. He frequently found himself humming as he paced the tiny, barely raised quarterdeck, his mind soaring free with ambitious and occasionally lascivious thoughts; even the monotonous drone of young Allwyn as he crouched over his books by the taffrail – 'two fathoms, two strips; three fathoms, three strips; five fathoms, white rag; seven fathoms, red rag' – failed to irritate him. Once during each watch he descended to the hold to check the alertness of the new sentry and the security of Armstrong's repair work and each time he returned to the deck filled with wonder at his luck.

The two ships rounded the north-eastern coast of Hispaniola and entered the Mona Passage under cloudy skies and, in the last twenty-four hours, strong south-easterly winds and a long, heavy swell. The port of Aguadilla on the north-western corner of Puerto Rico was the northernmost limit of the *Rosemary*'s cruising area and the frigate and the barque beat slowly back and forth along this latitude awaiting the appearance of the brig-sloop. The barque was a trim little ship with a flush deck, apart from the section aft of the wheel which was a mere gesture of a quarterdeck. Like the *Adroit* she was square-rigged on the foremast and mainmast and fore-and-aft at the mizzen, with a long, low boom projecting well aft over her taffrail. She carried two six-pounders astern and three three-pounders along each side and from the very first hour of his command Lamb had set to work those few seamen and Marines he could spare to overhaul, clean, chip and paint these sadly neglected guns. Her supply of powder, also, was not of the best – harsh, coarse-grained stuff with none of the finest sievings to sharpen it – and Lamb begged for a few kegs of the *Adroit*'s powder, obtained only after Slade had eventually brushed aside the gunner's pitifully thin excuses for having absolutely none to spare, no, not a single keg, sir. The quartermaster was a one-time gun-captain of vast experience and with the half-dozen gunners in his crew, Lamb was able to form gun-crews for both of the stern guns and three of the smaller guns, a total of some nineteen men. This was more than half his crew but he was confident that he could both sail the ship and man the guns if the occasion arose.

This was the slack season for the sugar-and-spice convoys and with the Mona Passage used almost exclusively by British merchantmen and the French privateers that earned a fat living from them, there was little in the way of shipping to be seen. On the morning of their second day in the Passage a ship was sighted approaching from the south-west. She was soon identified as the *Compiègne*, a smart two-decker captured in the Gulf of Lyons some four years earlier and now homeward-bound after three years on the West Indies station. The sun made a brief appearance as she drew near, shining on her taut, bleached canvas and her fresh black and yellow paint and sparkling from the gilt-covered, bare-breasted nymph dancing above the white foam at her bows. Lamb thought she looked a magnificent sight but he felt no envy for her officers, waving their hats from the quarterdeck. As a general rule, the larger the ship the more rigid and formal were the conventions and having had a taste of such a restricted, oppressive, largely silent existence as a midshipman, he waved his hat with a degree of smugness at having escaped from it. He caught sight of a figure waving a stick in the air and reaching for a telescope, he levelled it at him. It was Wheelwright, still in need of his stick, bound for home and a life on dry land. Poor sod! thought Lamb, with a twinge of compassion, and lifted his hat in an extra, personal wave for the unfortunate officer.

The *Rosemary* lifted her topsails above the horizon as the end of the forenoon watch and two hours later her captain, Lieutenant Wallace, was seated with Lamb in front of Slade's table, sharing the captain's last bottle of madeira. Wallace, a year or two older than Lamb and a trifle wanting in deference in Slade's eyes, gave a low whistle of surprise when he was told of the barque's cargo.

'God, sir, I can well understand why you did not wish to send her back on her own. I shall be only too happy to keep her company – in fact, I shall stick to her like a limpet.' He glanced at Lamb and smiled. 'Who knows, if we keep close enough, perhaps a little of your luck will rub off on to me.'

Slade gave him a cold look. 'Luck had little to do with it, sir. Far be it for me to be immodest but like most successes in action, it was the result of forethought, determination and leadership – qualities which are generally found to be proportional with one's years, captain.'

'Oh, I am sure you are right, sir,' said Wallace pleasantly. '"Forethought, determination and leadership" – I shall keep those words constantly in mind, sir.'

'The pompous old goat!' he said to Lamb as they walked away from Slade's cabin. 'You will not be sorry to be free of him for a month or two, I'll wager.'

Lamb laughed. 'He is not so bad – you saw him at his worst today. For some reason any captain or commander under the age of thirty seems to rub him up the wrong way.'

'Let us hope he never makes Commander-in-Chief, then, or we shall find all our ships commanded by dotards.' Wallace swung himself over the side and lowered himself lightly into his boat. As it pulled away he looked up and called, 'I will send those men across to you directly!'

Slade had requested – and Wallace had little choice but to comply – that ten men from the *Rosemary* be sent across to the barque in order that ten of Slade's men could be returned to the *Adroit*. Wallace was generous; he not only sent Lamb ten prime seamen – topmen and forecastlemen – but also his senior master's mate, a hard-faced, competent young man blessed with the name of Drake. Lamb was delighted; he could now allow himself the occasional bliss of four hours' sleep without interruption.

The two smaller vessels parted company from the *Adroit* at the end of the first dog-watch, the frigate heading east to sniff along the coast of Puerto Rico and the *Jeanne-Marie* and her escort beating their way south, close-hauled against the opposing wind. Lamb took his supper in a chair by the taffrail, his feet comfortably on the carriage of a six-pounder, his cold beef and French pickles washed down with half a bottle of her French captain's delicious dry white wine. Overhead the sky was hidden by thick cloud but to the west, over the unseen hills of Hispaniola, a thin ribbon of clear sky allowed the sun to dart its last rays warmly over the starboard rail of the *Jeanne-Marie*. To larboard, some two cables away, the two-masted sloop shared the same friendly rays, the light picking out the nine red-painted gun-ports above the broad, black stripe running along her side. The sloop was fitted out with carronades, short, squat twenty-four pounders that at point-blank range could blast a hole straight through a ship's side. She also carried a couple of long-guns fore and aft; the total weight of iron she could throw almost matched that of the *Adroit*, which had twice her rated number of guns.

Lamb swallowed the last of his wine and stretched, yawning. The past few days had allowed him little in the way of sleep and he knew that if he sat much longer he would doze off in his chair. He watched Drake striding the deck as he brought the ship on to the opposite tack, his voice curt and authoritative; if he was enjoying this taste of executive power he was giving no sign of it. Lamb rose and calling Allwyn from his trance on the other side of the deck requested him to carry his chair down to his cabin. It was a fine chair, covered in rich brocade and if the sea got up a little more the spray would do it no good. He moved across to the helm, blinking sleepily; his eyes felt as if they had dried up in their sockets. The ship's bell sounded the end of the last dog-watch as Drake returned to his place by the wheel.

'I shall turn in now, Mr Drake,' said Lamb. 'Call me if you think we need to shorten sail, otherwise at eight bells. Do not wander out of sight of the *Rosemary*'s lights – Captain Wallace would be most offended to find us shunning his company.'

'Aye aye, sir,' acknowledged the master's mate, without a trace of a smile at Lamb's light attempt at humour.

Lamb stretched out in his cot with a luxurious sigh, punched his plump pillow decorated with fine, French lace and closed his eyes, revelling in the prospect of four long hours of uninterrupted sleep. There should be no reason for Drake to call me, he thought drowsily; he gives every indication of being a competent, confident sort of man. His mind turned again, as it had a dozen times that day, to his share of the money from the silver. Let us suppose it is worth two hundred thousand pounds, he thought, with one-eighth to Sir John Dillforth and three to the captain. That will leave four-eighths for the rest of us and an eighth of a hundred thousand is – is – figures whirled around in his head and Mrs Mainwaring appeared, smiling. He slept.

At four bells in the middle watch the ships cleared the Mona Passage, or rather Wallace in his wisdom decided that they had done so. The night was very dark, without the slightest relief from stars or moon, and Lamb had taken over the watch in his tarpaulins in the middle of a heavy downpour of rain. The rain had ceased after an hour or so and he thought the wind had eased a little as he stood beside the wheel waiting for Wallace to signal a change of course to the west. A yellow flash and the sharp bark of the sloop's signal gun came from the darkness to larboard.

'Starboard the helm. Steer west by sou'west. Haul away, Mr Allwyn.'

'Aye aye, sir!' squeaked the midshipman enthusiastically from where he stood waiting between his two gangs of sail-handlers.

The ship settled on to her new course and with the wind comfortably over her larboard quarter and the heavy, irksome labour of constant tacking done with, Lamb sent the off-duty watch below. He paced the quiet deck, glancing from time to time at the lights of the *Rosemary* and occasionally giving a brief helm order. Overhead, ragged breaks had appeared in the cloud cover, allowing short-lived but brilliant shafts of moon-light to break through; the wind had noticeably decreased. Fair weather tomorrow, he thought – lighter winds and a few more hours' sailing-time to Port Royal. He moved to the mizzen weather shrouds and hooking an arm round a rope he stared out at the heaving, dark sea and the faint, unsteady lights of the *Rosemary*. He exercised no discipline over his thoughts during the long silent hours of the night watches; he was content to follow their aimless wanderings as they turned over and examined ancient memories, recalled past pains and pleasures and peered over tomorrow's horizons. He dwelt on San Domingo, a few miles to starboard, the long-established capital of an island torn by bloody uprisings and the scene of recent British failures to gain a foothold; he thought of Mrs Mainwaring and heard again her throaty gasps and her pleas for patience, her loud, shuddering cries; he reflected on the silver beneath his feet and of prize-courts and prize agents, of new uniforms and a bright, new sword, of a captain's epaulettes and a trim sloop on an independent cruise.

'Ease her a trifle,' he murmured, his eye on the *Rosemary*'s lights.

'Ease her a trifle it is, sir.'

Lamb took to pacing again, his hands behind his back and his chin sunk on to his chest, only half-hearing the sentry strike the half-hours. As the sky to the east showed the first, green hint of dawn Drake stood before him and the bell was sounding the end of the middle watch.

Drake had shaved, Lamb noticed; he looked trim, clean and alert. Lamb rubbed his hand over his own bristles as he handed over the watch, feeling decidedly unkempt faced with a man who had given up twenty minutes' precious sleep rather than appear on watch unshaved. Allwyn, frowsty-faced, blinking, dazed with sleep, almost cannoned into him as he stepped off the low quarterdeck. Lamb fended him off and gave him a vigorous shake.

'Have a care, Mr Allwyn,' he growled. 'Assaulting your captain is a hanging offence.'

'Yes, sir, sorry, sir,' said the boy, clapping a hand over a mouth that threatened to yawn into the captain's face.

'When you have unglued your eyes, kindly seek out Hart. I want coffee and shaving water at four bells. Understood?'

'Coffee and shaving water at four bells, aye aye, sir.'

As Lamb sought his cot Marine Blake was leaning beneath the lantern suspended from the timbers of the strong-room, his musket propped beside him, a finger absently exploring a nostril, his mind far away beside the Sea of Galilee, unaware that Sergeant Wolstenholme was treading stealthily towards him, hoping, joy of joys, to catch the Marine asleep at his post. The sergeant, hardened sinner that he was, had no liking for devout young men and when this devoutness was combined with total abstinence from tobacco and strong drink, Wolstenholme considered it to be his plain duty to make the misguided man's life as miserable as possible. Behind the sergeant trod Marine Baker, Blake's relief, no friend of Blake but even less of the sergeant and he clattered his musket noisily against the bottom of the ladder. Blake was instantly transformed into a picture of intent alertness, his musket in his hands and presented at the ready.

'Halt! Who goes there?' he challenged.

'Sergeant Wolstenholme,' came the response as that cruelly disappointed officer loomed up out of the darkness. 'Did I see you with your musket out of your hand just then?'

Devout Blake might have been, but he was no fool. 'No sarnt.'

The sergeant pulled and kicked at the timbers of the strong-room. Satisfied that it was still secure he peered around the shadowy darkness of the hold, sniffing at the stale air. He gave the sentry a suspicious glare.

'Have any of these kegs been tampered with, Blake?'

'Not while I been here, sarnt. You knows I'm temperance,' said the Marine, doubly indignant.

Wolstenholme gave a grunt, more of disgust than disbelief. 'All right, Baker, take your post.'

Baker watched the pair recede into the darkness with a sardonic grin on his long, narrow face. He waited until the hatch-cover had been hauled back into place and then removed his shako, revealing a small, tin pannikin resting on his thinning hair.

'Right, Billy my boy, it's time you had yourself a little wet,' he muttered. He peered at the tiers of kegs to starboard; he would sup from those this time. There was no sense in storing up trouble by emptying one keg when he could take a little from a lot without creating suspicion. A tiny hole and a pinch of oakum to conceal it and no one would be any the wiser. He removed one of Armstrong's brad-awls from his pocket and knelt at one of the lower casks. The tool slipped and he swore, sucking at a lacerated finger. That's what comes from working in your own light, Billy boy, he told himself. He lifted the lantern from its nail and placed it on the deck beside him. That's better, my son, you can see what you are doing now! He pushed the point of the brad-awl into the keg and began to bore, humming softly to himself as he worked.

'Four bells, sir! Four bells!'

Lamb opened his eyes to see Hart's blackened stumps bared

in a hideous semblance of a smile as the old seaman bent over him.

'Four bells, sir. A fine morning, light winds from the southeast, coffee and hot water on your table, sir, and I've broken out your clean rig.'

Lamb nodded by way of thanks, his two hours' sleep leaving him feeling more exhausted than he was when he came off watch. He swung his legs out of the coat and scratched his head, his mouth agape in the most enormous of yawns.

'Don't let it get cold, sir,' warned Hart sharply as he picked up Lamb's dirty linen and backed out of the cabin.

'No, no, off you go, Hart.' Lamb had not enough men in his crew to provide him with a full-time servant but the boatswain's mate had produced Hart, who professed to be familiar with a servant's duties and was willing to combine looking after Lamb's simple requirements with his own deck duties for the reward of a few extra shillings.

The shaving water was hot and the coffee strong and Lamb sampled both alternately, scraping at his stubble and pausing to sip at his coffee, an unaccustomed but delightful practice which pleased him beyond measure and as his blade removed his whiskers and the coffee warmed his stomach he felt his weariness receding and his spirits lifting. Hart had laid out clean linen for him and had blacked and buffed his shoes and when Lamb emerged into the sunlight of the deck he felt cool and clean, and as alert and refreshed as if he had slept for twelve hours. The *Rosemary* was still two cables to larboard, her hands busy about her masts and yards preparing to set the topgallant-sails and royals in order to make the maximum use of the light winds. Drake stayed on deck long enough to supervise the setting of the same for the *Jeanne-Marie* before he went below for his breakfast.

Lamb strolled the length of his ship, up one side and down the other, revelling in his command, breathing deeply of the golden, sparkling air and noting with an appreciative eye the freshly sanded and scrubbed deck and the neatly stowed hammocks along the bulwarks. He stepped up to the little quarterdeck and took his place on the weather side beneath the mizzen shrouds, gazing forward over the rich blue of the gently heaving sea to the hard-edged horizon, contentment bubbling through every vein. A shade less than six hundred miles to Port Royal, he mused, three days' sailing, give or take a few hours. The first thing I must do –

He was thrown violently to the deck. Stupefied with shock he scrambled to his feet, staring in disbelief as the bows rose high into the air, accompanied by the crunching, groaning sounds of tortured timber. The foremast sagged sideways with a crack like the report of a gun. The deck heeled sharply as the bow crashed down in an explosion of water, the ship's head forced away to starboard as if slammed by a giant hand. Lamb ran across the tilting deck to the larboard rail; leaning out, he saw the weed-festooned keel of a large ship subsiding sullenly beneath the surface as the barque scraped her way past, large bubbles rising and bursting from the hulk's disturbed interior like the belchings of an enormous leviathan. The barque slowed her wild rocking and wallowed in her own waves, the leaning sails of the foremast pushing her head around to point at the distant coast of Hispaniola.

There was no need to call the hands. Men were pouring out on to the deck, staring wildly around in bewilderment at the empty sea. Drake appeared, his shirt stained with a mess of of spilled burgoo.

'See to the foremast, Mr Drake,' shouted Lamb as he ran forward, pushing his way through the press of mystified men milling aimlessly about the forward hatchway.

'Stand aside! Stand clear, you men! Mr Armstrong, come with me.'

The main damage was right forward in the crew's quarters. A large section of the curving larboard bow had been pushed inwards, splintering the planks without holing them but allowing the sea to spurt through with every rise and fall of the bow. Lamb and Armstrong knelt in the water sloshing about the deck and examined the ship's wound.

'Well, it could be worse,' said Lamb. 'At least, the cutwater seems to be undamaged.'

'Yes, I can soon patch this, sir. Well braced, it should hold until we reach Port Royal. She must have struck a glancing blow on the downward dip, sir, to have been damaged this high, then rode upwards over the hulk's keel. She will have done her sheathing no good, I'm thinking, sir.'

'Perhaps so, but that is of small concern. Get to work here without delay, if you please, Mr Armstrong.'

Lamb made his way to the upper deck, muttering angrily to himself, his nerves still twitching with the sudden shock of the impact. Bloody hulk, floating about the bloody sea like a submerged bloody island, getting in the way of innocent ships! Why had it not sunk to the bottom, like any normal, well-behaved wreck? He felt such a violent anger towards the hulk that if it had still been in view he would have turned his guns on to it without a moment's hesitation.

Drake had removed the canvas from the foremast by the time Lamb reached the deck and the hands were busy unshipping the yards. The shock of the collision had broken the mast just above the foretop and snapped the foretopgallant stays and one of the backstays. The *Rosemary* came alongside, her rail lined with curious men.

Wallace's voice sang out across the narrow stretch of water. 'What the devil happened?'

Lamb shouted briefly back.

'Is there anything we can do for you?' returned Wallace.

'No, nothing, thank you. We can manage.'

Wallace waved and the sloop drew off to a safer distance. Lamb and Drake peered upwards.

'What is the break like? Can we fish it, do you think?'

'I think so, sir, without too much trouble – the upper part is still resting on the broken stump. If we double the fore and backstays and pull the mast upright, we should be able to make a reasonable repair, sir.'

Lamb nodded, feeling his spirits rising a little. Perhaps things were not so bad after all. 'I shall go up and take a look.'

He swung himself up into the ratlines but was halted by a sudden, loud cry from Allwyn.

'Sir! Sir!'

Lamb looked round, hearing the alarm in the midshipman's voice. The boy was pointing to the bare deck between the foremast and the main hatchway. What the devil was he – ?

'Smoke, sir!'

Lamb's blood went cold. God, no! He jumped to the deck and with Drake raced to the spot at which Allwyn was pointing. Thin, grey, barely visible tendrils of smoke were seeping upwards from the deck seams. He put his hand flat to the deck. This part of the deck was in the shade of the mainsail but it felt as warm as if it was in the full heat of the sun.

'Man the deck and head pumps, Mr Drake,' he said quietly, a cold, sick certainty in his stomach.

He walked quickly to the main hatchway and knelt to put an ear to the canvas cover. A faint roaring, interspersed with strange popping noises, sounded from the hold. There was now no doubt, as he had known from the first sight of that wispy tendril of smoke, that there was a fire roaring below his feet and the peculiar noises, like corks being pulled from bottles, were, he realized, coming from the kegs; the alcoholic gases, driven off the brandy by the heat, were exploding their casks and showering the hold with inflammable liquor, feeding the flames. My God! he thought suddenly – the sentry! He glanced up and caught the alarmed eye of the Marine guarding the hatch fixed on him.

'Lend a hand here,' said Lamb urgently and began to tug at the heavy grating beneath its canvas cover. As they lifted the grating from the coaming smoke burst from the opening and billowed across to the lee side of the deck. Men came running to assist and Lamb stepped back, his lungs smarting and his eyes streaming.

'Stand back there! Stand clear! Stand aside, you men!'

It was Drake, dragging a canvas hose. Water began to dribble from the nozzle and then increased to a fast flow as the men at the pump forced the water along its length. Drake directed the flow into the hatchway, crouching at the coaming, his head turned away from the dense, rolling clouds of grey smoke.

'Bend your backs, there!' Lamb shouted at the men working the pump. He looked around him. 'Where is that other hose?'

'Here, sir,' said Keo, dragging a flat, canvas tube forward, 'but I think the pump is blocked, sir. Leastways, it ain't working. Mr Armstrong is taking a look at it now, sir. It was working fine first thing this morning,' he added helpfully.

Jesus Christ, of all times! Lamb clenched his fists, silently raging. He controlled himself with a strong effort and knelt to squint through the whirling column of smoke into the hold. He caught glimpses of blue and yellow flames leaping high, roaring and crackling, and at their base a horrifying, raging inferno of fiercely blazing timbers, spread right across the width of the hold and as far forward as he could see. He stared transfixed, aghast at the speed with which the fire had spread and the savage hold it had on the ship's timbers; it was much too late now, for the sentry below, for the silver and for the ship. A sudden gout of flame and searing heat erupted from below, licking at his face and he fell back, coughing and choking, his eyes running freely and his brows singed.

'Replace that hatch-cover!' he shouted hoarsely. There was just a chance, the very faintest chance, of the fire burning itself out if it was starved of air but he knew that his order was a mere gesture to hope already gone; long before that happened the flames would have eaten their way through to the sea.

'Give Keo your hose, Mr Drake; he can play it on the hatch-cover. Get the boats into the water – the ship is done for.'

Drake stared at him for a long second, his hard face rigid. 'And the silver, sir?'

'Forget the silver – it is too late for that. The boats, Mr Drake!'

'Aye aye, sir.'

Lamb scanned the faces around him. 'Where is Arkwright? Pass the word for Arkwright.'

'Here I be, sir,' said the old gun-captain, now acting-gunner of the barque, pushing his way forward.

'Do you know how to flood the magazine, Arkwright?'

'Course, sir,' said the seaman, slightly offended. 'There's a water-tank just above – '

'Good. Go and do it, if you please.'

'Sir! Shall I go with him, sir?'

Lamb glanced down at Allwyn's anxious face, noting his urgent expression. Clearly, the boy was desperate to do something constructive, to play a useful part. Lamb hesitated but reflecting that the magazine was shielded from the hold by a stout, copper-lined bulkhead and the work of flooding should only take a few moments, he nodded.

'Very well, Mr Allwyn, off you go.'

The *Rosemary* had edged closer; not too close – Wallace had every captain's horror of fire and he kept his yards at a prudent distance. He bellowed at full voice to make himself heard over the gap.

'How bad is it?'

'As bad as it can be,' Lamb yelled back. 'Stand by to receive our boats.'

Wallace raised his arm in mute reply and sheered off out of shouting distance.

Thick columns of smoke were writhing at the base of the mainmast and steam was rising from where Keo was playing his hose. The roaring of the blaze below was clearly discernible, like an angry, caged animal snarling and clawing to break free.

Drake approached and saluted, his stony face grim. 'The boats are in the water, sir.'

'Very good. Get the men into them and pull for the sloop. You, too, Mr Drake. Leave me the jolly-boat.'

Drake frowned. 'With respect, sir, I – '

'Kindly do as you are damned well told!'

'Aye aye, sir.'

Drake saluted and turned away and Lamb went aft to his cabin, passing Keo staring angrily at the dribble of water coming from his hose now that the man at the pump had deserted it for the boats.

'Leave it now, Keo,' said Lamb. 'Get yourself into a boat.'

He collected together his log, chronometer, sextant and sword and his best hat and silver-buckled shoes; Drake was right, there was little point in him not leaving the ship with the rest of the crew but all the time the ship floated, all the time there was the faintest glimmer of hope for her, he felt he should stay with her.

Drake was in the act of lowering himself over the side when Lamb came back to the deck and he handed down Lamb's possessions into the boat. There came a sudden blast of heated air and the deck trembled. Lamb glanced round. A dancing column of flames roared out of the main hatchway.

'You'll not be long, sir?' asked Drake, giving Lamb a hard look.

'No, I – ' A sudden thought struck Lamb. 'Are Mr Allwyn and Arkwright in the boats?'

'Not this side, sir. They may be in the other – ' He pointed. 'Here is Arkwright, sir.'

Lamb turned to see the acting-gunner stumble from the forward hatchway, bent double, coughing, his hand rubbing at his eyes. Lamb strode forward and grabbed him by the arm, pulling him upright.

'Where is Mr Allwyn?' He gave him an impatient shake. 'Speak, man!'

Arkwright jerked his thumb at the forward hatch-way. 'He's still down there, I think, sir,' he wheezed in a hoarse whisper, scarcely able to speak. 'The smoke is so bleeding thick, sir, we lost touch. And we couldn't flood the magazine, sir – the stopcock was seized solid and then the smoke came pouring in – black as night, it was, sir – '

Lamb could have struck him. The useless fool! 'Get in the boat,' he snapped, coldly furious. 'Tell Mr Drake to make off before the ship goes up.'

He made his way to the forward hatchway. The heat from the deck, lifting and twisting from the furnace below, struck painfully through the soles of his shoes and the masts shimmered and danced in the distorted air. A burst of flame caught his eye as he lowered himself down the ladder; the flames from the main hatchway had caught the mainsail and in a trice had raced up to the royal topgallantsail. The smoke pouring from below was thick and choking and Lamb clutched his handkerchief to his mouth as he descended. He stepped off the ladder on to a body. Well, alive or dead, he had found him. He bent, fumbling in the darkness, and levered the midshipman's limp body into a sitting position, the smoke biting deep into his lungs. He struggled to raise the boy high enough to put over his shoulder but even Allwyn's light weight seemed to be too much for him. He lowered his head into the crook of his elbow, coughing uncontrollably, choking on the smoke, his head swimming. I am going to die here, he thought dully, me and this boy together.

'Let me help you, sir,' said Drake's voice in his ear. 'It's all right, I've sent the boat off, sir.'

The master's mate bent his knees and with a single jerk threw the body of the midshipman across his shoulder.

'After you, sir,' he wheezed courteously.

Bloody fool! thought Lamb but this was no place to argue about Naval conventions, even if he had the voice to do so. He fumbled for the ladder and scrambled up and out into the hazy, dirty sunshine, his eyes weeping and his lungs on fire. The mizzenmast was ablaze, he noted, without surprise; if the foremast had not been stripped of its canvas, that, too, would be in flames now. He bent with outstretched hand to assist Drake and his load from the hatch and for the second time that morning was flung to the deck, his ears deafened and singing from a tremendous explosion below. The deck reared and tilted, steeper and steeper, and as he was thrown into the water the thought crossed his mind that it would have been better had he not begged for those extra casks of Mr Winter's best gunpowder.

He went deep, pressed down by a mast or a yard and struggled frantically, terrified of being trapped. Suddenly he was rising, clawing his way upward towards the light, kicking at a rope that snaked itself around his legs. He broke the surface and sucked in a huge lungful of glorious, sunlit air before striking out away from the ship, fearful of being dragged down again by the suction of her plunge. The boats rose and fell on the long swell some way off to his left and beyond them he could see the sloop, her rail crowded with men. He turned on his back and looked at the *Jeanne-Marie*, the waves slapping at his face, lifting and dropping him as they passed. The barque was on her side, very low in the water, wreathed in smoke and steam, blue flames dancing over her corpse like pale ghosts. Lamb watched her settle, his ears ringing with the shock of the explosion, his mind stunned with the suddenness of her going and the loss of Drake and little Allwyn. He shook his head and brushed the water from his blurred vision, unwilling to believe the evidence of his eyes. She sank lower and lower, very quickly, until only a hint of green copper showed, and then that, too, was gone. Her mast ends rose briefly out of the water as if for a final salute and then dipped and disappeared.

Lamb was lifted by a swell and he stared at the dirty stain of filth and rubbish that marked the barque's going. The sea dropped him again, slapping water into his mouth and eyes. He spat. 'Oh, shit!' he murmured, and turning, struck out wearily for the nearest boat.

214